Just Add Spice

Carol E Wyer

Safkhet
Publishing

First published in 2013 by Safkhet Soul, London, United Kingdom
Safkhet Soul is an imprint of Safkhet Publishing
www.safkhetpublishing.com

1 3 5 7 9 10 8 6 4 2

ISBN 978-1-908208-22-4

A CIP catalogue record for this book is available from
the British Library.

Printed and bound by Lightning Source International

Typeset in 12 pt Crimson and Calamity Jane with Adobe InDesign

Find out more about Carol on www.carolewyer.co.uk
and www.facing50withhumour.com
and meet her on Facebook at
www.facebook.com/pages/Carol-E-Wyer/221149241263847

Carol E Wyer	*author*
Amber Gunn	*editor*
Kim Maya Sutton	*managing editor and cover artist*
Sally Neuhaus	*cover designer*
Walter Richardson	*proofreader*
William Banks Sutton	*copy editor*

The colophon of Safkhet is a representation of the ancient Egyptian goddess of wisdom
and knowledge, who is credited with inventing writing.
Safkhet Publishing is named after her because the founders met in Egypt.

Dedication

The characters in this book are fictional but the Hotel Volcán on the island of Lanzarote, is very real. I would like to thank the staff there, in particular the management, for letting us enjoy their generous hospitality while I was putting the finishing touches to this story.

Should you be looking for a wonderful holiday destination that offers tranquillity, charm and relaxation, then you will find it all at this wonderful hotel. It is the perfect retreat and very fitting for this novel.

I am also indebted to the team at Safkhet Publishing who are the most supportive and fun people to work with. It is a huge pleasure to be part of their family.

Lastly, I would like to thank my husband for putting up with me while I worked on this novel, ignoring him and the housework. He, of course, always manages to spice up my life.

What about you? Do you need to inject some spice into yours?

Carol E.Wyer

The windows in the old Golf GTI were almost completely steamed up, thanks to the activities of the middle-aged woman and the young man inside it. The sudden rapid barking of a dog in the distance made the woman jump. She was already sweating and aware of a rancid aroma pervading the car. It most certainly was coming from her partner–in–crime. He turned his head towards her and scowled.

"Hurry up, will you? I could have finished this twenty minutes ago."

Dawn shrank at the reprimand. He might have been twenty-five years her junior, but he oozed menace. His dark eyes burrowed into hers.

"It's not easy. My knees hurt from being in this uncomfortable position, and my glasses keep slipping down my nose, which makes it much harder to see. You wait until you get to my age. The world becomes all foggy, and then you start bumping into objects like doors and cupboards …" She trailed off. He continued to level his cold stare at her. She squirmed, then took a deep breath, and shoved her glasses back up onto the bridge of her nose for the umpteenth time. She scrabbled about again searching out the wires that had dropped down. "I should have stolen a motorbike. It must be easier than this. Or a mobility scooter," she mumbled.

"You're quite funny, you know?" he muttered, peering out of the window.

"Keep low. There's the old man from down the road, walking his dog. Don't want him seeing us."

They both dropped down in the seats until the pensioner had gone by. The dog stopped at the next lamppost and cocked its leg against it.

"Okay," he whispered. He drew himself up a little, huffed onto the passenger window steaming it further with his acrid breath and then drew a smiley face on it. "Dodgy knees and bad eyesight. Suppose that's why middle-aged women don't generally try to hot-wire cars."

She ignored the comment and continued to fumble with the wires. The smart arse lying next to her in the VW Golf, had been trying to teach her how to break into the car and hot-wire it. She could get in

1

the car easily enough, but the hot-wiring was proving impossible. In the darkness, she couldn't see which wire went where. Despite the specially insulated thick gloves he had demanded she wore to prevent shocks, she didn't possess the same dexterity as MJ. Her left leg was going numb again because MJ also insisted she stayed in the obligatory slumped stance to avoid detection by passing *Filth*—his preferred name for the police. At that moment, she was regretting getting herself into this situation. Her back ached, and her right knee was beginning to throb.

"Almost there," she whispered. At last, she had the correct wires grasped clumsily in her hands. She only needed to pull gently to ensure they would touch to get the car started, when a loud thumping on the roof of the car made her shriek loudly and drop the wires.

"You're supposed to be the look out!" she yelped at MJ.

MJ shrugged his shoulders. "They must have sneaked up on me when I dozed off with boredom," he replied and grinned at her, revealing brown-stained teeth. "You've taken so long, it's not surprising you got caught. It probably took less time to build the car than you to hot-wire it," he added and smiled again. "Still, you didn't do too badly. It took me a few months to learn how to do it properly. My cellmate was very patient."

A face appeared at the driver's window.

"For goodness sake! Have you two not finished messing about in my car yet?"

Dawn took in a deep breath, which was probably a mistake, given the sour smell pervading the car. She opened the door and crawled out.

"Sorry, son. I thought I'd have cracked this by now, but I can't get the hang of it. I can't get the wires to touch. It's like threading a needle and missing its eye with the cotton every time. My eyesight must be even worse than I suspected. I'd better get some new lenses for these glasses."

"I need my car to collect Phoebe from her friend's, so soz, but you'll have to give up. Hi, MJ!" he added as MJ slunk out of the car with one stealthy, feline movement. They tapped fists together in a show of camaraderie.

"I think I'll have to forget it altogether," Dawn continued, pulling off the gloves and handing them back to MJ. "I don't think it would be viable for a woman my age to hot-wire a car like this. I'd need to be slimmer, younger, and a lot more flexible."

MJ nodded in agreement.

"Don't worry. I have faith in your devious mind. You'll come up with another idea. You'd better get off home. Dad will be getting suspicious. I'll drop MJ back off at his place, once he's put the car back together," he added, surveying the mess of wires hanging out.

Dawn nodded. "It's all right. Your father thinks I'm at a special meeting with the writing group. I told him we needed to do some research for our writing. This classifies as research. I must say I thought it would be easier than this. It seemed simple enough, according to the internet, and MJ has been a very good teacher."

MJ looked embarrassed by this compliment and pulled out a scruffy packet of tobacco from the back of his jeans, which hung low on his scrawny backside.

"I might have to try a different tactic now. MJ explained tonight that these old cars are the only cars you can hot-wire these days. The new models are impossible unless you have the actual key for them. I'll have to work out a different way of stealing a car."

Her son grinned back at her. "Yeah, right, research. I hope that's all it is. I don't want to have to visit you in jail."

She smiled and hugged her son, then waved goodbye to MJ, who had wandered off away from them both, pulled out some cigarette papers, and was rolling a long thin cigarette.

"Cheers, MJ. Thanks for trying to help."

"S'okay. Anything for the Big Man," he mumbled, seeking out a well-used lighter from inside a jacket pocket. "You did okay, really. Another few lessons and you'll get the hang of it."

The Big Man—her son, Dan—grinned again.

"Night, Mum. Don't worry, I won't tell Dad you were here."

Dawn drove back home along dark lanes. The radio station was playing songs from the seventies. She liked seventies' music and was soon singing along loudly to Abba's 1976 hit, *Dancing Queen*. Most people of her generation remembered 1976 for its long hot summer. Dawn remembered it for an entirely different reason. Memories like falling snowflakes in a storm swirled around her as she drove. That summer had been spent at the small nursing home near the village where she lived, watching her mother battle cancer and, just days before her sixteenth birthday, slip away from her forever.

Her father also left her that day in August. He withdrew into himself and became reclusive. In spite of her tender years, she knew she had to help her father, Jack, and focussed on him rather than wallow in her own grief. She nursed her own broken heart and did her utmost to help her father mend his.

At first, local well-wishers in their village dropped by to offer sympathy and support. The village was not large and most people knew her mother as she had worked at the local store. Little by little, they ceased their visits, embarrassed, or found it too difficult to communicate with her father, who suddenly went from quiet and reclusive to angry. It fell upon Dawn to help him. She was the only person he would engage with. She ceased being a fun-loving teenager, and instead became his carer and companion, shunning her contemporaries to stay at home and help him.

Time healed. Gradually, they felt able to talk about the woman who had been such an important part of their lives. They shared memories and tears. Jack became less angry and more resigned to the blow life had dealt him. It took a few more years before her father felt he could face the world—and dating—again. Dawn was just about to start university when he announced he was seeing a woman. She was a work colleague. Apparently, they had shared lunch together a couple of times. Dawn couldn't have been happier for him.

She went to Birmingham University to study English in the hope of becoming a journalist and met James Ellis at the Fresher's Ball. A mature student, he was a few years older than her and was studying accountancy. They became "an item" that same day, seeing each other regularly during the first two years she was at university. Dawn didn't make it to her final year though. She fell pregnant and abandoned her studies to become a mother and a wife.

The day baby Elisabeth came into their world was one of tears of joy and sorrow; tears of sorrow that her own mother couldn't be there to meet her namesake, and tears of joy as they watched the tiny miracle, weighing only six pounds three ounces, grasp Dawn's thumb. Like her namesake, she left Dawn broken and torn. This time, it took much longer for Dawn to heal.

Four weeks after arriving home to their rented apartment, baby Elisabeth was discovered lifeless in her cot when Dawn got up to feed her, wondering why the baby hadn't woken her earlier.

The verdict was cot death. Dawn couldn't focus on anything for months. She blamed herself incessantly, wondering if she could have prevented it. If only baby Elisabeth had slept with them in their little bedroom, instead of the nursery they had decorated especially for her ... if only she had woken earlier and picked her up to feed her before this happened ... the "if onlys" plagued her.

Nurses and doctors assured her that there was nothing she could have done. Dawn couldn't comprehend why it happened. She didn't want to have children for a long time after that. It took endless counselling to help her recover. For months, she couldn't look at babies in prams without filling up with tears. She attempted some distance learning to finish her degree course, but she had lost the momentum and found working at home alone too difficult. She ended up working part-time in the local town library for a while to help with the income. She had little recollection of those days. Both she and Jim changed, and neither wanted to suffer that sort of pain ever again. Jim had been stronger, but his hurt was buried deep within him. He never spoke about it. They weren't, she mused, the hedonistic days that newly-weds should enjoy. They were dark days. In 1985, she discovered she was pregnant again. She was thrilled and terrified in equal measures.

She made sure baby Daniel would never suffer the same fate. She kept vigil over him almost twenty-four hours a day until she was too exhausted to watch over him. For the first six months of his life she barely slept, but as he became stronger and bigger, she began to relax.

She remained a full-time mother even when Dan was at college. Jim's salary by then was sufficient for all of them all to live on, although there was not much left over for luxuries. Dan filled the hole in her heart caused by the loss of Elisabeth, and even though he no longer lived at home, she experienced a warmth that nothing or no one else could give her whenever she thought about him.

He had recently moved into a rented flat himself with his long-term girlfriend, Phoebe. Next, it would be marriage and then a family of his own. Dawn was no longer needed to support and protect him. All she had left now was her love for him. She felt useless. She no longer had a role to fill. Dan's departure had left her empty again.

Dawn drew up to the old ramshackle house they had lived in for over two decades. It needed work, but like many of the plans they had made years before, these too had been shelved. Lack of energy and money meant the house was looking tired and dated, much like Dawn felt about herself.

She opened the door into the kitchen. The casserole she had left for her husband was still on the top, untouched. A used breakfast bowl was beside the sink next to an open packet of Shredded Wheat. On the oak kitchen table stood a Hayter lawn mower. It was in pieces, and a variety of dirty parts were strewn about the table top. Grease stains leaked out from under various screws and plugs. There had been no effort to cover the table with newspaper. She slammed her handbag onto the kitchen top.

"James Ellis," she called. There was no response. She stomped into the sitting room where she found her husband, Jim, sprawled on the settee in his work jeans, watching a documentary about Keynes and the economy.

"There's a lawn mower on the kitchen table, and you didn't eat the casserole I left you," she began. Jim was firmly engrossed in the documentary and oblivious to her entry. Whenever there was a programme on the television about the economy, financial institutions, or corporations, he became completely absorbed by it. Jim had been "retired" from accountancy for a few months, but he still maintained an interest in all things financial. The firm he worked for, Chilternz, had been taken over by a larger company, who had their own experts, and so redundancies had been made. Jim was one of the unfortunate casualties who found himself without a job. He was "too old" to consider securing another position, and even though he had sent out hundreds of CVs, he had yet to be invited to an interview.

Dawn stood for a while and received a grunt of recognition for her patience. She sighed. She may as well have been invisible. He would not communicate with her until the programme finished. In fact, if he carried on working on the lawn mower, he wouldn't notice her until it was time for bed, and even then he would probably not realise she was there. Jim had suddenly started to fall asleep as soon as his head hit the pillow.

She grabbed her glasses from her bag in a huff and stormed upstairs to her office. It used to be her son's old bedroom, converted now into a sort of study. Dawn spent most of her free time here working on her project—her first novel.

It was thanks to her son that she had started writing. Dan had suggested she try her hand at it. He had seen an advert in the local paper and taken it to his mother.

"With me gone, you'll need something to fill in your time," he joked. "If you don't fancy this, you could try getting a job in the supermarket. Or, I could just come round for my meals every other day and bring you my washing, if you prefer!"

The creative writing class was just what she needed. She had joined immediately. This was a chance for her to try writing her very own book. Led by award-winning author, Blake Ryder, she was now one of a small group of people who hung on his every word and hoped to get enough tips and coaching to help with their own journey to publication.

It was Blake's fault she had been out attempting to hot-wire a car instead of preventing her husband from turning their kitchen into a garage.

"You need to live, breathe, and act like your characters," he gushed, while waving a half-eaten Garibaldi biscuit at the group. Dressed eccentrically, at that first meeting, he was sporting a striped neckerchief and a silk waistcoat. The group waited for more words of wisdom. A large raisin stuck to his front tooth made him look like a wild pirate. "It's like a method actor." He continued waving his arms theatrically. "A good actor becomes absorbed by his role. He, or she, gets into their character's mind. First, they think like the character, and then they begin to act and behave like the character. They make up legends for the characters. They envisage that character's whole life: where they came from, what their family is like—everything. That is what makes them act so well. It's the same for an author. They become the character."

"If you want people to believe in your characters, you need to make them credible. Whatever they do or say, you must have lived it too. Your characters must have a back story and a life, even if you don't share that with your readers. They have it because they are real. Earl Bashkov would never have been so popular if I hadn't got into his head," Blake finished and sat down.

Dawn was spellbound. Earl Bashkov was as well-known as Hercule Poirot. He was an eccentric Russian detective. Dawn had read the Bashkov series before joining the class and had become a huge fan. Blake was a genius, as far as she was concerned, and she hung on his every word. After all, Blake had been published by a big publisher and was on best-sellers' lists. He should have known what an author needed to do to get noticed in the world of writing.

The problem for Dawn was that her chosen protagonist was quite wacky and got up to all sorts of behaviour completely alien to Dawn. She had an imagination, but creating a character like hers had sent it into overdrive. The woman had her own agenda. Hence, Dawn had been trying to see if it would be viable for her character to steal a car.

She stared at the computer screen. It was incredible what you could find on the internet these days. There were detailed videos on YouTube of how to hot-wire a car, although she didn't fancy sitting in one, laptop propped on the dashboard, attempting to follow the instructions of the apparent twelve-year-old, who was giving the tutorial. Hot-wiring was trickier than she thought. Besides, you could only hot-wire an old car like her son's. There must be an easier way to steal a car, especially a modern one. She fired up her laptop to check her information and was soon lost in the technical world of tumblers, pins, and levers.

Cinnamon Knight ground the stub of her Benson and Hedges' cigarette into the pavement with the heel of her Prada leather motorcycle boot, where it now joined a small pile of tab ends. Strategically placed in a shop doorway, she watched the top left window of a block of flats opposite. She had been there almost two hours. Rain beat steadily on the pavement, drumming against the gutter with constant thuds, but this did not deter her. Her patience was rewarded as the light blazing from the window was finally extinguished. She sauntered across the road to the BMW parked in front of the block of flats along the kerbside, sandwiched between a Peugeot 205 and a C Class Mercedes.

Dressed completely in black, face partially obscured by her North Face hooded jacket; she was almost invisible next to the dark car. It took only a minute to fiddle with the lock, open the door, and slide into the car. She lowered herself down in the driver's seat, casting a cursory glance out of the window. The streets were empty. The weather was on her side and no one was braving the downpour, not even the old man at the end of the road who rarely missed taking his dog out for an evening stroll.

She leant forward and pulled off the cover below the steering wheel with one deft movement. Extracting the screwdriver from a neat case, she stabbed it into the ignition lock. A quick fiddle, one sharp twist, and the car burst into life; the persistent thudding of the rain against the pavement hid the initial coughing of the engine. She pulled away from the kerb swiftly and headed up the road at speed.

Pushing the hood away from her head, she checked her face in the rear-view mirror. That'll teach him to mess about with women, she thought. No one, but no one, messes about with Cinnamon—the rat!

The rat in question was Alex Wells, an advertising agent from Manchester. He had met Cinnamon in a bar eight weeks earlier. For Cinnamon, it had been the first time she liked a man since the terrible experience with her ex-husband.

Her husband of twenty years left her for a younger woman. Not just any younger woman but the younger woman who had moved in next door to them and who was, Cinnamon believed, her best friend. The woman, Jessica, had certainly hoodwinked Cinnamon.

Jessica was one of those easy, cheerful, and vibrant people who gave the impression they really were interested in you. Cinnamon, in desperate need of an understanding friend, unburdened a mountain of emotions on this woman. She was the first person in years to breach the invisible armour that Cinnamon wore to protect herself.

Cinnamon missed the signs. Blinkered by friendship and trust, she didn't recognise what was going on under her nose. She never imagined that Geoff would leave her, let alone have a torrid affair with the woman next door. She didn't realise until she found Geoff waiting for her when she returned from Waitrose one lunchtime, his suitcase by the door.

He had fallen in love with the feisty, go-getting harlot next door. They were moving down south where Jessica had been offered a promotion and would be an area manager for a cosmetics company. Geoff had already applied to work at the London branch of the firm of accountants he worked for, and together they were going to start a new exciting life.

Cinnamon could pinpoint the exact moment when a switch flicked in her head, and she threw off the mantle of respectability she had been wearing for all those years. It was the moment she looked out of the window and saw Jessica, who had been sitting behind the wheel of her company Audi, lean forward and give Geoff a passionate kiss as he clambered into the car. The memories flowed back, opening the wound in her heart once more. Cinnamon Knight, gunned the throttle of the BMW and headed at high speed down the M6. It didn't matter if the speed cameras along the route caught her zooming along at 110mph. The Rat would be the one to be fined. He deserved more than fines.

After a string of meaningless one-night stands, which had left her with nothing but self-loathing, Alex Wells had charmed her. He convinced her it was possible to love again and enjoy a relationship. For a short while, she was reminded of the possibilities that might have lain ahead: possibilities that might have included a normal caring relationship. Just when she thought she could have become the 'old' Cinnamon again, she spotted him exiting an Italian restaurant in Birmingham. She had been at the hairdresser's. She hid among the shoppers and observed him. He walked casually out onto the street and wrapped his arm around his companion, a woman at least ten years younger than Cinnamon. He kissed her and murmured something into her ear. She nodded and smiled back at him. Red mist descended once more before Cinnamon's eyes. Without any thought, she followed them to a hotel, where she discovered that they had checked in as Mr and Mrs Wells.

She had planned her sortie that night with care. A phone call to Alex's office, pretending to be a new client, had determined he was expected back in Manchester to work at Head Office for the next two weeks. She travelled up by train and waited patiently near his apartment until she saw him return home. She was skilled at waiting: she had accomplished what she wanted.

She revved the engine again, spinning the wheels, as she tore away from the lights. She was going to leave the car abandoned in Birmingham. There wouldn't be much evidence of it by the time the sun rose the next morning. Alex would be distraught. He loved this car. It was a special edition M3 in an unusual colour, specially chosen by him. It had been fitted out with the most expensive sound system and extras. He had lavished much money and time on it. It was, without doubt, very special to him.

A tight smile played over her lips. She glanced at her reflection in the rear-view mirror, tossed back her long raven-coloured hair, and narrowed her eyes as she sped on. Alex was lucky. She could have done worse. The anger she had been attempting to contain for years had been unleashed. She had plenty more revenge to wreak. This was just the beginning.

Blast Alex! She had spent five years trying to forget Geoff and what an emotional wreck she had been when he left her. One selfish action by Alex Wells brought back all the bad memories.

She dumped the BMW in the middle of Birmingham, door wide open, its keys in the ignition. Someone would make off with it, change the licence plates and respray it. That would be the last he would see of it. Served him right. He'd mourn its loss, though. It wouldn't be easy to find one exactly like it to replace it. It had been pimped. He had even chipped it so it went faster than other cars. In fact, he had spent a fortune on it. Still, it was only a materialistic thing, she thought. That wasn't much to lose. In fact, compared to what Cinnamon had lost over the years, it was nothing. She dialled the number of a taxi firm and asked to pick her up, then walked up a street and waited at the arranged point at a bus shelter. She lit another cigarette and reflected on her life so far, a life she kept trying to escape from. Just when had she become so hard, so embittered?

Memories of a young Cinnamon struggled to the surface of her mind: images of a pretty girl playing on a swing, a good-looking man pushing her. Laughter. "Higher Daddy!" The memory flickered like a dying match and disappeared to be replaced by another bleak colourless memory of her mother, Tina, crying.

That was a turning point. Cinnamon was two weeks away from her thirteenth birthday. Her head was full of the thoughts of getting the Bontempi organ she had been promised and maybe some proper make-up. Her mother had hinted Cinnamon might be allowed some as she was nearly thirteen. Cinnamon could not wait to be grown up. Thirteen sounded so grown up.

She had been watching an episode of a new show, *Multi-coloured Swap Shop*. She wanted to know if she could phone in and swap her old dolls, as she was getting too old for them. She wandered into the kitchen, where she found her mother at the kitchen table, head in her arms, weeping softly.

A few terrifying minutes passed by, during which her mother could do nothing but shake her head and cry, Cinnamon learned that her father had been killed a few hours earlier in a car accident. Tina was not the same from that day onwards. She shut herself away from everyone, including Cinnamon. She started drinking. First, it was vodka after work; then, vodka before work. And finally, vodka and wine instead of work.

After one particular bout of serious drinking, Tina revealed something that hardened Cinnamon's heart even more. Her father had not been alone in the car when it crashed. He had been with a female passenger: a woman for whom he had just left them both. He had been heading to his new lover's home when the car had been hit by an oncoming lorry, and he was gone, not to live in the next town, but forever.

Money wasn't a problem. Her father had taken out an insurance policy, which paid out handsomely. His elderly parents died later that same year, through grief, her mother said, and left a generous inheritance, which ensured Cinnamon's mother need never work again. Instead, she made it made it her mission to become intimately acquainted with every bottle she touched.

Cinnamon grew up, but not how she had imagined she would. She went from being a carefree girl to carer and companion in one fell swoop. She also lost what little confidence she had and transformed into a reclusive teenager. As well as the usual angst that accompanies growing up, Cinnamon feared someone would discover her mother's drinking habits and take her away. She didn't dare invite anyone to their home. Fortunately, Tina was also an only child, whose parents had died, so there was no one to bother them. Cinnamon started at a new senior school that autumn, where she kept herself to herself, barely registering the existence of her fellow students at the all-girl's school. The other girls thought she was crackers and avoided her. There was something about her that guaranteed they didn't mock her. Her cold stare blanked them all, and she remained friendless, burying herself in schoolwork and ignoring the others at break times. She spent weekends hidden away in her bedroom listening to pop music and reading. She became an avid reader. Books allowed her to escape from the nightmare created by reality.

She managed for such a long time. She cooked, cleaned, and looked after her mother. Her mother's moods were difficult to handle. One minute, she would be quiet and calm, the next weeping, or, worse still, yelling at Cinnamon and behaving like a mad woman. Cinnamon tried to keep her mother away from the alcohol, but what could a teenager do against someone who was hell-bent on self-destruction? Her mother managed to get down to the local shops by taxi while Cinnamon was at school and went home with shopping and booze. Cinnamon found vodka bottles hidden at the tops of cupboards, in the toilet cistern, and under her mother's bed. She turned a blind eye to most of it. She knew her mother would never recover. She had a shattered heart. Cinnamon dreaded experiencing that sort of pain.

Her valiant efforts to keep their small family unit together were in vain. Just after her sixteenth birthday, she returned from a trip to the shops to find her mother had taken a lethal cocktail of pills and alcohol. A note beside her read:

Cinnamon, my darling girl,

You have been the only thing good in my life, but you deserve better than this. I hope you find happiness and are able to put all of this behind you. None of this has been your fault. It was weakness that started the chain of events. I am sorry I am not stronger. You are strong. Stay strong. I hope you find love. But be very careful who you give your love to. Remember, whoever has your heart also has the power to hurt or destroy you.

Your loving mother. X

It took another full year for Cinnamon to come to terms with what happened and take control of her life. She decided that a job would be good for her and found a position in a local library, where she could remain safely hidden among the books. It was too late for her to transform into some sort of social butterfly and begin to make friends. She was socially inept and painfully shy.

Geoff Sullivan was studying accountancy at university. He was at home for the summer vacation and had gone into the library to get some books to help him with some retakes he had coming up. The emerald-eyed Cinnamon caught his attention. He tried to ask her out, but she refused. It took several visits and all of his charm to persuade her to go to the cinema with him to see Monty Python's *Life of Brian*. They laughed all the way through it. It had been the best evening of her life.

Cinnamon stubbed out her cigarette. She wished she had never met Geoff. The taxi she had ordered was approaching, its headlights glowed eerily in the gloom. It pulled up to her where she stood.

"All right, luv?" asked the taxi driver. Looking at her face, he didn't question her, just noted her address and set off once she had clambered aboard.

She sat back in the seat. There was a faint aroma of kebab. The driver had worry beads hanging from his rear-view mirror and no doubt a photograph of his kids above his sun visor, she mused.

She closed her eyes and willed the unwelcome thoughts away. They came anyway, uninvited. It would have been different if there had been any children. More images rose like bubbles in a glass of champagne, each racing to the surface before bursting. Her mind whirred unrelenting, determined to drag up memories.

She had adored Geoff. He rescued her from her reclusive prison, and for that she was grateful. He introduced her to a life she hadn't thought possible. His parents were warm and welcoming. Their house was bright and filled with love. She craved being part of it. She handed her life over to Geoff. She cared for him. She ensured he had everything he could wish for. She lavished him with gifts and attention. She made herself indispensable. She went around to his parent's house every evening after work and sat with them all, some evenings washing up with Geoff or helping prepare the meal with Geoff's mum, Sarah. When Geoff went back to university for his final year, Cinnamon stayed with him every weekend and phoned him every evening. She sat quietly on his bed reading while he studied, and helped him by testing for his examinations, typed up his essays, and ensured his bedside didn't look like a tip.

He proposed to her at the leaving party. Fuelled by alcohol and affection, he dropped to one knee outside the bathroom and asked her to be his. She accepted the Coca-Cola can pull tab he used in absence of a ring. She kept that ring pull all the years they were together.

She sold the old house she had shared with her mother and purchased a new one for her and Geoff with the proceeds. There was more than enough money for the newly-weds and Cinnamon wanted for nothing other than a child to love to make their relationship complete.

She opened her eyes. They were going past Lichfield. That was where they used to live. She shut her eyes again. She couldn't let the thoughts take over. She instinctively drew back from the images of her sobbing over lifeless tiny bodies. No, she wouldn't go there. She refocused on Alex Wells and hoped someone had driven his precious car away by now. Men— who needed them? She fumed for a little longer. Most of them were double-crossing bastards. She would fix that. She would make it her mission to ensure all cheats were dealt with appropriately. Yes, that's what she would do.

Cinnamon looked at the taxi driver's eyes in the mirror, but did not know that the driver was taking in every detail about her. He noted his passenger's icy expression as he glanced in his rear-view mirror. He wondered why she was out on her own at such a late hour. She hadn't been drinking. Maybe she had rowed with her boyfriend or husband and stormed off. She was a good-looking woman, but she had a steely determination about her. She looked fierce, like one of those Gladiator contestants he watched on television. Now, this was a woman you wouldn't want to double-cross. She looked like she would do you some serious damage if she was angry with you. He would keep quiet. He learned a long time ago that staying silent was a good option when faced with an angry passenger. He would be glad to get this one home, collect his fare, and get some shut eye. Heaven help whomever she was annoyed with; he wouldn't want to be in their shoes.

Dawn felt considerable empathy for Cinnamon. It was obvious Cinnamon had lost control and was about to go wild. Some voice deep within Dawn joined in. The mundanity of her own life was suffocating her. She wanted to be free of all shackles like Cinnamon and just be herself—no not herself, be wild. She understood why her character had chosen to transform into a dark creature, one that refused to be beholden to anyone.

Dawn understood Cinnamon's complex character. Cinnamon spoke to her when she was writing and revealed her innermost thoughts and fears. Dawn could see her face clearly when she shut her eyes. Cinnamon was as real to her as her own family. Cinnamon accompanied her everywhere and watched. Sometimes she commented and other times advised. Cinnamon had been with her for a long while, waiting for Dawn to write the book. Dawn could hear the low, sultry tones of her voice when she spoke, she could see every emotion that flickered across Cinnamon's face as she battled with her inner demons. Dawn could see Cinnamon every time she looked at her own reflection.

Dawn ached to be like her character. She had the courage, strength, and willpower that Dawn lacked. Unlike the middle-aged Dawn, she had remodelled herself. She had transformed in ways that Dawn could never manage. Through gruelling exercise and a strict regime, Cinnamon possessed the enviable figure of a twenty-year-old. Dawn sucked in her stomach. It made no difference. The muffin top still hung over her jeans. She really should take up some form of exercise, but she just couldn't make the effort needed. An invisible hand held her back from attempting any exercise or opened a packet of *Wine Gums* for her to chew on while she typed. She decided it didn't matter anyway if she were out of shape. Jim didn't care how she looked. The last time she had made an effort, put on a new short skirt, and done her hair and make-up, Jim hadn't made any comment at all, preferring to stare at the cupboards and stating he might be able to get some reclaimed tiles for behind the stove top.

There was no passion in her life. There had never been any passion. Companionship yes, but no passion. She and Jim rarely made love. When they did it was merely perfunctory. After a couple of drinks, there was a chance Jim would wrap an arm around her in bed, kiss her when he came to bed, kiss her ear noisily a couple of times and run his hand over her body in a clumsy attempt to arouse her. He seemed to have forgotten how to awaken any desire in her, or maybe he too couldn't be bothered to make an effort any more. He might even have managed a couple of wet slurps on her cheeks, and then, believing her to be as ready for sex as him, he would attempt to mount her. She just let him. If she pushed him away, he would sulk and then only be more randy by early morning. *There is nothing worse than bad breath, creaking joints, and a horny man at three in the morning when you really want to be fast asleep,* she decided. He hadn't made any attempt in recent months at all. In fact, they hadn't had sex since before he had been laid off.

Cinnamon was passionate in a way that Dawn was not. She was a vixen, hell-bent on letting men know who was boss. Dawn was quite pleased with the opening of her book. Cinnamon was exciting, sexy, and dangerous, quite the opposite of her creator. Cinnamon wouldn't have put up with lawn mowers on her kitchen table. Cinnamon wouldn't have let any man ignore her. Dawn suddenly recalled a story Dan had told her. It was about a recent stag party and a stripper who ended up surprising them all. Sucking on the end of a pencil, Dawn drafted the next chapter of her novel.

It was very late when she went to bed, having completed the latest chapter. Jim was fast asleep and didn't hear her slip quietly between the sheets. He was making that puffing sound he usually made just before he burst into rhythmical snores that would increase in decibels until Dawn felt like screaming. She was tired. Her eyes were sore from staring at the screen, and she needed some rest before Jim decided it was time for them both to wake up.

He was one of those "early to bed and early to rise" people. At about five o'clock he would start to become restless in bed, which would inevitably waken Dawn. He would then yawn noisily several times and huff as if he didn't fancy another day on the planet. Some short time after that, he would throw back the covers and tumble out of bed, clumping about the bedroom, opening wardrobe doors noisily, and then running the bathroom tap for ages and flushing the toilet several times. He was oblivious to Dawn, who was still bleary-eyed from tiredness.

Age was creeping up on him. She glanced at him. Light cast from the digital alarm clock glowed blue across his face. His mouth was open, and he was dribbling slightly. She prodded him gently in the side to encourage him to move off his back and onto his side, where he might not make that irritating puffing sound.

Dawn pulled the covers up to her chin and nestled into the warmth of the duvet. The puffs turned into gentle rumbles. Dawn burrowed further under the duvet. The rumbles became louder. Dawn gave him a prod. The rumbles stopped. Dawn sighed and covered her head with the duvet. Sleep wasn't far away. She edged towards it relaxing and welcoming the night which would envelop her and leave her refreshed. She began to drift, floating towards that comfortable oblivion.

She was woken from the almost dream-like state by an almighty snore. Jim was at full volume. She shook him gently. Nothing. He continued to snore. She tried to move him. No way. He was out for the count. She hid her head under the duvet and fumed. She needed some sleep, for goodness sake. It was 3am. She needed those two precious hours.

Cinnamon suddenly appeared from nowhere. She was in Dawn's mind, whispering to her. Cinnamon wouldn't have listen to this holy row. She would have given him a sharp kick. As soon as the thought entered her mind, Dawn's leg shot out involuntarily and caught Jim's sharply on the tender portion of his calf muscle. The snoring stopped instantly. Cinnamon winked at Dawn. Dawn snuggled down again. A few minutes later, the rumbling began once more. Cinnamon leapt up and grabbed the Tempur pillow from under Dawn's head. It was weighty and sank in the middle. Straddling Jim with her long, strong legs, she placed the pillow over his head and prepared to hold it over his face. Dawn shook her head. *Too much, Cinnamon. He'll suffocate.* Cinnamon blew a strand of hair away from her nose, nodded, and got off Jim. Dawn leant across and instead pinched Jim's nostrils together until he started spluttering. As soon as he started coughing, she feigned sleep. Jim coughed some more, then got up for a drink of water. When he returned to bed, he turned over onto his side and dozed back off.

Dawn smiled quietly in the dark and held her thumb up to Cinnamon, who disappeared again into the recesses.

The closing movement *O Fortuna* from Carl Orff's *Carmina Burana* was reverberating around the room. Paint covered her hands, and flecks of vermillion stood out on her forehead. She didn't mind. She was totally absorbed in completing the second canvas, which had occupied her for more than a month.

The first painting was framed and propped up against the wall. It was a swirling mass of Byzantium, purple taupe, deep Tuscan reds, and greys. Wild spirals of colour mingled into lesser spirals of darker shades finally leading into jet. It was a moody piece that caused discomfort. The more one examined it, the darker it seemed to get; it was inescapable. The colours twisted and turned, trapping and dragging the viewer into the depths of the painting.

In contrast, this latest effort was inviting. It, too, was painted on glass. It had taken Cinnamon some time to master the technique of painting backwards onto the glass, but the effect was remarkable. This painting displayed spiralling colours which melted into one as they rotated away from the eye. Whereas the first painting left you sucked dry and depressed, the second piece gave off a feeling of warmth, painted in hues of rich reds, magenta, bronze, and burnt sienna. A hint of light pink illuminated the entire painting, creating an aura. The viewer once transported into this painting emerged with a sense of well-being.

Framing now completed, Cinnamon lifted the painting and stood it next to its sister. She had taken up art after several months of utter torment. When Geoff left her, she had crumbled. All the fears of loneliness and desolation that had been with her since childhood had surfaced and drowned her. For a while, she became insane. It had taken psychiatrists, doctors, and finally therapy to help her recover. Art had been part of that therapy. She had a natural talent, and art was the best medium for her to release her inner torments.

She found she could lose hours at a time when she was working on a painting or drawing. Time became irrelevant. She would forget to eat or rest. She had transformed one of the bedrooms in her house into an art studio. It faced south and was inevitably light. It was here that she would mix paints, try out new mediums, or draw.

These were the first paintings she had attempted on glass. She didn't paint them directly onto the front of the glass. Instead, she worked from behind the glass so that they had a natural protective front when mounted. The glass enhanced the colours and gave more depth to the pictures. They could almost be photographs on high-gloss paper with the sheen they emitted.

She was satisfied with them. Most of her work ended up in a cupboard, but these were pleasing enough to mount on one of her walls.

Cinnamon was content enough when she painted. She never craved the company of other people; in fact, she preferred to be alone. Some people were like parrots or monkeys— they needed to belong to a tribe or a community, she believed. Others, like herself, were happy prowling outside that community, like a lone wolf or a bear. She had been a bear long before Geoff, and once wounded, had returned to her solitary existence.

She moved to the house in Yoxall shortly after she left hospital. The village was quiet, and people were not nosey. She managed to live within a community who actually knew nothing about her. One or two villagers may have known her by sight, but she had maintained a low profile, situated as she was, away from the main thoroughfare.

Her house was her fortress. There she could spend hours painting, reading, or listening to music. She switched off the Bang and Olufsen sound system. She cleaned her brushes at a sink installed in one corner of the room. Leaving them to dry, she gazed again at the paintings. She opened a drawer from under the large worktable in the centre of the room and pulled out some small labels. She took out a calligraphy set and a bottle of black ink, then sat down to write the names of her sister paintings.

How much longer would this pain last? Every time she thought she had it under control, it would rear inside her, burning her, twisting in her stomach. Alex had broken through defences she had put in place and, in deceiving her, had set her back once more. She was better but she wasn't cured. The pain was still inside. She needed more than just painting to help her.

She had been such a fool since Geoff left. As soon as she was able, she had embarked on a series of disastrous relationships. She threw herself at every available man and bedded them. The psychiatrist had explained it was partly in retaliation but mostly because she had no self-worth. She had sought out men as lovers, confusing sex with love. The result had been a gradual breakdown, and for a while, she despised herself.

Therapy, followed by meditation, yoga and ultimately exercise, made her stronger. Superficially, she was healed. Inside, however, was a different matter. She had been thinking about it since she returned from ditching Alex's car. She needed to find a way to make herself feel better. The answer manifested itself more clearly in the early hours of the morning. She would try and help others so they didn't become wounded like she was. She would hunt down those who chose to hurt their loved ones.

She wrote with care. Her writing was large and precise. Cinnamon was used to taking her time. She had known what she would call these painting before she even began them.

Two small white cardboard squares, dated and signed with her name, were now ready to put on the back of the paintings. The first, which she put on the latest painting, was called *The Power of Love* and the other placed on the moody slate-grey and purple painting, *Infidelity*.

The unremarkable woman wearing a baggy cheap black cardigan and calf-length skirt attracted little attention from the morning shoppers gathered in the coffee shop. She was glued to an open copy of Thomas Hardy's *The Mayor of Casterbridge*. Cinnamon preferred it that way. Her dark mane of hair was scraped back in a scrunchie, twisted into an undefined hairstyle, half ponytail and half old-fashioned bun. Her piercing eyes were now shielded by plain dark-framed glasses with clear lenses. There was nothing wrong with her sharp eyesight, but somehow the glasses and librarian garb made her invisible to others and afforded her an anonymity she required. It was thanks to this anonymity that she could sit and eavesdrop without anyone taking a second look at her.

She had just read the passage in the book where a drunken Michael Henchard sells his wife, Susan, and baby daughter, Elizabeth-Jane, to Newson in an auction and was quietly fuming. She hoped he suffered a terrible fate. She would want to wreak horrible revenge on a man who thought so little of her as to sell her.

Her musings were interrupted by soft sobs coming from the table in front of her. One young woman wearing a concerned expression was attempting to comfort her friend, a woman in her late twenties whose face exuded unhappiness. Cinnamon's antennae went up, and although she pretended to be lost in the world of Casterbridge, she listened to the conversation playing out before her.

"He left his phone behind this morning. It was on the kitchen top. I didn't intend to pick it up, but it looks exactly the same as my phone, and I was in a hurry, so I automatically grabbed it and raced off to work. When I was on the train, it vibrated, so I opened the message." The woman paused to gulp and wipe a large tear rolling down her nose and threatening to plop into her latte sitting untouched in front of her.

She stared at the phone and read out the message that had upset her so much:

Morning, you naughty boy. I hope you managed to sneak in last night and not get caught out. Glad you liked my new baby-doll outfit. Next time, you get to wear the furry cuffs and get coated in chocolate. Still can't walk straight. See you at the weekend if you can get away. Love you Baby. x

She scrolled through the phone. "There are lots of messages. He always calls her "his little doll" and she always tells him he is her "baby". There are photographs too. She looks like just a doll. Her face is all pale, and she has the most beautiful long blonde hair. No wonder he fancies her. Look at me. I can't compare to that. I don't resemble a golden-haired Barbie doll like she does. I'm plump in comparison. I can't believe it. We've been together for seven years, and I had no idea he was having an affair."

"You have to confront him. Show him the phone," urged her friend.

"I can't do that. He'll say I was prying, and I had no right to take his phone to check up on him. He'll use that against me and make it seem it was my entire fault. He's good at that. Besides, I have no other evidence as such. You don't know him. He can get very mad about his privacy, and he'll take it out on me and Chelsea."

"Don't be silly. You're just overwrought because of this. He wouldn't hurt you and Chelsea's only six years old, for goodness sake."

The woman's silence said more than words. Cinnamon recognised that look of pain in the woman's eyes. She was a victim of abuse. Her friend hadn't picked up on it, though, and was more focused on the apparent affair.

"You need to do something, Charlotte. You can't let this continue. Have it out with him. Isn't there someone who can help you?"

"No, I don't think there is. I need to think. Maybe this affair will blow over. I'll put the phone back on the worktop and hope he doesn't realise I've seen the messages."

Cinnamon didn't listen any more. Two more customers had come to the next table and were discussing what to wear on Friday, to some party. She closed her book quietly and left the café where she stood hidden from view until Charlotte and her friends, left. She followed them.

Richard Tomkins was drinking beer from a can and watching television when the doorbell rang. His wife had gone out into town to visit a friend. They would no doubt sit about drinking wine and complaining about their lot in life. He palmed their daughter off on his mother for the night, hoping he could take advantage of the situation and visit his beautiful Barbie-doll mistress, but she had cried off when he had phoned earlier. She had been elusive and said he couldn't come round. He was still irritated by that. He might give her an extra-hard session next time he saw her to show her who was boss.

He dragged himself away from the football, can in hand, and answered the door. On the doorstep stood a huge live rag doll. It had an enormous head which was simpering in a coquettish grin. It was hideous. The doll carried a large CD player and held out a card.

On the card he read "A special present for my baby from his doll to say sorry—enjoy it, lover." He relaxed a little.

"You'd better come in," he grinned. Must have been from his Barbie. That woman! She was so full of surprises. What had she conjured up this time? He instantly forgave the earlier brush-off.

The doll nodded and put her CD machine down on the ground. She pressed the start button, and stripper music played. She shrugged off her coat to reveal a baby-doll nightdress with black panties, fishnets and Christian Louboutin high-heeled shoes.

Bloody hell, this one was a fit piece, he thought, feeling a familiar rise in his trousers.

The doll wiggled seductively and then skipped around him, making him dizzy. It was slightly uncomfortable seeing the large head with huge eyes staring at him. Fortunately, his eyes were drawn mostly to her firm rounded breasts, which needed no support. God, he could suckle hard on those. He hardened some more.

The doll bent over revealing silky white flesh between her stocking tops and her bottom. He groaned inwardly. God, this woman was a tease. Before he could react, she pulled out a large ruler and tapped it against her buttocks. He grinned wolfishly again and attempted to take it from her. She waggled her finger and gestured to his trousers.

"Oh, I get it. I've been a naughty boy and need spanking," he said, tongue moistening his lips.

The doll nodded an affirmative. She gestured again. He needed no encouragement and dropped his tracksuit bottoms to reveal a pair of boxer shorts and a magnificent erection. The doll feigned surprise by putting both hands to her mouth, and then pointing at him. He grinned again.

"I'm a proper man," he claimed. "Want to see what I mean?"

The doll nodded and flicked the ruler. He obliged and bent over the sofa. The doll whacked him gently, then a little harder, then harder still.

"Ow, careful. That last one hurt. You won't want to make me sore and angry. You won't like me when I'm angry," he commented.

The doll skipped forward again and rummaged in her bag. She pulled out some oil.

"Ah, that's more like it," he said, relaxing once more over the arm of the sofa, ready to be massaged.

The doll went behind him and doused his backside in oil, rubbing firmly into his cheeks and gradually moving her hands so her fingers slightly entered his anus.

"Ooh, that's nice, Doll! You can push harder if you want," he groaned. Instead of obliging, the doll returned to her bag. The machine was playing *Baby Love* by Diana Ross. She extracted something he couldn't see and moved closer to him. He could smell her perfume now. It was musky. The see-through nightdress clung to her breasts. Her nipples stood out under the material.

"Look, you're really sexy, and you're driving me crazy with desire, Doll," he said, "but the head is freaky. Could you take it off?" The doll nodded, then waggled the soft satin mask and black fur handcuffs, which she had extracted from her bag, at him.

"Okay, I get it. You promise you'll take the head off, if I wear the blindfold?" The doll nodded her grotesque head once more and shook the cuffs at him. He laughed and obligingly put his hands behind his back to be cuffed. She did so, then expertly tied the mask so he could see nothing. Leaning over the arm of the sofa again, he heard her remove the horrible rag doll head. He detected a muffled thump as it slipped onto the carpet. He bet she looked fantastic; actually, he didn't care what she looked like. Her body was all that interested him. He couldn't see her anyway, and that made it sexier. He was now reliant on his other senses, which only served to heighten his desire.

He felt breasts push into his back as she wriggled into him. The fabric of the baby doll nightie tickled him and aroused him further. He felt her breath on his neck and her fingers tracing lightly over his features seeking out his mouth. He felt her fingers gently pry his lips open. He opened his mouth to suck on them and found a lollipop being inserted. It was raspberry flavour. He sucked greedily, wishing it was the nipple of her breasts in his mouth.

She went back to massaging his buttocks in soft regular movements, in ever decreasing circles, until she found that place between his anus and scrotum. She gently probed. His breathing quickened.

He wanted to tell her that he would explode all over the settee, but the lollipop prevented him. She must have realised what he wanted because she rubbed her body up behind him, leant forward, and extracted the lollipop.

He groaned as she immediately went back to her probing. Her fingers were strong and urgent now. He wouldn't be able to contain himself soon. In, out, in, out, in. He yelped suddenly. She had pushed too hard that last time. She went in a long way too. He wasn't used to that. It wasn't what he liked. It also felt sharp. Was she using her nails? The probing now wasn't so pleasurable; in fact, it was a bit uncomfortable for him, and it was beginning to make him feel vulnerable.

Almost immediately, she placated him by pushing him forward and attempting to straddle him from behind.

"Like it rough, do you, you dirty doll," he began. "Let me out of these cuffs, and we'll see who can be the roughest."

It was the last thing he said.

Cinnamon struck the side of his jaw with a carefully aimed chop of her hand, making him lose consciousness immediately. The next Richard Tomkins knew, his wife was standing in front of him open-mouthed. He was tied to a kitchen chair, naked, apart from a baby's bonnet and a bib. His mouth was taped up and a lollipop stick was extruding from it.

As his wife saw him for what he was, Richard realised that the lollipop no longer tasted of raspberries and knew exactly what the hideous doll had been probing his backside with.

On the other side of Birmingham, a woman was staring at her reflection in the mirror. She wasn't sure how it had happened, but earlier that day, a large rag doll had barged into her apartment and smacked her in the face. She was forced to stare at her reflection in the mirror while the doll took a pair of scissors to her long hair and chopped it brutally. She had been given a message too from the doll, who had hissed at her before it left. "Stay away from other people's husbands, or you'll lose much more than your hair."

Dawn had spent most of the night in her office. She enjoyed writing about Cinnamon's outrageous behaviour. Now, she stood in the bedroom. She glowered at the middle-aged woman staring back at her. That woman had neglected to look after herself over the years. Her breasts weren't too low-slung, but there and again, she had never been blessed with large breasts, so they couldn't fall too far, or they would just be completely flat. They now hovered halfway down her chest, above a rounded belly that, in turn, hung over hips, once considered voluptuous, now just classified as wide. The tops of her legs had thickened over the years too, and if she turned sideways, she could see that gravity had indeed had a bad effect on her buttocks.

This woman was in dire need of a shake-up. Dawn didn't feel like sorting her shape out, though. She was used to looking like this. Wasn't this normal for women of her age? Besides, who would she be shaping up for? Jim didn't care what she looked like as long as she didn't balloon to enormous proportions and block his view of the television.

She attempted to suck in her belly once more. Only the top part of it moved, creating a strange silhouette. She gazed at her reflection once more. Cinnamon looked back at her, toned, slim, upright, and glowing with health.

"You want to be Mrs Blobby for the rest of your life?" Cinnamon asked, raising one eyebrow.

"No, but not everyone is as disciplined as you. Besides, it's only because of you that I exist."

Dawn had decided that she couldn't write about a gutsy, kick-ass, gorgeous female, who could drop-kick a grown man in a swift, Lara Croft move, and not even break into a sweat, if she knew nothing about kick-boxing other than what she learned from the internet. She had phoned up her nearest fitness centre to rectify that situation.

The Stay Fit Health Club had refused to let her sign up for kick-boxing classes. She had to be checked out by the staff first to ascertain her fitness levels and then undergo an exercise programme until the staff felt she could cope with the high-impact classes. She didn't need an exercise programme to work out her level of fitness. She hadn't done any exercise since school days, when she used to forge her own notes to get off PE lessons. She was always active and walked a lot in her youth, but somehow jogging or going to aerobics hadn't interested her. Up until she hit forty, her figure had been decent enough, so she hadn't felt the need to expend energy, not when she had a family to look after, a house to keep clean, and meals to cook.

A diminutive female instructor, kitted out in tight lycra shorts and a bright canary yellow t-shirt emblazoned with the name of the health club, was chatting to a tall Ralph Lauren model type when Dawn entered the gym, tugging at the bottom of her baggy sweatshirt in the desperate hope it would cover her large rear. In front of her was a bewildering array of machines. Mirrored walls threw back the reflections of toned bodies pulling on rowing machines, marching on step machines, and running on treadmills. In one corner, a lithe woman dressed in a short halter top and tiny bottom-clinging shorts was performing strange manoeuvres on a vibrating round plate as an instructor, also dressed in a canary yellow t-shirt, encouraged her.

The female instructor caught sight of Dawn tugging again at her sweatshirt and looking nervously around. She finished her conversation with the young man who immediately plugged buds into his elegant lobes, increased the pace on his treadmill, and began to run more intently, with a practised easy gait.

"Hi, you must be Dawn," the instructor said. Dawn wondered what information this girl had been given in order to make such an assumption. *Hey, watch out for an out-of-shape Telly Tubby to appear at 11am. She'll be so huge, she'll be dressed in voluminous tracksuit bottoms and an extra-extra-large sweatshirt. She won't be our usual trim sort in skimpy modern kit.*

27

"Eleven o'clock appointment? Dawn Ellis?"

Dawn nodded dumbly. "I'm Kiera, your instructor." Kiera's smile reached not only her very white teeth but touched her large hazel eyes. "Don't worry. It's always a little daunting at first, but we're a friendly bunch, and you'll soon get the bug."

"The bug?"

"The exercise bug. I bet in a couple of months we won't be able to throw you out of here at home time. Now, let's get started. We'll go into the office first to do the stats and tests. You won't be seen by any prying eyes in there."

Dawn followed Kiera's pert bottom into the office where she answered questions about her eating, drinking and smoking habits and her current exercise regime—none.

Kiera weighed her, measured her, and gave her the bad news about her body fat. Technically, she was in the obese category; however, Kiera convinced her it wouldn't take much to tone her up and transform her fat into muscle.

Next, she was fitted with a heart-rate monitor and was escorted to a treadmill. An hour and a half later, she confirmed what she already knew, but ordinarily refused to admit—she was a middle-aged woman who needed to do something about her body before it was too late. She signed up to four weeks' personal training with Kiera and explained that afterwards, she wanted to be able to learn kick-boxing. Kiera assured her that after four weeks training with her, she would be ready to kick ass in more ways than one.

Red-faced through exertion but determined, Dawn returned to the changing rooms to shower . Cinnamon gave her the thumbs up in the mirror as she peeled off her soaking wet clothes.

"You'll soon have a backside like Kiera's," she encouraged.

"Just one that didn't touch the back of my knees will do for me," replied Dawn and grabbed her towel.

Jim was still out when she returned home, her face still glowing. She made a cup of green tea and fired up her laptop. She already felt more like Cinnamon. She started typing. She had an idea of what Cinnamon might be getting up to.

The show had been quite enjoyable. Cinnamon enjoyed a trip to the theatre. She headed back to her car past the illuminated windows of shops that had been closed for some time. The streets were empty in the pedestrian precinct. As she made her way up to the car park, she was aware of a commotion in an alleyway leading from the shops. She slowed her pace.

"No, don't do that. I don't want to do that," slurred a female voice.

"Course you do. You've been after me all night. Come on. It's just a bit of fun," replied a male voice.

Cinnamon stopped by the entrance to the alleyway. The rest of the precinct was deserted.

"Shaz is getting married," slurred the voice again. "I'm gonna be the best bridesmaid. She's sooooo lucky."

"Yeah, you told me. That's enough now. Shh."

Two figures were in the gloom. A young girl, about nineteen, wearing a very short skirt and tight top was being held against the wall by a tall man. The girl could barely stand up and was unaware that the man had lifted her t-shirt and bra and was groping her breast hard while kissing her neck. His other hand was up her skirt, and he was struggling to pull down her knickers.

The girl surfaced to semi-consciousness. "No, don't do anything. I've not done it before. I want to be like Shaz and have a real boyfriend," she protested.

"I'm your boyfriend now," grunted the man and continued fumbling with her knickers.

The girl tried to push him off, but he was stronger and certainly more sober. He held her back against the wall with his hand on her breast. She slumped and began to cry. The man continued regardless.

Cinnamon moved silently into the alleyway.

"Leave her."

"Get lost. It's none of your business. Nosey cow."

Cinnamon closed the gap between them to stand directly in front of the man. He gave her a menacing look.

"I said, leave her. She's obviously had too much to drink and doesn't know what's happening."

"Shaz is getting married," sobbed the girl. Her eyes were unfocussed.

"Come on, sweetheart," said Cinnamon holding her hand out to the girl. "Let's get you home. Your mum will be wondering where you are."

The girl nodded dumbly.

"Who do you think you are? Get lost, you old bag," the man spat, still holding onto the girl's wrist.

Cinnamon moved in a flash. Before he knew what had happened, she had dragged him away from the girl who collapsed against the wall. She twisted his arm behind his back and pinned it into him causing him to scream.

"It doesn't matter who I am. I told you to *leave her alone*. She's drunk, and she shouldn't be persuaded to do things she might regret. If you want to ask her out nicely, when she is sober, then that's your business. At the moment, she isn't in a fit state to know what's going on. I'm guessing you're part of the reason she's drunk. I bet you plied her with drinks all night. Don't answer me. I'm going to drop your arm and take this girl away until she is sober enough to tell me where she lives. You, meantime, are going to buzz off, Sonny. If you decide to hang about, I'll break your arm, and maybe your neck too if you are a persistent pain in the arse. Got me?"

The man nodded, face screwed up in pain. He wasn't much older than the girl.

"I suggest you learn some manners if you want a girlfriend," hissed Cinnamon and dropped his arm.

The man rubbed it gingerly then slunk off. Cinnamon helped the girl to her feet, and stumbling, she accompanied Cinnamon back down the pedestrian arcade. They made it to the McDonalds restaurant where Cinnamon ensured she drank plenty of water until she sobered up a little.

It took a while until Cinnamon worked out that the girl had come into town with a group of friends to celebrate an engagement. The girls had all enjoyed a drink at the pub and then she had been approached by a young man, who began to chat her up and bought her some more drinks. She had only asked for orange juice, but she suspected he must have put something in it because the rest of the evening had become a complete blur. Her friends left the pub without her. She couldn't recall what happened after that until Cinnamon arrived. Cinnamon listened to the girl's ramblings. A mobile rang. It was the girl's. It was her mother.

"No, I'm okay, Mum. Don't cry. I'm fine. I forgot what time it was, that's all. No. I'm in McDonalds with a friend." She looked up. Cinnamon mouthed her name. "She's called Cinnamon. Yes, that is a nice name, isn't it? I'll be back in half an hour. I'll get a taxi. Yeah. Love you too."

The girl introduced herself as Naomi and thanked Cinnamon. "I don't know what would have happened if you hadn't found me. I'm so embarrassed. I shall make sure I never accept drinks again from anyone I don't know."

Cinnamon saw her to the taxi and then went to get her car. Good thing she had been around. Naomi seemed like a nice girl. Alcohol, she decided, had a lot to answer for.

Dawn stood at the stop of the concrete staircase leading into the museum and shook her umbrella vigorously, in an attempt to shake off some drops of water. It was hammering down with rain. The day had not begun well and threatened to continue badly.

Earlier that morning, Cinnamon suggested that rather than waiting for her next exercise class, Dawn should try doing some keep fit at home, in an effort to speed up her progress. Dawn had agreed that was a good idea. Her exercise kit was in the wash, so she settled on doing her exercises in her knickers and bra. Jim announced he was going out so she wouldn't be disturbed or, indeed, be ridiculed by him.

As soon as she heard the back door shut, she turned the radio in the bedroom up loud, and to *Pump up the Volume* began to do a few star jumps followed by frantic jogging on the spot, whirling her arms around like a windmill. She was soon breathing heavily. Cinnamon tutted. "I think you are supposed to warm up slowly. You'll keel over dead at this rate." Dawn took a ragged breath, turned the radio station over to something less energetic, and clearly heard an urgent knocking on the back door. Someone was there. Blast! She probably hadn't heard the knocking, thanks to the music. It was probably Jim. He had only been gone a short while. He had no doubt left his house keys behind again. He was always doing that.

She turned off the music, and the knocking continued, even louder than before.

"Coming," she yelled and dashed to the door. Opening the door, she saw it wasn't Jim. It was a post lady with a large box.

"Sorry, this has to be signed for. It's for Mr Ellis." she said, handing the box over to Dawn, taking in her underwear and flushed face at the same time. "I didn't interrupt anything, did I?" she asked.

"No, no, no!" replied Dawn with a nervous giggle. "What must you think?"

"It's not for me to comment. I see all sorts of things doing this job."

"I was, er, exercising," continued Dawn.

The post lady raised one eyebrow.

"I was. I'm trying to get fit, so I can learn to kick-box." The post lady's face was unreadable. She proffered an electronic pen attached to a grey machine by a plastic coil. Dawn put the box down then tried to suck in her stomach, maintain an air of dignity, and sign her name on the machine.

"Umm, where is Bill, our usual postman? Is he okay?"

"Oh yes. He retired last week. I've taken over the round. I'm Viv. Some call me Vivacious Viv. Don't know why, though. I feel done in half the time. I've lived in the village all my life. I live down the other end. I've been waiting for this round to come up for years. It makes my life a lot easier. I don't have to travel far when my shift is over, and I know quite a lot of the people in the village." She took the machine from Dawn and gave her a friendly smile. "Enjoy your *exercise* then. See you again. Bye."

Dawn didn't have the heart to go back to her dancing after that. She checked the parcel's sender. It gave nothing away. It would be the parts for the lawnmower Jim had been working on. She left it for him in the hall. Instead of exercising, she spent half an hour going through her underwear drawer throwing out all the grungy pairs of white-grey knickers. Fancy being caught in a pair of bright red pants with "I'm a Sex Kitten" written on them.

The day got worse. Jim got stuck in a lengthy queue at the DIY store and returned home later than arranged. Dawn was then late leaving home for her writing class. She couldn't find a parking spot on the road near the meeting place and had to use the supermarket car park, some distance away. Running down the high street to get to her writing class, she spattered dirty water up the back of her best boots and managed to get soaked down one side, when a four-by-four drove through a huge puddle, splashing her with a small wave of water. She wasn't in the best frame of mind when she arrived at the class. She hated being late.

She pushed open the large door, dropped her umbrella into a large pot by the table advertising guided tours, and then clattered up the wooden stairs behind the shop, dropping her notebooks as she went.

The monthly writing group was assembled on the second floor of the Samuel Johnson Bookshop and Birthplace Museum in Lichfield. It was an appropriate place for writers to gather. The building had a grand feel to it. The museum had a superb collection of manuscripts, books, paintings and prints from the eighteenth century.

Samuel Johnson was born in that very building. He was a writer and philosopher and became most famous for *A Dictionary of the English Language*, which gave an insight into the language of his day, and was the basis for later English dictionaries. It seemed fitting that they should be attempting to start their writing careers there in the same wonderful house.

Dawn breathed in the scent of wood and polish. She pushed open the door to the Wood Library and, apologising for her lateness, took up her place on a chair towards the back of the room, notebook in hand. She could hear the sounds of the market taking place outside. Muffled cries from vendors combined with the mellifluous tones of her tutor, Blake, soon relaxed her.

She took a few minutes to gaze at her fellow writers. She was always too busy taking notes, or hanging onto every syllable from Blake, to actually pay any attention to the others. Next to her, wearing a stylish turban, Turkish-style trousers and a dark maroon silk scarf over a lighter maroon silk blouse, sat Geraldine. She looked like an extra from an Agatha Christie drama. Elegant, with immaculately groomed nails and expertly applied make-up, Geraldine oozed class. Dawn suspected she was a widow and had been married to someone rather wealthy. Geraldine wasn't ostentatious and only someone who knew a lot about fashion and jewellery would have recognised that Geraldine sported a £15,000 Jaegar-LeCoultre watch under the cuff of her blouse and carried a Marc Jacobs purple Carolyn Crocodile handbag, costing approximately £18,500.

Her dress sense may have been tremendous, but the confident air that should have accompanied it was absent. Geraldine scurried rather than walked, and she appeared to be very nervous. At the first meeting, she was most anxious to explain she was having trouble with writer's block. She had come along to the group to see if it would help kick-start her writing again. At each session, they were given a writing task to complete as homework. Geraldine reminded them all before they left not to expect her to hand in any homework. She was, after all, just there to shake up her writing muse.

Seated right in front of Blake Ryder was Dotty. Her real name was Dorothy Fields; however, she insisted everyone call her Dotty, and not Dot. Dot reminded her of a character in *Eastenders*. As it happened, she was the complete opposite of that character, Dot Cotton. They may both have been a similar age, but Dotty had rosy cheeks, curly ginger hair and was three times the size. She looked like a friendly farmer's wife. It transpired she used to be a dinner lady at the local school. She had been retired for a year and was ready for a new challenge. She hoped to write a book with recipes in it. Not an ordinary cookery book, but one that had a story woven around the recipes. She brought in freshly baked cakes every meeting. Dawn's stomach gave a quiet rumble making her wonder idly what would be on offer today.

Blake was talking about the importance of being grammatically accurate. She put aside her thoughts to listen to the subject but was immediately distracted again. Jason, an attractive man in his late thirties arrived. He tapped lightly on the door, mouthed 'sorry' at Blake, and settled next to Dawn. She looked up to give him a smile and was surprised to find her stomach did a little flip. His deep chestnut hair had fallen over one dark hazel-coloured eye. That day, he had a fashionable amount of chin stubble which suited him well. His white t-shirt accentuated his muscled chest. He smelt of citrus and spice. He looked delicious—yes, delicious, that was the word. Feeling a warmth creep up her face, she pulled her gaze away.

Jason was one of those men you couldn't help staring at. He was just gorgeous. The first time they had all met Jason was sitting next to the youngest member of the group, Paige Willett. Paige had an arresting cleavage and eyelashes like tiny black fans. They were the longest eyelashes Dawn had ever seen, and framed Paige's azure blue eyes perfectly. No red-blooded man could have resisted shooting lustful looks at Paige. Even the oldest male in the group, Harold, was drawn to her magnificent chest on several occasions. Paige didn't mind. She thrust her assets out, sat with a straight back and a coquettish look on her face. Blake spent the first half an hour of that class talking to Paige's breasts before reluctantly dragging his gaze away to include the members of the class. Only Jason failed to notice Paige. Even when she sucked the end of pencil repeatedly, with plump red lips, making Harold almost drop his notepad. Jason, however, didn't seem to pick up on her sensuality. Unlike everyone else in the room, including Dawn, who wished she looked half as good as Paige. In fact, Jason seemed to be more focussed on Blake or Colin, who had a lot to say about libraries at that meeting, leading Dawn to conclude he might be gay.

Jason nodded at Dawn. She was staring at him again. She smiled back. Oh Lord, now he would think she was flirting. She dragged herself back to the conversation. Geraldine was complaining bitterly about the abuse of the apostrophe. She was fed up with seeing signs advertising goods or products with apostrophes in the wrong place. She declared she always wanted to scrawl on such signs with a large red marker pen. Colin nodded in agreement. Harold shouted "Hear, hear!" Blake took back control, nodding in agreement. He told the group he was going to give them all a grammar test, to make sure they were capable of writing accurately and to help give them pointers if they made mistakes. He then threw a glance at Dotty, who took her cue and announced that she would get some tea and cake ready to help fuel the brain cells for the test.

Jason leaned into Dawn. She caught the heady smell of his aftershave.

"Just like being back at school," he chuckled. Dawn sniggered.

"I wonder if we get to mark it ourselves or have to hand it into Sir," she replied.

"I'll do yours, if you do mine," said Jason.

"Deal, but be nice to me."

"I think we'll be able to come to some reciprocal agreement," he whispered.

Dawn felt a flush creep up her neck. She hoped he was gay or she might have been tempted to read more into that statement.

Checking she had milk, tinned sardines, and four bottles of Guinness, Dawn headed off to the car. She tried to visit her father at least once a week. He was fiercely independent, so she didn't want to make him feel too mollycoddled by her. Dan always tried to drop by once a week too and sometimes took his grandfather out to the pub for a pint.

Jack Cresswell still lived alone in a one bedroom cottage in the village of Alrewas. He had moved there shortly after Dawn and Jim had moved into the village nearby so that he could be close to his only family. Set back from the main road, the cottage was small but charming. Roses curled around the front archway to the front entrance.

Dawn parked on the roadside. She hated parallel parking, but there was no option here. Good thing Jim couldn't see his Volvo stuck out at an angle, she thought as she pushed the door to and alarmed it. She trotted up the front path. Her dad had been gardening again. There were neat pots of multi-coloured pansies by the door. Pansies had been her mother's favourite flower.

She didn't need to knock. Jack was waiting for her by the door, balancing on a walking stick. He beamed at her arrival. She dropped the bag of shopping onto the floor gently, hugged him, and then held him at arm's length to check him over. It was their ritual. She always made sure he wasn't looking thin or had not let his standards drop. Satisfied that he looked well, she gave him another hug, picked up the bag, and headed for the kitchen.

"I brought some of that marmalade you like, too," she said as she unpacked the bag, putting the shopping into the cupboards. She took note that he was running out of porridge.

"Have you got your list for this week?" she asked.

"All done," he replied placing an envelope on the worktop.

"You did put porridge on it, didn't you?"

Her father winked. "Of course I did. I can't be without that. It's what keeps me going. I swear by it. I'm sure it's helped me get to this ripe old age."

Jack was seventy-nine and sprightly with it, even though his legs had become frailer with age, and he needed the walking stick when he was tired. His eyes were still bright and from what she could gather so was his brain.

"I see you completed the crossword again," commented Dawn.

"It was very easy today. I finished it in fifteen minutes."

Dawn smiled at her father. He only bought the daily newspaper daily for the puzzles.

"I'd expect nothing else from a Mastermind champion!"

"It was only a pub quiz," said Jack.

"Nevertheless, you won it. And, I didn't know you were fan of Douglas Adams' books. You answered every question on that particular special subject."

"Always enjoy a well-written book, Dawn. You know that. I think you inherited your love of reading from me. By the way, I have a Terry Pratchett you might like to read. I thoroughly enjoyed it. Remind me to lend it to you."

She made a pot of tea for them both. He still liked a proper brew in a pot. She carried the cups and pot through to the lounge on a tray, along with a plate of his favourite Bourbon biscuits. The lounge was immaculately tidy. Logs were set up in the fireplace, ready to light later when it got colder. Dawn put the tray down on the side table near two armchairs. A large photograph of her mother watched them both from the same table.

"I told Mary Harper I couldn't do her garden. She was quite disappointed. I'd love to help her, especially now that Cliff, her old man, has passed on, but I have enough to do with my own and the other two ladies'," he said after he had sat down.

Her father was quite the local gent. When the weather was better, he helped local ladies with their gardens. He mowed their lawns and planted out flowers for them. He loved gardening. He didn't charge much for his time. As he had explained when Dawn told him he should charge for his services, "We're all pensioners and we don't have a lot of money for extras. As long as they make me a brew, bake me a cake, or give me enough money for a pint of beer, that'll do me. Besides, it keeps me fit and active, and those ladies keep me on my toes."

She was proud of her father. He had recovered from the tragic loss of her mother and although he was a late starter, he was there for her when she lost Elisabeth. He patted her hand and let her cry. He hadn't asked any questions or told her to try and get over it. He just held her and let her sob. He understood exactly what it was like to lose someone who meant the world.

"That cheeky Laura Marks asked me out last week for a dirty weekend in Blackpool," he announced.

Dawn spluttered some of the tea she had just sipped.

"Don't be surprised," he joked. "I'm quite a catch in these parts, you know. I have all my own teeth … and I can dance."

It was true. Her father could dance. He attended regular ballroom classes where all the single ladies would fight over him. He swore it kept him youthful.

"Are you going to take her up on her offer?" she asked.

"No, am I heck. There was only one woman for me … your mother," he said picking up the photograph nearest him and tenderly stroking it with his forefinger. "I realised that a long time ago. I like women, and I certainly enjoy their company, but I could never get involved with anyone other than Elisabeth." He touched his lips in a silent kiss and pressed them onto the photograph. "You know there isn't a single day that doesn't go by when I don't think about her or miss her. I talk to her every day and tell her what we've been doing. She's still part of my life. I just can't see her." He paused for a while. "What I'd give to see her again," he whispered.

Dawn leant across and put her hand on his knee. "I know, Dad. But she's still here in our hearts."

He pulled out a pristine white handkerchief from his cardigan pocket and blew his nose. His eyes looked rheumy, and Dawn was mindful of how fragile life was.

"Anyway, enough of this," he said suddenly. "What's it to be? Scrabble or backgammon? I have to warn you, you will be beaten. I am hot to trot at the moment."

"You got that expression from Dan, didn't you?"

"Oh yes. Talking of 'hot', haven't you got something to confess to your poor old father?"

Dawn looked confused.

"Dan dropped around on Monday night after work. He mentioned something about you, a young man, and hot-wiring a car." Her father raised his eyebrows at her.

"Little wretch. I thought he'd keep quiet about that. It was nothing. I was trying to see if it was viable for a woman like me to hot-wire a car, for a book I am trying to write."

"Ah! That explains it. A book, eh? Is it chick lit?"

"What do you know about chick lit?"

"You'd be surprised what old ladies leave lying about in their gardens on benches, tables, and the like," replied her father smiling. He picked up a Bourbon biscuit and dunked it into his cup. "Ah! You can't get a better dunker than a Bourbon," he said satisfied.

"No, it's not chick lit. It's sort of psychological. It's a bit of a mishmash of a Marvel Comic super heroine and a screwed up woman."

"Based on you, then," he joked.

She tapped him playfully with her fingers.

Tea finished, they set up the Scrabble board where her father trounced her soundly and ended the game by playing 'zealous' into a triple-letter score.

After lunch, her father was looking a little tired. He would no doubt have a nap after she left. He didn't protest when she said she should be going.

"See you next week, Dawn. Thanks again for all the shopping."

"It's a pleasure, Dad, as always. It's easier for me to buy it when I get ours than for you to struggle out on the bus and try to bring bagfuls home. Now, take care of yourself and watch out for that wicked Laura Marks. Don't want you being whisked off to the Pleasure Beach or anywhere else, for that matter."

He hugged her by the door. "You're a good person, Dawn. You remind me a lot of your mother. Good luck with that writing. I think it's a corking idea you're writing a book. It's about time you did something for yourself. Let me know how it goes. By the way, Dan said he's taking me out to the arboretum next weekend for a little walk and lunch with him and his girl, Phoebe. I'm a lucky old sod really."

She made sure she had pocketed the shopping list and clambered into the Volvo. She blew him a kiss and waved before she turned the key in the ignition. Her father was watching by the door and stood waving. He continued to wave long after she had driven out of sight.

"If a reader can't engage with a character, then your novel or story will be doomed from the off," Blake announced in a theatrical fashion. "Your character needs to have appeal. Readers must empathise with or detest your character. Evoke some emotion in your reader, even if it is hate or fear. Take Shakespeare. Mark Antony and Hamlet were heroes, but they were heroes who were tragically flawed, which made them appear more human. Your main character can't be perfect. They need to have a flaw ... or possibly an illness. Modern-day characters must appeal to today's modern audience," he added looking suddenly deflated by his words. He shoved a piece of chocolate muffin into his mouth, crumbs falling onto his notepad.

A few moments later, he looked up again. "I think you would all benefit by making your character as realistic as possible. What I propose for your homework this week, is to put up a profile for your character on Facebook or Twitter and see if you can attract any followers or friends. Make your profiles as convincing as possible. We could have a little competition to see who can attract the most attention and friends. Don't tell us who they are —just see if you can convince others they are real. Engage in conversations as if you were that person."

There was immediate confusion in the room.

"What's Twitter?" asked Geraldine.

"Stupid place where people write pointless rubbish and fill up spaces with hashtags," replied Colin, slamming his own notepad shut.

"I'm on Twitter," offered Harold. "I don't understand it, but I am following my favourite authors. I find out when they are releasing books or doing signings. I follow Stephen Fry. He's jolly amusing."

Colin stared coldly at Harold. "It's rubbish. People spend far too much time on the internet. They should be reading books. No wonder libraries are closing all over the place when children would rather see who is trending on their mobile phones than read a good book." With that, he scraped back his chair, stood up, and declared, "That is not the sort of homework I wish to undertake, Mr Ryder. I shall write a poem or a short story instead. That would be far more productive."

Blake pushed back his hair which was beginning to fall across his face. "Whatever, old chap. It's not compulsory. I'm just here to help you guys get ahead, and be able to swim in the vast ocean of writers, who are also trying to become recognised. Times have changed you know, and you have to keep up with modern technology, social networking, and DIY marketing. It's a fag, but it has to be done."

"No, it doesn't. And I, for one, don't intend to become an internet junkie like everyone else today," Colin huffed. With that he put on his hat, wished everyone a 'good afternoon', and left, shutting the library door quietly behind him.

Blake watched his departure with little interest. It was true. You had to keep up with technology. It was dog-eat-dog out there, and now, even *he* spent endless hours attempting to promote his old-fashioned detective books to a world that hungered for teenage vampires and erotic literature.

People like Colin would not survive. The old ways had died. You could no longer send your script to a publisher, who would eagerly sweep it away, offer you a ridiculously large advance, and then market your books. Nowadays, the Big Six favoured celebrities and sure bets. They had no choice. It was getting tougher for publishers, just as it was getting harder for everyone.

These people in front of him would probably fail just like he had. He was a dinosaur. One only had to look at all the indie authors who were taking over the charts. They all had blogs and Facebook pages with thousands of 'likes'. They tweeted about what they were doing to their adoring fans. Blake had tried to get his share of internet fame, but his fans were probably people who didn't use the internet or social networking sites. How he loathed the way the world had changed. If traditions had been maintained, he shouldn't have been doing this to earn a living: advising and cajoling housewives and retired folk? He should be sitting in the southern Spain outside his new villa, enjoying royalties from his books, not earning a few quid here and there to keep him going and trading off his past success.

Besides, Colin was writing stuff that kids in the fifties and sixties enjoyed. Children today had sophisticated tastes. Poems and stories about eating worms were old hat. Yet, he felt sorry for Colin. Christ, the poor man ran a teddy bear shop and still lived with his mother! He hadn't really adapted to an adult world, whether that was through choice or not. He wanted the world to be as he had known it as a child. And, he wanted children to enjoy childish pleasures he had known, including literature when it had seemed to be somehow more innocent. Blake felt sorry for Colin, because Blake felt sorry for himself. He too was a has-been.

He forced a smile. Dawn was looking directly at him with concern etched on her face. She was a pleasant woman. She lacked confidence, though. That was for certain. After the first class, she had waited until everyone had left, then coyly asked him to sign one of his own Bashkov novels for her. He gave her a friendly wink and continued to address the class. "Well, you don't have to do this homework. I feel it could be beneficial. After all, when you finish your novels, you are going to have to get used to these social networking sites, and what better way to kill two birds with one stone than by pretending to be one of your characters? If you don't fancy having a go, then write a two-hundred-and-fifty-word flash-fiction story. Continue from this start..." He paused, as he thought up a suitable beginning. His pupils scribbled furiously on their notepads. "The seagulls were circling now, their cries getting louder and louder. I watched as their numbers grew until the sky grew dark with them..."

Blake slumped in his chair as the class ended. Dotty fussed about, clearing up the half-empty biscuit packets. Geraldine raced off first, claiming she needed to get started on the flash-fiction exercise while she had so many ideas in her head. Chances were, she wouldn't manage it. The woman hadn't written anything since the class begun a few weeks earlier, coming up with various excuses for not bringing any homework in. Blake wondered if she could write at all. Still, he wasn't there to judge. It had been some time since he had put pen to paper too. He just didn't have the heart any more.

The group packed up. Paige, Craig, and Margaret were swapping Facebook details. At least they knew what Facebook was. Dawn thanked him, wished everyone a nice weekend, and scuttled away. Jason followed her. Blake nodded goodbye to him. He couldn't make Jason out. He was a good-looking guy who didn't seem to realise it. Most men with a terrific physique like Jason's would have been flaunting it in front of the women there. Blake certainly would have. Jason always seemed to have his head down and didn't speak very often. He could have been one of life's observers. It would have been good for his writing if it were the case.

Craig left next. He was the class clown. Blake wasn't too sure why a car salesman would want to take writing classes, but he learned a long time ago to be surprised by nothing. His attention was suddenly drawn back to the room by a cough.

Harold loitered near the window, as he did every session. Blake groaned inwardly. If the wretched man wanted him to look at his screenplay again, he would hit him over the head with his notepad. It was the same every time he visited this group. Harold had been writing his screenplay for twenty years and had only managed to put together a couple of scenes. It wouldn't have been too bad if he didn't insist on sharing his progress with Blake every session. Harold would collar Blake, make some comment about how his project was coming along, ask to show Blake what he had done, "to make sure I am on the right lines", and then would spend a further half an hour revealing what amounted to only a few lines. Blake hadn't the heart to shoot him down in flames. He should have. The script wasn't badly written, but so far was beginning to sound exactly like the plot of Top Gun.

Harold, however, didn't stay behind to show him his play. He only wanted to check on how to produce em dashes and en dashes on his keyboard. Blake was dashed if he knew and told him to Google it, as he had to rush off. As he left, he noticed Jason climbing into a bright red MG driven by a rather attractive piece. Lucky sod, he thought. Well, that would certainly explain why Ms Willett couldn't grab his attention. Now, why would a man like that be a member of a writing group?

Frustration didn't begin to cover it. Dawn was fed up to the back teeth with being ignored. The night before, she had tried to interest Jim in some sexual activity, but he rolled over and ignored her. It had been months since they had last made love. She wouldn't have minded, but since she had begun exercising, she was beginning to feel better about herself and her body. She felt she should be attracting some attention, especially from her husband. He seemed to be the only person she knew who hadn't noticed she was looking trimmer. Even Jack had commented on his last visit that she was looking more like her old self.

What was she supposed to do? Sit on the kitchen sink stark naked? Jim wouldn't have blinked an eyelid if she had done. She wasn't a highly sexed person, and to be fair, she often just wanted to get it over so she could get some sleep, but this complete blank was making her depressed.

She stood up straight in front of the long mirror and turned sideways. She looked in decent shape for a woman of her age. Okay, she was definitely not slim, but she could have been called curvy, and in the dim lighting, stretch marks or wobbly bits weren't noticeable. What could she do to get Jim's attention?

"It's his age," commented Cinnamon from the bed. She was sitting on the edge of it, filing her long, painted nails. They were a deep maroon colour and matched her lipstick. Dawn looked at her own broken nails and made a mental note to file and paint them later that day. "His libido has dropped. His hormone levels have dropped, like yours have, and he's discovering he can't perform certain activities like he could. It's not just his age. It's probably all related to being thrown out of his job. He's been emasculated. That has affected his physical prowess and, consequently, his ability to perform in the bedroom. Let's be truthful here, he's never been that great, has he? Not that you'd know what 'great' is. He is ignoring you, rather than try to start something he is worried he might not be able to finish. Check it out on the internet. He's got physical difficulties due to stress and anxiety."

Dawn reflected on that for a while. It made sense. Jim had changed dramatically since he gave up working. He was much more short-tempered than he ever used to be, and he seemed to be dispirited. She dressed and fired up the computer. There was plenty of information on various health websites. Three hours later, she was convinced her husband was definitely depressed and that the depression was due to being unemployed. She needed to help him. First things first, she needed to make him feel masculine. Cinnamon hovered about all the time she was online. She kept whispering in Dawn's ear. In the end, Dawn gave in. She typed the word Viagra into Google and read some of the pages that came up.

It took no more than a click of a button for the deed to be done. Cinnamon yawned and stretched. "That should sort you both out. Now, what shall I get up to? I feel like having my own night of torrid sex with a good-looking man. Could you write me a nice scene, please?"

"Cinnamon, if I could muster up the imagination, I would, but at the moment I'm stumped. You'll have to have a night off. I can't do sex scenes. I am in an angry mood anyway, so I can't even fire up any faded memories."

Jim clattered about downstairs. He was still working on the lawn mower, and Dawn had given up asking him to move it.

"It's not like you use the kitchen much, is it?" he complained when she nagged him to take the machine outside. "It's cold out there. Besides, I don't have the space to put all the bits and pieces. I could just leave it if you prefer, and we'll let the grass grow up around the window instead," he had argued.

Dawn threw in the towel. There was no getting through to him these days. It was so much easier when he used to be out at work or off with workmates. Since he had been at home, he had done nothing but mess up her days. She now sat in her office holding a cigarette out of the bedroom window. Jim would go ballistic if he knew she had taken up smoking. She took a drag and immediately started coughing.

"Cinnamon, you're going to have to give up the cigarettes. They are disgusting and don't really help with stress. Besides, it's not healthy to smoke, and you're obsessed with your health," she decided after a few minutes.

"I am not obsessed with my health; I am obsessed with being strong. I can give up the cigarettes. I can give up anything. It's you who needs to give them up."

"Good, because I am writing them out of the story. You'll have to get rid of your frustration in different ways," said Dawn, stubbing out a half-smoked cigarette and crumpling up the remainder of the packet.

"Please yourself. You're writing this story, not me." Cinnamon stretched again and sat down beside her.

"We'll soon see how strong you are, my friend," said Dawn. "First though, I need to do my homework."

This whole Facebook and Twitter thing was beyond Dawn. She had wasted an entire evening trying to set up a Facebook page for Cinnamon. She wanted to write a book, not start conversations with strangers on the internet. She was happy being anonymous. If she had wanted friends, she would have made some real ones before now. She was content enough with her own company. She had been alone for many years. She wasn't one of life's socialites.

What was she supposed to say to these new online buddies anyway? She appreciated that Blake was only trying to get everyone to create lifelike characters and get this group to employ new technology to help them become successful as writers, but she just couldn't comprehend the appeal of Facebook or Twitter.

Cinnamon was as real to her as any living person she knew, she mused. Cinnamon had history. She was everything Blake said she should be. She was flawed, although not tragically so. Dawn had no intention of killing her character off. Readers could sympathise with Cinnamon. Dawn had read enough novels to understand the importance of credible and likeable characters. It was much easier to enjoy a story if the character was likeable or dislikeable; a reader became a sort of voyeur into their lives and, in some cases, felt part of the story.

She could hear Jim in the bathroom cleaning his teeth. It was 8.30pm. Honestly, the man would soon be going to bed mid-afternoon. She would work for a couple of hours before she turned in. Dawn opened up the Word document she had been drafting for her book. She had an inkling of an idea of how she could convince her readers that Cinnamon was likeable, and at the same time, reveal some of her tragic past.

Cinnamon strode out of the newsagent. Ripping the cellophane wrapper from the new packet of cigarettes, she didn't, at first, register the face of the woman who barrelled into her. It was the squeal of alarm that made her look up, and into the flushed face of her nemesis, Jessica.

Before Jessica could race off, a strong arm whipped out and grabbed her by the wrist. She was powerless. Cinnamon's grip was vicelike. Jessica gulped.

"Cinnamon, is that really you? You look … fantastic … really fantastic … amazing, in fact. You've lost so much weight, and well, I didn't recognise you." She licked her drying lips. Cinnamon's eyes narrowed. Holding on tightly to Jessica, she marched across the road. Jessica scurried alongside, stumbling to keep up with her.

"I know we have a lot to catch up on, but could you slow down? In fact, could you stop, please? I can't keep up with you."

Cinnamon stopped abruptly by a bus shelter. Checking no one was in sight, she pushed Jessica roughly into it.

"Why are you here?" she snarled.

"My auntie," puffed Jessica. "She's sick. I had to come to visit her. She lives in the next village. I nipped out to buy a couple of magazines and to get some fresh air. What are you doing here? I thought you lived in Lichfield."

"I sold that house after you stole my husband. I live here now."

"About that—"

"Shut up. Someone is coming."

"Look, Cinnamon. We probably need to talk about ... you know what."

Cinnamon stared hard at Jessica. She lifted the packet of cigarettes and flicked the lid then tapped one out into her long fingers. Slipping her hand into her pocket, she extracted a silver lighter and, with one click, lit the cigarette now held by two crimson lips. She inhaled deeply, nodded to the person walking by the shelter, then pushed the packet of cigarettes and lighter back into the pocket of her coat. She took another lengthy drag then casually blew smoke into the air. She looked into Jessica's eyes, making her squirm. "Okay. Talk. But not here. You can come to my house."

With that, she grabbed Jessica's wrist again, and together they paced up the road. They crossed over a small bridge, under which a swollen stream hissed and bubbled. Cinnamon traversed the road and dived up a track on the right, hidden behind a large Victorian house, and then veered left, down a rougher track. At the end of that track, hidden among tall pine trees, stood an imposing black and white house.

"Is this yours? Gosh, this place is much larger than your old house," commented Jessica.

Cinnamon ignored her. She stepped up to the front door and rooted deep in her coat pocket for her keys. There was a loud bleeping as the door swung open. Jessica found her hand dropped as Cinnamon punched in a code to disarm the alarm. Jessica took in the huge entrance. Cinnamon was clearly not short of money. The hall was simple but tastefully painted. An impressive wooden staircase rose ahead of them. She walked inside. To the left was a living room. Again, painted in simple tones of grey and cream, it looked classy. It was furnished minimally. Modern silver, grey-and-bronze-coloured curtains framed the windows. A marble coffee table stood in front of two enormous cream sofas. A large fireplace dominated the room. Above the fireplace was an attractive modern mirror and reflected in the mirror was a stunning painting. Jessica squinted to see the reflection more clearly. It looked like Jackson Pollock's Convergence. Jessica loved art. She had studied it at college. In those days, she had wanted to be an artist, but life had blocked that choice for her. She was very keen on abstract expressionism and had even been to a Pollock exhibition taking place at the Tate in 1999. Although the painting looked authentic from this distance, she realised it must have been a print. Funny that Cinnamon liked that type of art.

Before she could ask about it, she was shoved towards a door on the right. It opened into a kitchen where cream cupboards and dark marble tops gleamed. A large cream Aga stove stood at the far end. Jessica had always wanted an Aga. A beautiful dark oak table was placed in the centre of the room. Heavy bespoke oak chairs were set around it. The table seemed out of place. Jessica couldn't work out why, and then it hit her—there was nothing on the table, neither indeed on any of the work tops. There were no bowls of fruit, food processors or ornaments that make a kitchen cozy. The table was bare. There was no runner or tablecloth. There was no flower arrangement, nothing, not even candles. The impression was one of a kitchen with no heart. It was smart but soulless. Jessica doubted if Cinnamon had ever cooked in here.

Cinnamon pointed to a chair. Jessica pulled it out, noting how heavy it was, and sat down.

"I don't know where to begin, Cinnamon."

"How about why you pretended to be my friend for four years," growled Cinnamon opening a cupboard behind Jessica. She took out a porcelain ashtray which she clattered onto the table. "My best friend? My only friend? Or, how about telling me when it was that you began having an affair with my husband? Did you fancy him first and decide to become my friend to get to him? Was your friendship for real, or was it all an act? Did you and he laugh behind my back together marvelling at how gullible I was?"

Jessica's mouth opened and shut. The hurt and anger were palpable.

"Okay, let's—" she began.

Cinnamon threw open a drawer and rummaged about in it. Before Jessica could say another word, she felt her hands being tugged behind her. Grasped firmly together, she couldn't move them. She yelled out, "That's enough, Cinnamon. Pack it in or I won't explain anything. Leave me alone. Let go of my hands. You're hurting me. Stop it! What's the matter with you? You were never like this. You're barking mad."

The protests were in vain. In an instant, her hands were tied firmly behind her, binding her to the chair and restricting movement.

"Right, now we'll do some proper talking, my bestie," spat Cinnamon appearing in front of Jessica and lighting up a cigarette. "And, I want answers."

Dawn yawned. It was late. She had to get some sleep. She had a training session in the morning with Kiera, and she needed to be on form. Cinnamon would have to wait until tomorrow, yet Dawn felt she should keep typing and unveil Cinnamon's dark secrets. A muffled cough reminded her that Jim was in bed. It wouldn't be long before he would get up again. She had better turn in for the night. She saved her document and turned off the laptop.

"Night, Cinnamon. Be nice to Jessica."

She was sure she heard a voice replying, "For the moment…"

"Well done! You have lost five pounds," crowed a satisfied Kiera as Dawn stepped off the scales. Dawn returned her smile. She had only been working out for three weeks, but she already felt stronger and fitter than she had done in a long time. Kiera's enthusiasm was infectious. Dawn had quickly adapted to the demands made on her ageing body and now, when Kiera put the treadmill speed up a couple of notches or gave Dawn a heavier weight to work with, Dawn would oblige and try harder.

It hadn't been easy. After the first session, Dawn thought she would never be able to move again. She had an acute case of the DOMS, as Kiera explained—delayed onset of muscle soreness, thanks to working muscles which had, hitherto, been enjoying a very long holiday. After the second session, during which Dawn had squeaked with pain every time she attempted a sit-up, Kiera had given her a sports massage. It wasn't quite what Dawn had expected. It was anything but relaxing and had made Dawn shriek expletives each time a sore spot was pressed, but it did the job. Later that same night, after luxuriating in a scented warm bath, Dawn felt much better.

Kiera had since shown her how to stretch thoroughly so she wouldn't experience similar pain again. Dawn now did the stretches at home every morning and night, and they were certainly making her supple. She could almost touch her feet without bending her knees, and her calf muscles no longer felt like they would snap if she ran down the street. Kiera had been a miracle worker. Dawn had gone from a middle-aged flabby woman to one who now took more pride in her physique. It was astonishing how little time it had taken. Dawn had surprised herself at how determined she had become to get fit. She was convinced Cinnamon was urging her on with the same determination she possessed when exercising.

"You're the ideal client," continued Kiera as they went into the gym together to do some warm-up stretches. "You don't moan, and I can push you to work harder. I wish all my clients were like you. It's been fun working with you. In fact, your stamina levels have improved so rapidly, you'll be able to start kick-boxing lessons next week."

"Excellent. I am dying to learn some of the moves."

"Yes, well, there is one slight problem. I won't be teaching you those moves," said Kiera as two bright spots appeared on her cheeks. "The doctor said I'm not to do too much high impact stuff now," she continued and gave Dawn a knowing look.

"Oh my goodness," whispered Dawn, "you're expecting, aren't you?"

The look on Kiera's face confirmed Dawn was right. "It's early days yet, so I haven't broadcast it. Keep it to yourself for now. I don't want everyone to know."

"That's fantastic news. Congratulations. I'd give you a hug, but that might make the others wonder what was up."

Kiera giggled. "So, if you don't mind, I am going to let you be taught by our very best martial arts expert. He has trained in Thailand and has lots of awards. You can start one-on-one with him, so you can learn the basic moves and then join the regular class on a Friday morning. They are a tough bunch, but very friendly. You don't mind working out alone with a man, do you?"

"No, as long as he's gentle with me."

"Oh, he's a perfect gentleman. I promise he'll be able to teach you more in a few lessons than I could teach you in a couple of months. He's not here at the moment. I'll introduce you to him when you come next time."

The training session went well. As well as a session that involved jogging, cycling, rowing, and leaping up and down on small step, holding weights until she was bright red, could go. Dawn wished she didn't sweat so much, but when she watched herself lifting a barbell in the mirror, she was secretly pleased with the rapid progress she had made. She stood taller, and that, in turn, made her appear slimmer.

Kiera watched over her ensuring she didn't injure herself, coaxing her to attempt one more set of repetitions. The session completed, Dawn thanked Kiera who sent her off with a wave. "See you on Thursday," she called out as Dawn was leaving, "You're looking good from behind, Dawn. Those buns have lifted. We'll make a supermodel of you yet!" Dawn affected a model's walk and swaggered out of the gym to the sound of Kiera's laughter.

She turned the corner to go to the changing room and caught sight of someone she knew. Coming towards her, one arm draped around the shoulders of a stunning female instructor, was Jason from her writing class. She was going to say 'hello' to them. She had seen the woman before. She had dropped in to the gym on her way to an exercise class. Kiera had pointed her out. She was called Agniezska and came from Poland. Apparently, she taught an extremely popular spinning class. Dawn suspected the class would be stuffed full of admiring men. She was mesmerised by Agniezska when she saw her. She was very tall, raven haired and possessed an aura that attracted attention. Dawn could imagine her as a Bond girl. She would have made a fantastic Eastern European spy, who could steal any man's heart. Jason was engrossed in a conversation with Agniezska, who was smiling warmly at him. Best not to embarrass him in front of what was clearly his girlfriend, she decided, and scuttled off out of their path into the female changing room before they noticed her.

Well, what a dark horse Jason turned out to be. He probably worked out here, too. That would certainly account for his rather muscular body. Yes, she had noted it. There had been several opportunities to take in his physique. This would have also explained why Jason hadn't noticed blonde bombshell, Paige Willett, who fluttered eyelashes at all the men in the writing group. Her suspicions that he was gay were obviously incorrect. Besides, who would look at Barbie Doll, Paige Willett, if you were with a woman like Agniezska? She might mention something to him when she next saw him at the writing class. Tell him what good taste he had in women or something witty, if she could think of anything.

Showered and changed, Dawn rushed off, forgetting Jason and his beautiful friend. She had shopping to do, and joy of joys, she and Jim were supposed to be going to the DIY store together to choose some paint for the back door, then she had to get the weekly shop. I mustn't forget Jack's list Oh, to have a life less ordinary! Cinnamon wouldn't be busy doing such menial tasks.

Viv stood on the doorstep grinning wildly. Her electronic signature pad stuck out of her coat pocket, and her hands were behind her back.

"Morning!" she trumpeted when Dawn opened the door. "Got something for you, all the way from Canada." A rather small packet covered in sticky labels appeared. Viv gave it a little shake as she handed it over, beaming at Dawn again.

"Now, let me see, what might it be? A tiny can of maple syrup, perhaps, or maybe a small model of a beaver, or some super-duper pills you can't get in Boots?" she joked. "What would you order online from Canada?" She asked, waggling her eyebrows in a comic fashion.

"Ha ha, nothing special, just some pills, some pills for women, you know for older women, to assist with …" She tailed off wondering why she was being so defensive. Viv always liked to tease. It was guilt that was making her so prickly. She backtracked as she tried to scrawl her signature on the pad. "Bet you thought I was getting something for Jim," she said, then immediately wished she hadn't spoken. Was that a look of confirmation that fluttered across Viv's face?

Viv took the pad from her and shoved it back in her pocket. "Hope they, you know … make you feel better," she said with a wink.

Dawn mumbled her thanks. As soon as she shut the door, she leant against it and groaned loudly. Her words would have confirmed Viv's suspicions. She would know what was in the package; after all, the woman had been doing this job for years. She must have delivered packages just like this to other houses. Oh Lord, what if she told anyone in the village? It could get back to Jim. He would be humiliated. Worse still, Dan might get to hear about it. It would be dreadful if his parents were the laughing stock of the village. What would he think of his frisky parents? Dawn hadn't thought this through. She should have just laughed it off at the door and agreed with Viv that there was a tiny beaver or a miniature brown bear in the parcel or jewellery from a Canadian friend. She could have handled this differently. Dash it all! Now she felt guilty.

She shook the parcel. It didn't rattle. She checked the labels. The parcel was fairly anonymous. Her heart eased its thumping. Perhaps Viv had no idea what was in it. The more she thought about it and looked at the packet, the more she convinced herself that Viv could not have known for sure that it contained Viagra pills. She took it upstairs to the bathroom, where she opened it. It was Cinnamon's fault she now held little blue pills in her hand and was planning on turning Jim into a sex machine.

On cue, Cinnamon appeared as Dawn hovered over the toilet, considering flushing the pills down it.

"Ah! Those'll put some lead in his pencil," she drawled.

"I'm not so convinced. I did some more research online. Some of these things aren't safe. What if they are Chinese fake pills and are made up of blue paint and lead? Or, what if they make his heart beat too fast and he dies of over-exercise?"

"Or, over-sexercise," suggested Cinnamon and snorted. "Of course he won't drop dead. It'll give him a night to remember. And what about you? When was the last time you had a wild passionate night of sex … or any sex that lasted longer than twenty seconds? Oh, all right, thirty seconds," she added thoughtfully as Dawn shot her a look. "Come on, Dawn. If you're that worried about it, cut the pill in half or quarter it, just to test it out. You need to remember what it's like to have such a fantastic night of raw sex that you drip sweat and can't walk straight for a week."

"Sometimes, I can't believe the things you come out with," Dawn huffed, adopting a prudish tone.

"Fine. Don't bother then. See if you can add some spice to your life and our book by using your imagination. Let me guess, the next chapter containing a sex scene will go something like this … Cinnamon coyly lifted her nightgown to reveal her secret area. He looked lovingly at her, tracing the contours of her body with his fingertips, making her tingle in anticipation, then he leapt on top of her and rode her hard. After thirty seconds she cried out as she climaxed … blah, blah, blah. Do you even remember what an orgasm is? Or foreplay?" With that, she disappeared.

Dawn mumbled to herself and slipped the pills into her make-up bag. Cinnamon was right, as usual. At her age, she should be able to conjure up sex scenes from experience. Jim was in for the surprise of his life.

Jim was out. This was the first time since he had been forced out of work that he had gone out on an evening. Before, he had often gone out and left Dawn watching television with Dan. Today, he had spent half an hour in front of the wardrobe staring at his clothes, sighing in an infuriating manner. Dawn was working in her office and could hear him chuntering in the bedroom. He was clearly in a strop. Drawers were being slammed shut. In the end, she couldn't concentrate, so she stomped out to see what the problem was.

Trousers, shirts, and ties were strewn over their bed in a pile. Jim was hurling a grey suit on the floor in annoyance when she entered the bedroom.

"What's the matter?"

"I haven't got anything to wear!"

Dawn clasped her hand to her mouth to stop the squeal of laughter from erupting. This was too much.

"None of this stuff will do," huffed Jim. "Look at these." He held up a pair of smart dark blue trousers.

"They are very nice—" she began but was shot down with a steely glare.

"No, Dawn, they are not very nice. They are very smart. They are a very, very smart pair of Oscar Jacobsen trousers that cost me almost a month's salary. They are a pair of useless, very smart trousers that I can no longer wear. Let's face it. I'll look a complete prat dressed in these and a Jaeger shirt down the local pub, won't I? They are very smart clothes for a man who had a prestigious job, a man who had worth, a man in employment, and well, I … don't … go … to … work anymore."

He tossed the trousers onto the pile now forming on the bed. "And these," he dragged out a pair of beige slacks, "they are useless. And these," he continued to pull out items of clothing in a frenzy, "all bloody useless. Just like me!"

Dawn wasn't laughing any more. In fact, a cold hand was

squeezing her heart. Jim was about to have a meltdown. She had to do something. She hurried forward and seized a pair of blue corduroy trousers and a soft blue shirt.

"These'll look good. You can wear these. We'll go through the wardrobe and get rid of the clothes that are no good anymore. I'll bag them up, and we'll take them to the charity shop.

Jim stared at her, calming slightly as he took in the corduroy trousers.

"Okay," he replied and turned back to the pile, picking up the beige trousers he had just thrown down, smoothing them back down and putting them back on the hanger. He looked wistfully at them and back at the pile. "We'll throw some stuff out. Not tomorrow. Maybe next weekend."

Dawn was relieved Jim had gone out. He needed to get away from the house that was rapidly turning into a prison. A night out with an old work colleague, who had also recently retired, would be just the thing for him. It was incredible how circumstances could change someone so rapidly. Jim hadn't been the same since he had lost his job. Cinnamon hadn't been the same since her husband had walked out on her. With Jim out for the night, she could write in peace and let Cinnamon face her demons.

Jessica's arms were still tied behind her back. Cinnamon was prowling about the room. She thumped the wall with her fist.

"You duped me, you bitch," she growled.

"I didn't dupe you," sobbed Jessica. "We were friends. You were... my... best friend."

"Liar! How dare you lie to me, even now!" She pulled Jessica's hair hard, dragging her head backwards, making her yelp in pain. "You were the only person I confided in. I trusted you. I told you secrets and innermost thoughts no one else knew. There were even things I hadn't told Geoff. I didn't tell him about my mother. He didn't ever know the full extent of that. He knew I had lost my father in a car accident, but he didn't know about my mother's breakdown and the drinking. I didn't ever share that part of my miserable life with him."

She let go of Jessica's hair and lit yet another cigarette, inhaling the nicotine deeply. Jessica seized the opportunity and blabbered,

"Cinnamon, when you told me about that, I felt so sorry for you. I think it was dreadful your mum went to pieces after your dad died. You were only thirteen … how could you look after someone who only wanted to drink? It must have been terrible lying to everyone, pretending everything was fine, looking after the house and you both and never daring to invite anyone home. I can't imagine how lonely you felt."

Cinnamon exhaled and levelled a cold stare at Jessica. "You have no idea how lonely. Once I met Geoff, I thought loneliness would never feature in my life again. Do you know what it is like to have no friends at that age? It's the time in your life when everyone is talking about boys and laughing and growing up together. Have you any idea what it is like skulk about on your own, or to be left out of everything? I bet you had plenty of friends. I bet you went out to dances and parties and tearooms. I was only invited to two parties. I had to turn them down. I couldn't leave my mother on her own at night. She was always blind drunk by evening. I couldn't even invite friends back to my house, in case they discovered my drunken mother lying in a pool of her own puke or piss," she spat. "Everyone thought I was a freak." Cinnamon paused to regain some composure, but memories set her off again in a further rage.

"You, who had a perfect childhood with a mother and a father who were completely normal, can't possibly imagine what it was like to look after someone who actually hates you? They hate you for trying to keep them alive. My mother would scream at me until I gave her back the bottle I had hidden. Do you know how many nights I stayed awake crying, and yet hoping that in spite of the terrible temper and hurtful comments, she would still be there in the morning because I was terrified of what would happen to me if they took her away? No, of course you don't. You made all the right noises when I told you about it all, but you didn't really comprehend the pain it caused me. If you had understood, you would never have taken away the one person who loved me."

Cinnamon marched around the room. Jessica's eyes were open in fear. She struggled against the ropes that bound her hands. Cinnamon picked up a kitchen chair, turned it around, and sat on it facing Jessica. Slowly, she continued, lazily waving a knife at Jessica.

"Geoff saved me. When he asked me to marry him, I couldn't believe my life could be so happy. Did I tell you how we met?" Jessica shook her head. "I fell for him the first time I saw him, you know. It was at the library where I worked after my mother died. I knew straight away we were made for each other. People talk about love at first sight. We experienced it. I pretended I wasn't interested in him, but all the time he talked to me that first time, my heart hammered against my ribcage so loudly, I thought everyone in the library could hear it. I gave in after he asked me out several times. I knew he was right for me, you see. He had persisted. He had really wanted me. He needed me too. You could tell he did, by the way he looked at me, like a big puppy. He couldn't live without me. He and I became inseparable. I slept with him on our third date. He told me then he loved me. I knew our love would last forever. You know he proposed to me when I was nineteen?"

Jessica turned her head away. "It wasn't quite like that, Cinnamon. I know you're going to hurt me, but I have to tell you that Geoff didn't see it that way. He told me all about it. He got drunk at a party, and you kept going on and on about getting married, asking when would he propose. He said you told him you thought you were pregnant. In the end, he popped the question. He was just drunk. By the time he had sobered up the next day, you'd told the whole street, his family and all his friends. He couldn't really get out of it."

"No. That's not true," replied Cinnamon, twisting the knife about and teasing the tip of the blade against her thumb. "That can't be true. He loved me. I did everything for him. I went round to his house every evening. His parents really liked me and let me stay over most nights. I helped his mum get dinner every day, and I stopped by and did cleaning for her. I gave him everything I had. I loved him and he loved me. I'm going to leave you here to think about what you have just said. When I get back, I expect you to have changed your mind."

"Don't leave me like this, Cinnamon. Think about how much fun you and I had. Think of our friendship—"

Cinnamon opened the kitchen drawer again and removed a gag. She marched to Jessica's chair and tied it swiftly around Jessica's mouth.

"Friendship we HAD Jessica, until you decided to run off with my husband. MY husband, who I had cared for, adored, and helped when he was still training to be an accountant, with money from my inheritance. I supported that man for the first few years with my money. He wouldn't have been half as successful if it hadn't been for me. This is the same man, MY husband, who sobbed with pleasure when I bought us our house with the rest of the money and told me I was the best person he could have hoped to meet. The very same man who cried with me when we lost our first child, and who wept all week when we lost the second. MY husband who held me tightly when I was told that I couldn't have children and told me it didn't matter because we would always have each other. The man who I looked after for over twenty years was my husband, my lover, and my friend, Jessica, not just a drunken boy who fell into a relationship with a girl who fancied him. You know a lot about me, but you don't know him. He worshipped me, and you, you hussy, stole him when he was vulnerable. You chased after him … you, with your tight clothes, Jessica Rabbit figure, and flirtatious ways. He was temporarily attracted to you; that was all. If I had not been feeling so low about my life at the time, I would have spotted the signs and fought you off."

"You're no match for me now though, are you? I've changed, Jessica. I'm not the shy, anxious woman who ate comfort food all day and worried what to prepare for my husband's dinner. I'm not the same woman who spent hours choosing patterned curtains and matching sofas, who arranged flowers every day, and tried to make his home perfect. I'm not the doormat who thought if she did everything that he wanted, life would be fine. No, I am different, and that is bad news for you."

Cinnamon picked up the chair and shoved it back under the table. She strode to the door, where she turned back to look at Jessica and waved the knife at her.

"I have something important to attend to. You will have to wait until I get back. It'll give you a chance to get the facts right in your head. Then, I'll decide how this will end."

With that, she slammed the door shut, locking it behind her, leaving Jessica wriggling impotently against her bounds.

"Forty-nine … fifty!" counted Kiera as Dawn performed crunches on the large blue ball. "Well done. Four weeks ago you couldn't manage five reps. Look at you now."

Dawn wiped the perspiration from her forehead with a small

towel, chugged some water from her new plastic water bottle, and nodded. "Okay, what next? You're not going to make me do that damn plank thing again, are you? There is no way I can suck this blubber in for an entire minute," she added, bunching her stomach flab with two hands and wobbling it. Kiera chuckled. "No, I thought you might like to start on some boxing moves. Your new trainer will available in a moment. He's just finishing the kick-boxing class. He said he'd like to meet you and volunteered to take half this training session with you. I'll go with you to the studio. There's a punch bag in there, so you'll be able to get rid of all that pent up rage you have."

"I don't have any rage."

"Course you do. So far, you have spent all session complaining about Jim's lawn mower being in the kitchen again and how he leaves used dental floss lying on the sink. You need to thump something. Come on."

"Good thing I put on my new exercise kit, then," retorted Dawn, tugging at her figure-hugging exercise top. "I'll look professional."

"Suits you. Red is a good colour for you."

"Yes, it matches my eyes," retorted Dawn.

"Yeah, right!"

They stopped outside the studio door. Three stragglers from the class came out, faces glowing. Agniezska strolled out behind them, hair swept back in a neat long ponytail, looking as if she had strolled through a supermarket, rather than be part of a high-impact class.

"Hello, Kiera. Ah, you must be his new victim," Agniezska said looking at Dawn and gave a deep sensual laugh. "He is a verrey demanding man. Good luck. I go to spinning class now." Her obvious accent gave away her Eastern European roots.

"Does she always look like that?" asked Dawn.

"Yes, pretty much. She seems to have the ability to exercise all day and show no evidence of it. It must be in her genes. She takes more classes than any other staff member. She's extremely focussed. When she isn't instructing, she often participates in other classes. She used to be in my step class. I have never seen anyone with so much energy as that woman. All the men adore her. Little do they realise they'd never stand a chance with her, though. Ah, here he is, our very own *Karate Kid*. Hi, Jason!"

Dawn's feet turned to stone. Her mouth opened and shut. She pulled at her tight red top and squirmed uncomfortably. In front of her, dressed in an instructor's yellow t-shirt, attempting to remove a headset and microphone, was Jason from the writer's class.

"Jason!" squeaked Dawn. "I had no idea ..."

Jason looked just as surprised. "Me neither. Are you my new student?"

"Well, since you two already know each other, I'll leave you to it and go and check the swimming pool levels. He's very good, Dawn. You'll soon pick up the techniques. Oh, and Jason, be gentle with her!"

Kiera exited the studio.

"Right, well, we'd better get started then. Kiera told me you were desperate to learn a few kick-boxing moves. Thought we'd begin with a few punches and get that technique sorted first, then move on to the legs next session."

"So, this is your proper job, then?" asked Dawn.

"Just part-time. I come in three times a week for the kick-boxing class, and now and then I take on one-to-one clients like you. Two of the classes are in the evenings, so that gives me plenty of time for my other job."

"What's that?" asked Dawn as Jason moved off to put on some music.

"Oh, nothing very interesting," replied Jason. A loud thumping beat interrupted the conversation, and Jason returned instantly, adopting a professional tone as he stood beside Dawn facing the mirror. "Okay, let's get started. Shoulders back. Let's get you warmed up again. We don't want to rip any muscles, do we?"

The session went too quickly. One minute, they were marching around the studio getting warmed up, and the next, Dawn was thanking Jason and scuttling out of the studio to have a well-earned shower.

It had been exhilarating. First, she had learned how to throw punches at her reflection. Then she had donned a pair of large gloves and followed Jason's lead in a type of boxercise dance. The gloves transformed her. She changed from meek and mild Dawn to a woman who would take no nonsense from anyone. Jason and she managed co-ordinated dance moves involving upper cuts, jabs, and hooks, in time to the music. The weight of the glove made the punches harder to throw, and she was soon sweating with the effort.

As soon as Jason was satisfied she had grasped the correct

technique, he turned the music off and guided her to the large punch bag hanging from the ceiling in the corner of the room. Holding the bag firmly, he got her to repeatedly hit it. She gave it all she could and battered the bag. It wasn't long before she couldn't even lift her arm to throw another punch. "Good, well done. You're quite strong. Okay, let's do some stretching, and then I'll pad up and you can try hitting a real person."

He grabbed a pair of gloves and held his hands up facing her. "Hit my gloves with alternate punches. Left … right … go on … harder."

Dawn hadn't got the energy to hit hard. She tapped feebly at his gloves, barely able to lift her arms. Jason laughed. "Wimp!" he chuckled. "I think you are done, lady. Next time, we'll progress from this, and I'll show you some kicks."

Dawn pulled off the gloves, now sticky inside, and shook her hands.

"Come on, you need to cool down and stretch those arms."

He walked her around the studio, slower and slower until her heart rate dropped. Then he stood next to her again, so they were both facing the large mirror, and together they stretched their triceps, biceps, and shoulder muscles. Jason didn't converse with her. He was too focussed on the moves. "Excellent," he finally said. "I think you show promise." He tidied the gloves away in a cupboard at the back of the studio, and checking the room was acceptable for the next class, he picked up his water bottle and took a swig. "So, why do you want to learn kick-boxing then?" he asked. At that moment, Kyle the Kiwi and senior gym instructor appeared at the door.

"Mind if I have a word, Jas, please? I'm not interrupting, am I?"

"No, it's fine. I was just leaving. See you next session, Jason. Thanks very much."

Dawn felt different somehow. She couldn't explain it any more than that. The training had been effective in many ways. She felt happier and somehow more relaxed. She bumped into Kiera in the changing rooms, who was getting ready to take the aqua aerobics class and was shimmying into a fetching blue swimsuit.

"Someone has had a good dose of endorphins," she remarked. "You look … alive." Yes, that was how Dawn felt—alive.

Jessica twisted frantically against her bindings. Blasted Cinnamon had gone too far. It was one thing to be upset about your husband leaving you, and quite another to kidnap the woman he chose to run off with. If only Cinnamon knew the half of it. The trouble was, she believed firmly in her own version of events.

In spite of what Cinnamon said, it hadn't been a wonderful relationship. Geoff always felt trapped by her. Geoff spoke about his relationship with his wife, the second time he and Jessica had gone out. He had done so with sincerity and a great sadness. Jessica had felt deeply for him.

The problem, he confessed, was that Cinnamon had always had such power over him. She had suffocated him with love. In return, she expected devotion and loyalty. He had tried his best. Cinnamon, however, wore the pants in the house. She made all the major decisions. He blamed himself for being lazy or weak. He shouldn't have let her creep into his life the way she did, taking it over until he felt little more than a puppet.

His openness touched Jessica. He didn't blame Cinnamon at all. He blamed himself. The more he revealed, the more attracted she became to this sensitive man.

He hadn't recognised the problem at first. Well, he was young, flattered that a pretty girl like Cinnamon would be interested in him. She wheedled her way into his family's affections. They, in turn, put pressure on him to take his relationship with her more seriously. At the beginning, it was fine. They didn't even have to struggle financially as newly-weds. As luck, or now with hindsight—bad luck, would have it, Cinnamon inherited a large fortune from her grandparents. She used it to buy a house for them, furnish it, and pay for all their living costs, while Geoff struggled at university, then college, taking endless examinations. Cinnamon ensured his life was comfortable. It was only later after he got a position with a good company that he understood the problems with the arrangement he had. Cinnamon was the one who controlled everything, from what they ate, to what he wore to work. It was like living with a strict parent. He felt financially impotent. Even though he earned a decent salary, he didn't feel he was the breadwinner. Cinnamon had plenty of money, most of which was invested in shares and earned them a reasonable income each year. His salary wasn't needed. He saved most of it for the rainy day he knew would happen. As time passed, the situation became worse. He tried to explain to Cinnamon, but she shushed him and told him he contributed more than enough by just loving her.

He never found the right time to tell her they couldn't go on together, that he needed to break free, feel independent, be … a man. After she lost the babies, she suffered a minor breakdown and became clingy and needy, crying daily on his shoulder. He tried to understand her desperation; after all, he was suffering a loss too, but Cinnamon got increasingly depressed and withdrew into herself. He worried that she would do something crazy if he wasn't there to support her. She might have even contemplated suicide, given how low she sank after she subsequently discovered she couldn't have any children. Geoff often saw the way she looked at young mothers with children. There was a hunger in her eyes, and it saddened him. Cinnamon had a lot of love to give, and had they been blessed with children, he was sure things would have turned out differently. Geoff hadn't been able to hurt her further by abandoning her.

As she became increasingly depressed, she lavished more attention onto Geoff. The more she did for him, the more he hated it. Somehow, he couldn't tell her. Years floated by, and he became accustomed to his situation. He buried himself in work and put up with the smothering. It was only after they celebrated twenty years of marriage that he realised he had been living a complete lie for too long. He wasn't sure he loved Cinnamon. In truth, he hadn't even fancied his wife in years.

Jessica hadn't considered Geoff a catch when she had moved next door to him and Cinnamon. She was freshly divorced, having come out of a turbulent relationship with a man who had spent more time in the pub than at home and was enjoying life as a single woman again. She was more drawn to her melancholy neighbour, Cinnamon. If ever someone needed a friend, it was this quiet creature who worked part-time in a local library and who lived solely for her husband. Jessica tried repeatedly to invite Cinnamon around for a drink. Eventually, one dark grey afternoon, Cinnamon turned up at her door with a box of Marks and Spencer's chocolate biscuits, and a friendship began.

It took Jessica quite some time to uncover much about Cinnamon. The poor woman lacked confidence. Every sentence seemed to begin with 'Geoff this' or 'Geoff that' to start with. Eventually, they enjoyed a decent relationship. Although Jessica preferred the light-hearted company of her work colleagues or her girlfriends, Cinnamon became easier to talk to. She became less reserved and on occasion would come and watch a film with Jessica, eat popcorn, and have a glass or two of wine. It was thanks to one such night that she learned Cinnamon and Geoff hadn't had sexual relations for several months. She made some crack about getting a Rampant Rabbit, and they laughed it off.

In her mind, Geoff Ellis was off limits. That was until the night Geoff became her personal bodyguard. Jessica arrived home late one evening to find her front door ajar. In a panic, she raced around to Cinnamon's house. Cinnamon had gone to bed early with a migraine, but Geoff told her not to worry, he would go around and see what state the house was in and make sure no one was still inside. He grabbed a large poker from the fireplace and marched around to her house. She called the police and followed him outside, sobbing. After a while, Geoff emerged, walked up the driveway, and enveloped her in a friendly hug. "It's okay. There's no visible damage, and no one is in there. I'll come in with you, and you can check to see what has been taken."

He held her hand, and together they entered her home. Other than the television, nothing seemed to have been removed. The thieves had somehow managed to break in through an open window in the utility room and let themselves out through the front door, so no damage had been done. Geoff gently led Jessica to the settee, where she sat shaking with shock. Within a minute, he had found a glass and filled it with brandy he had discovered in the kitchen. He patted her hand. Jessica looked into his face and suddenly saw him for the man he was: a kind, strong, sincere man who cared about people. That was the moment it started.

They waited for the police. Geoff chatted about films, books, television, and generally kept her mind off what had happened. After the police left, he stayed, joining her in a glass of brandy. Eventually, he left her, telling her to bolt her door and giving her his mobile number in case she needed him. "They were probably just kids who wanted stuff to sell for money for drugs or something. They won't come back, but if you are at all frightened, give me a ring. I won't turn the phone off, and I can come back over in a jiffy."

The next day, she saw Geoff coming home from work and thanked him again. "Maybe I could invite you both over for a meal or a drink?" she suggested.

"Cinnamon is a bit low at the moment. I don't think she'd be up to any company. How about a quick drink at the pub, just the two of us?" he replied.

It snowballed from there. Jessica couldn't explain it or justify it. It just happened. They were two people attracted to each other by a force neither could ignore nor escape, regardless of the consequences.

The front door slammed shut. Cinnamon was back. Jessica wondered how she should handle this. She really needed to get away. Cinnamon was unbalanced, and who knew what she might have been capable of.

Music boomed out of the speakers, resonating against the walls in the exercise studio. Dawn felt it vibrate through the very fibres of her body, making her heart thump faster, consuming her and making her work hard to its incessant beat.

Jason and Dawn worked in synchronisation to a choreographed routine they had started last session. Dawn now knew the moves in advance and could change in time to the music and at the same time as Jason. They moved as one, punching out to the left in a series of sharp jabs, straight into a series using the right arm, box-stepping to get into position then changing into a mad frenzy of upper cuts. The music changed tempo hitting the 150 bpm they needed, and they jogged in place with aggression, guards up, boxing gloves protecting their faces, until Jason yelled, "Forward, forward, kick, flick, punch, punch, kick and back!" Dawn gave it her all, fired up by the music and adrenaline.

"And ... march!" Jason threw his gloves onto the floor and raced off to turn off the music for their personal workout routine. "Those Prodigy tracks always get the pulse racing," he commented, as he collected the large black pad ready for Dawn to launch some kicks at him. "Feel warmed up enough?"

"Good and sweaty," she replied.

"Okay, let's try a few of those kicks we had a go at last time. Try to flick your foot as you bring it up. Get some power behind it. You're trying to disable me remember, not show me your new sparkly shoes you bought in the sales!"

He demonstrated. His leg kicked forward, darting out dangerously quickly. It could have easily hit a grown man in the chest, propelling him backwards.

"Your turn," he offered. "Aim a bit lower, though. I don't want you doing your back in or falling over. Aim for my leg."

Dawn threw all the energy she could muster into her kick and aimed it at Jason's knee, where he was holding the large pad.

"Too feeble. Come on, Dawn, this is kick-boxing, not line dancing!"

Irritated, she aimed again and could feel the pad move.

"Better, much better. Okay, again. Aim a bit higher. Kick that pad, Dawn. It's you or him. Mr Pad will get you if you don't prevent him."

She spent the next half hour following the moving pad as it was raised and lowered. Jason made her alternate legs when she began to weaken, then when she couldn't aim straight and strong, he let her punch at the pad.

"I'm the enemy, Dawn," he announced, just as fatigue threatened to stop any further efforts. "This is your chance to go into combat. Come on, hit me. Kick me. Throw whatever you fancy at me. Don't worry. You won't hurt me. Think of someone you'd really like to hit and then use that anger."

Cinnamon appeared from nowhere, dressed in a black workout top and dark combat trousers. Her hair was tied back in a long ponytail, and she looked amazing. She put her guard up to defend herself from any blows Jason might attempt to throw. Her reflexes were sharp. She wasn't tired. She wanted to hurt someone ... Geoff.

Cinnamon took over from the exhausted Dawn and kicked out in a flurry of well-executed kicks, which would have found their mark had Jason not had well-honed reflexes. Like a wild fury, she attempted to shin-scrape Jason, knock his knee caps out and jab him in the throat. Then, as suddenly as she had arrived, she disappeared, leaving Dawn drained. Suddenly, Dawn couldn't lift either of her arms or legs. She was spent. She shook her head.

"No ... more ...," she wheezed.

"Wow! Excellent job! You're a quick learner," he effused. "You nearly got me. I would be worried if I got in a match with you. You show huge promise," he continued as they walked around the gym slowly, trying to bring Dawn's pulse back down to normal. "So," he added as he helped her stretch out her hamstring by pushing on her leg as she lay out on the floor, "why kick boxing? Want to sort out the Old Man or just terrorise people?"

Dawn smiled weakly. "My novel," she replied then yelped as Jason stretched her leg further than she thought it would be possible to push a grown woman's leg.

"I didn't hurt you, did I?"

"No, more surprised me."

"Breathe in … and … out," he said. He helped her to her feet. "That sounds intriguing. Is it about ninjas or something similar, then?"

"Uhm, well, it sounds a bit daft now that I'm telling you, but it's about a woman who is a cross between a Marvel Comic heroine and an avenging angel. Weird, I know, but it's deeper than that. It's a mixture of psychology and how life and circumstances can change you."

"Does she wear a costume like Wonder Woman?" he asked grinning. "I had a thing about her when I was younger. Other boys fancied Pamela Anderson or Page Three models. Me, I liked Wonder Woman and those blue knickers. Or what about Catwoman? I mean the original Catwoman. Did you know she first appeared in a 1940s Batman film? She was a burglar in that film and called The Cat. Best bit was, she had a whip!" Jason's eyes twinkled. "I had an old poster of the film on my bedroom wall. She looked like she'd keep a young man in check. Catwoman was played by Eartha Kitt in the 1960s, then Michelle Pfeiffer played her in *Batman Returns*, and of course, Halle Berry played her in the *Catwoman* movie in 2004. It flopped at the cinema. Can't understand why. I watched it four times!"

"You're a film buff?"

"Only certain films. I like adventure and comic heroes. Seen all the X-Men films. Love Superman and Batman. Catwoman was my favourite character in those films. I wouldn't mind fighting that feisty alley cat."

Cinnamon whispered that she wouldn't mind getting in a grapple with Jason, with his clear eyes and enigmatic smile, but Dawn told her to put a lid on it, and go and take a cold shower.

"What about you? What are you working on? I had you down as

one of those guys who write science fiction, or now I know about your job, maybe you write war-type books?"

Jason laughed

"My latest story is about a lazy, irreverent slacker, Po, who is overweight and who is completely crazy about Kung Fu but has to spend his days working in his family's noodle shop. He is unexpectedly chosen to fulfil an ancient prophecy, and his dreams become reality when he joins the world of Kung Fu, studying alongside his idols, the legendary Furious Five."

Dawn laughed. "Isn't that the plot of *Kung Fu Panda?*"

Jason grinned back. "Busted! But it was a great film. I saw it fifteen times. He's not a big fat panda ..."

"He's THE big fat panda," Dawn continued and laughed. "It starred Angelina Jolie, so I had to watch it. I love that woman. If I could be anyone else in the world, I'd be her."

"You sort of remind me of her when you are training. You're pretty determined. I'll have to start calling you Lara Croft," he joked. "So you like similar stuff to me, then? I can't help it, I love cartoons. Pixar films do it for me too. I cried like a baby at Up."

"Me too. I bought the DVD and watched it on my own with a bottle of wine and a large box of tissues. I used the whole box."

"Lara Croft wouldn't have cried. You are like her, but definitely more feminine."

Dawn blushed again.

At that moment, Agniezska opened the door to the studio and waved a towel at Jason.

"Sorry, Jas, we haff meeting in office, ten minutes ago. Hurry!"

"Gosh, I'd completely forgotten about that. I have to go, Dawn," he said gathering up the gloves and throwing them into the cupboard. "Great work today, by the way. I hope it helps with your book. See you on Friday. Make sure you take a long warm shower. We don't want you injured."

With that, he dashed off, the studio door clattering behind him.

"How interesting. He is a surprise, isn't he? Has a rather unusual taste in films, like your own. Batman, eh? I wonder if Agniezska dresses up as Catwoman," said Cinnamon out loud. Dawn giggled.

Jessica had both hands wrapped around a mug of tea. Cinnamon sat opposite her oozing menace. She hadn't said a word since she returned. She came in, thrown a ready-made ham and cheese sandwich down onto the table, filled up the kettle and set it to boil. She then removed the gag, untied Jessica's hands, and gestured for her to eat the sandwich.

"So, tell me everything," snapped Cinnamon, her eyes fully focussed on Jessica's face. "I think I deserve to know why you did this to me."

Jessica had decided to tell her the whole story. There was no point in hiding any of the facts. Cinnamon had to be told. She looked like she wouldn't put up with half-truths. Well, after the way she had been treated, Cinnamon was jolly well going to get the truth in its full glory. She wouldn't spare her feelings. What harm could Cinnamon actually cause her? Besides, she had an ace up her sleeve should things turn nasty.

"This is going to sound so clichéd, but I really didn't intend for it to happen. It just did. We were both missing something in our lives," began Jessica. Cinnamon's eyes narrowed. "I needed someone whom I could count on, and Geoff, well, he needed to be freed."

She told Cinnamon her version of events, ignoring all the scowls. Credit to Cinnamon, she didn't interrupt once. She listened to everything that was said until Jessica finished her monologue. She had been honest. So what if Cinnamon didn't like the truth? Jessica was feeling more confident now that she wasn't trussed up. This wasn't some weird television drama. They could talk like adults; after all, she wasn't the first woman in history to fall for someone else's husband.

Outside, a dog barked. Cinnamon sat in silence, digesting the information she had been given.

"He told you all of this?" she asked after a while. The harshness had left her eyes. Her demeanour was less aggressive and had been replaced by a melancholy.

"Everything," replied Jessica quietly. "I'd never have got involved with him if I had thought for one minute that he loved you. I don't blame you for hating me. I can't tell you how sorry I am I hurt you. I can't explain any of it, except I was sure he and I were right for each other."

Cinnamon regained her composure and snorted. "Spare me your apologies."

"I am sorry I hurt you, but I am not sorry I left with Geoff. Look at you, Cinnamon. You are transformed. You look incredible. You look years younger and absolutely stunning. Geoff leaving you was a good thing."

Cinnamon looked deep into Jessica's eyes without blinking. "No, it wasn't," she replied simply.

"You didn't need to be so dramatic and tie me up. I'd have told you over a glass of wine or a cup of tea. You gave me quite a scare for a while. I thought you had turned into a raving lunatic and were going to do away with me, chop my body up, and bury it under the patio," she laughed. "Anyway, you need to know something else. Geoff and I have split up."

Jessica rubbed her hands up and down the mug as if to warm them. "He left a few months ago. Turned out he couldn't take responsibility after all. How ironic is that? He wanted to be a man, and when he had the chance to be one, he flunked."

Silence descended again as Jessica struggled with her next words.

"I have a child now. We had a child. Geoff, well he didn't seem to be able to cope with fatherhood and did a bunk. He pays maintenance but doesn't want anything further to do with us."

Jessica's eyes filled. "Shows that you weren't the only one to make a mistake, eh?"

Cinnamon wasn't listening. Her eyes had darkened.

They sat in silence for what seemed like an eternity. Cinnamon reached for her cigarettes and lit one.

"When did you take up smoking?" asked Jessica.

"When do you think? This doesn't change anything, you know. I still hate the fact that you didn't have the guts to come and tell me what was going on while we were friends. However, I can see why it happened. Geoff can be persuasive when he tries. No, I don't forgive you, but I can understand better where the fault lies. You are both culpable, but he is to blame more than you." She stubbed out her cigarette only half smoked and crushed the rest of the packet under her fist. "I think it would be for the best if we didn't meet again."

"I have no intention of staying around here. I only came to see my auntie. I'd better get back to her now. Thank goodness it's only been a few hours. She'd worry if I were away any longer. My mother has got Charlie, so I need to go home tonight."

"Charlie," repeated Cinnamon.

"Yeah, he's one and a half. He's great. I love him to bits. He's the best thing in my life," she continued.

Cinnamon pushed back her chair abruptly. It was over. Jessica realised that she was being released. She couldn't think of anything further to add.

"Uhm, good luck, er, with everything. You do look phenomenal, you know?"

The door shut fast behind her, and she wandered back up the road. It felt surreal. Had she really spent three hours in captivity? She shook her head in disbelief then reached for her mobile phone to let her mum know she'd be back home that night.

Leaning against the front door, Cinnamon took large gulps of air. She wrestled to control her feelings. She wouldn't give in. She had cried too many tears in her life. It was better to focus her energy on her anger. How dare that low-life Geoff walk out on a child? She would hunt him down. She would hunt down the son of a bitch and make sure he regretted that particular decision for what remained of his sad little life.

It seemed to be a fairly normal shop. Against the black backdrop in the window was a dummy's torso dressed in a cream camisole top and matching French knickers. Peering through the door and into the dimly lit shop, she could make out a girl standing behind a counter, browsing through a glossy magazine. She took a deep breath and went in.

"Hello," she said, trying out a confident tone that wouldn't belie how she felt. Without looking up, the girl managed "Hiya!" In normal circumstances, Dawn would have been irritated by such ambivalence, but today it suited her. In fact, it would have suited her to be completely invisible or wearing a large brown paper bag over her head.

She wanted to get an idea of saucy outfits she could write about. She couldn't have Cinnamon dressed in a large pair of greying M&S

knickers. Did people still wear Baby Doll negligees? Her own night-time attire consisted of a large t-shirt that reached to mid-thigh and sported the slogan 'Animal in Bed'. She just wasn't sure which animal she was—probably a hippopotamus. Sometimes she wore pyjamas, especially when it was cold, and during winter, she even wore thick socks. She always had icy-cold feet, and Jim complained if they got close to his own, so the socks were essential. She had never owned any seductive underwear. Practical knickers were to be found in abundance in her underwear drawer. One year, Jim had bought her a black lace bra-and-knicker set, but it had been scratchy and brought her bum up in red spots, so she abandoned it in favour of softer cotton. As for thongs, there was no way she was going to try and wear an outfit that resembled a piece of dental floss, not with her enormous bum cheeks which would spill over the sides of it, doing her no justice at all.

Her eyes darted around the shop taking in the rails of pale pink underwear. Nothing racy in the underwear department here, she thought. She moved further into the gloom of the store where she alighted upon some red basques embroidered with black lace and matching suspenders. The store stretched further back than she had imagined, so she made her way into another area. Here, she discovered shiny black corsets, fishnet stockings, and whips. She picked up a whip and tried to imagine herself in the outfit. She would have looked like a plump Zorro, especially if she wore the mask she spotted on the shelf. She pawed a crotchless skirted thong. Some of the lingerie was genuinely sexy. Maybe she could get away with an outfit to wear and excite Jim.

She shuffled past the Rampant Rabbits. She knew what they were but had never held one. The Powerful One? The Thrusting One? The Little Slim One? The Just Ears One! They were too much for her to take in, and a childish urge to giggle rose up in her throat. She moved away and bumped into a stand on which were dressing-up outfits. She pulled out the Hottie Hostess. Somehow, she couldn't envisage Jim and her playing at pilots and air stewardesses. If they played that particular game, Jim would want to order a gin and tonic, recline his seat, then doze off after a good hot meal. Officer Naughty … Miss Mafia … Sex Kitten … Kitty Playsuit. The latter came complete with cat mask. Suddenly, she thought of Catwoman and of wearing this outfit for Jason. A vision of him on a bed as she paraded in front of him flickered across her mind. Cinnamon smiled gleefully. "That's it. At last you're getting the idea. Add some sexy high-heeled shoes to that image, and don't forget to purr. Now, all you need would be some chocolate body paint which you could lick off his—" She was jolted out of her reverie by a voice.

"Can I help you, madam?"

Redder than the corset she had passed earlier, she turned around, Kitty Playsuit in hand, to face the shop manager, a young man in his late thirties.

"Er, no ... that is ... I'm just looking for fancy-dress outfits for a party," she stammered, thrusting the garment back onto the rail. "For my son's girlfriend," she floundered. The manager nodded. She noticed his name badge: "Roger". She stifled a grin.

"Maybe she would like to come into the shop herself, when she has a moment, and we'll advise her," Roger suggested. "Or she could try looking at our online store if that would be easier," he continued meaningfully.

She nodded, thanked him, and scurried past the girl on the desk who was still gazing at her magazine. "Biya!" she managed to say. Dawn rushed off, blinking into the bright daylight and barrelled straight into a woman passing by.

"Oh, I'm so sorry," exclaimed Dawn.

"Not a problem," replied a voice she knew. Dawn looked up into shining mischievous eyes that danced with humour. "I expect you are in a bit of a hurry to try out your new purchase, eh?" said Viv.

"Well, I read them, and I don't know what all the fuss is about," huffed Geraldine.

Colin looked aghast. "It's ... Mummy porn!" he spat.

"And?" challenged Geraldine.

"It's sordid," he replied.

The rest of the group kept their heads down. Dawn attempted to stifle a giggle, while Jason, who was next to her, seemed to making notes, and was wrestling with a huge grin.

"At my age, it's not so much porn or fantasy, more reminiscence. It's the closest thing I'll get to the real thing again," said Geraldine bluntly. She was clearly enjoying Colin's discomfort. "Grow up,

Colin. The world isn't all snails, worms, and playing conkers in the playground. The world has changed. It's grittier. People like reading about reality. Your stories are far more fantastical in this day and age than these books."

Colin looked downcast.

"It's not to everyone's taste though, is it?" interjected Dotty, taking pity on Colin. Geraldine could be such a cow some days. There was no need to shock Colin like that.

"No, but boy, oh boy, does it sell books," voiced Margaret, getting into the conversation now that it was no longer a spat between the two most vociferous members of the group. This latest Zee Zee Bagor novel is all over the newspapers. I was in Sainsbury's yesterday, and copies of Hot and Lusty were flying off the shelves. Women were fighting each other to get a copy."

"Did you get yours?" asked Craig, the cheeky Essex car salesman.

Margaret blushed.

"Ah, you did then. Lend it me when you finish it, will you?" he laughed and blew her a kiss.

"Part of the success of Hot and Lusty is the mystery surrounding the author. No one has managed to track her down or interview her yet. Mystery sells as much as sex it seems," commented Blake as he stacked up a pile of papers he had marked for the group.

"I bet she's over eighty years old and has a face like a slapped arse," said Craig.

Jason spluttered loudly while Margaret and Dawn giggled.

Blake coughed politely. "We would all love to be the next Zee Zee Bagor, but for the moment I think we should concentrate on the art of writing good books. There is not always a need to put sex scenes into our stories or books, but if you do, then they should be charged with emotion, realistic and …" He paused for effect. " … exciting. Women—and men—want to read gripping material, whatever it is. I am not in favour of it being pornographic though. Romance is always welcome. Look at the number of books Mills and Boon sell each year. What lady doesn't like the idea of being romanced, wooed, and cosseted? Geraldine! Are you alright?"

Geraldine coughed several times. "Yes, thank you, Blake. I don't wish to contradict you, but not everyone believes in red roses, candlelit dinners, walks along an icing sugar beach, or happy-ever-after swooning stuff. That's almost as bad as Colin's nostalgia for a lost youth. Some realistic grit is a welcome change."

Colin looked at Blake sympathetically and continued to doodle on his notepad.

"So, enough of the rapid rise and success of Zee Zee Bagor and Hot and Lusty," he said tugging at his cravat. "We have our own writing to deal with. Now, last time I set a challenge. Who had a go at writing a modern fairy tale? We don't have time to listen to everyone's because the discussion over ran somewhat today, but if we could have a couple of volunteers? Who would like to read out their stories?"

Colin sat up importantly, a large sheet of A4 in front of him. No doubt it was another of his poems. He waved his hand to attract attention. Dawn could hear Jason groan quietly.

"Yes, Colin. Let's hear what you have written," said Blake.

Colin puffed himself up and began to read:

Red Riding Hoodie dressed in a cloak,
Stopped in the woods for a quick smoke.
She really ought to quit, she thought,
to appease Nan, the worry wart.
She crushed the tab under her feet,
Then chewed mint gum to smell all sweet
'Twas then she spied old Wolfy boy,
Lurking afar, face full of joy.
No doubt he had a cunning plan
To gobble up her poor Old Nan.
She swiftly pulled out her iPhone 5.
She'd make sure Nan stayed well and alive.
She raced off then to Gran's back door
Where she spied splodges of bright red gore.
Inside, though, Nan smiled all brightly,
Wearing nothing but a nightie.
"Thanks for the warning text," said Gran.
"He was no match for my large pan."
Wolfy was flat out on the floor.
Pearly whites shattered, gums all sore.
Poor old chap was then removed.

Now in a zoo, he eats minced up food.

Moral: You are never too old to embrace technology and smoking occasionally saves lives. (But best not to try it!)

Jason sat back, pencil in his mouth. Dawn noticed his long eyelashes. "That was good, Colin," he said.

Others took up the call.

"I liked the iPhone 5 reference. Very witty," added Margaret.

Colin looked even more pleased with himself.

They spent a while talking about rhyme and rhythm and discussing nonsense rhymes.

"So, we have time for one more person," said Blake. "Who would …?"

Geraldine raised her hand. "Actually, if no one minds, I have something I'd like to share with you."

Dawn shoved her own effort back under her pad. Gosh, Geraldine had written something at last. She sat back to listen but part of her brain was mulling over an idea to help her book have more grit.

Geraldine sat up straight in her chair. She tapped a silver nail against her pearl-white front teeth, which, on that day, were smeared with fuchsia-pink lipstick. She coughed lightly.

"As you know, I've been suffering from writer's block now for six years. I joined this group in the hope it would help me overcome my …" She coughed again. " … erm, difficulties. Last night, I went out with some friends I haven't seen for a while, and we had rather a jolly night at Swinfen Hall. I'm afraid I got rather squiffy, and to cut a long story short, I slept like the proverbial log. I had a rather superb dream which I put down to the Dom Perignon, and when I awoke, I just had to jot this down for you all. I think I may have finally beaten the block."

She looked up briefly. A smile fluttered across her enhanced lips which she licked. Another slick of lipstick stuck to her teeth. She opened her Moleskine notebook, smoothing it down carefully to ensure she didn't break the spine. She tinkled a gold charm bracelet on her hand and then caressed the page. Head bowed, she read her piece in earnest, nervous at first like a school child who has been asked to read in class but with more confidence as she became enthused by her own writing :

Elvis was washing up when his brother called to him. "Elvis, get your round fat arse in here, double quick, boy. We've got us a problem!"

Elvis removed his apron. It was his favourite apron. It was bright pink and had his name spelt out in large silver sequins. He had always been good at cooking. His Mama had made sure he could cook from an early age. She had tried to teach all of them, but his two older brothers had not been interested and had preferred to go outside and play baseball, or as they got older, mess with car engines outside on the drive.

He folded his apron. No matter what, he couldn't abide untidiness. Jackson was probably yelling about nothing as usual. He was always one to get worked up. He yelled at the television every time his beloved Yankees lost a match, or at Washington, the third brother, accidentally picked up and drank his can of beer.

Those two were so lazy. They left the place in such a mess. It really was a pig sty. Elvis sighed as he took in the stinking pair of trainers that had been plonked on the cream woollen carpet. They'd left two muddy stains on the pile. He'd have to vacuum it again or use the stubborn stain remover.

Really, these two were getting worse. He wondered for the umpteenth time when they would finally move out of his house. He was heartily sick of them. They treated him like a servant, ate all of the food, and did nothing to contribute to the housekeeping. Jackson was an alcoholic, and Washington; well, Elvis wasn't sure what he was. Maybe 'pervert' described it best. Poor Mama! She would have turned in her grave if she could see how they had turned out.

After their mother died, she had bequeathed each of them enough money to purchase homes and become independent. Jackson had squandered more than half of his wealth at the Casinos in Las Vegas, leaving himself only enough for a rough patch of land and a very dodgy wooden cabin. Recently, it had been condemned as unfit to live in. Washington had fared better, but when his wife of two months walked out on him, taking more than her fair share of his wealth, he was left with little to invest in bricks and mortar.

He had decided to self-build and had employed some cheap labour: immigrants from over the border. The result was shoddy work, cracked ceilings, uneven floors—all in all poor quality. Ultimately, the place fell to pieces. He had lost all of his back wall and his new kitchen. Both the houses needed major repair work and the brothers were residing at Elvis's home whilst the work was going on. Thanks to them wasting their earnings on bars, floozies, and gambling, progress was slow, and Elvis, the youngest but brightest of them all, was left to look after them.

Elvis was an IT expert. His house had every gadget imaginable. Apart from his love of cooking, he adored anything to do with technology.

He wandered through to find his eldest brother, Jackson, in front of the 52-inch television set, playing on one of his computer games.

"I can't get to the next level on this Mario game. Sort it out will you? It's really frustrating. And we've run out of popcorn." Jackson grumbled as he shoved the control at Elvis and sat back, eyes glazed from the beer. Washington was staring at a porn site on Elvis's laptop, mouth open and lips twisted in a disgusting smirk. Elvis shuddered. What a pair of slobs.

A couple of hours later, Elvis was sitting alone quietly. Well, not so quietly. One brother was unconscious on the sofa, drooling and making revolting snorting noises. The other had skulked off to one of the spare bedrooms. Elvis didn't even want to think about what he might be doing. A fair wind was howling outside. He hadn't been able to watch the news or weather forecast that evening. What with looking after his brothers, pandering to their every whim and baking a wonderful date and walnut cake for tomorrow, he had been fully occupied. He logged on to a local weather website. Triangular red weather alerts filled the screen. Hurricanes were headed this way.

Elvis was prepared for such events. His electronic storm shutters were soon on his windows. He shook Jackson to wake him. Jackson belched loudly but drifted back to sleep. He gingerly knocked on Washington's door, but after several attempts Washington told him to **** off!

"But there's a hurricane headed this way," Elvis yelled through the keyhole. "It could cause damage."

"Don't care. You're a clever little arse, and your house is hurricane-proof. Bugger off and hide if you must, scaredy cat! Now, leave me alone."

Elvis tried to wake Jackson one more time, but Jackson just farted and slept through the shaking. He tried lifting Jackson but it was impossible. He weighed a ton.

Elvis gave up. A roar was approaching, a terrifying sound. He lifted the cellar trap door and raced down the stairs to the secure cellar, which housed provisions, water, an emergency generator, and a spare bed. He could hear the wind raging outside. The hurricane had approached far more quickly than he had expected. Surprisingly, the noise didn't prevent him from sleeping soundly.

Morning broke. The hurricane had passed. Birds sang outside. The generator hummed and Elvis turned on his television to check the morning news. The news was full of the terrible hurricane, which had mercifully missed most of the region touching only a few homes before turning northwards and heading out away from populated areas. Named 'Wolf' it had been a category four. Elvis turned off the television and mounted the stairs. He gingerly opened the cellar trapdoor. His jaw dropped open. His house had completely disappeared. There was nothing left apart from a heavy wooden table which was upside down and under which was a squashed filthy trainer.

Moral of the story: Not even bricks and mortar can withstand a proper bad Wolf.

Geraldine looked up. She was met with silence. Blake broke the silence by applauding. The others took it up one by one. Dawn smiled at Geraldine. It wasn't that the story was fantastic, what was important was that Geraldine had broken through the block. She had rediscovered her love of writing, and she would go on from strength to strength. Geraldine waved her hands in front of her face like fans.

"Thank you. Thank you everyone for being patient and letting me witter on. It's been such a help coming here. Without you all, I think I would still be in a drought and unable to write. And I so wanted to be able to write some stories to read to my grandchildren." She stopped as a sob threatened to choke her. Blake got up, walked over, and placed an arm around her shoulders giving her a friendly squeeze.

There was little more to be gained by others reading their pieces that day. It was Geraldine's day, so the biscuits were brought out, and they all sat around chatting about the latest episode of Dallas which most of them had watched the night before. The general consensus was that it wasn't as good as the eighties' series.

Dawn hesitated for the umpteenth time. She chopped the pill in half with the vegetable knife, looked at it, and chopped it in half again. She put it into her pestle and mortar and ground it into powder. Scooping it up again with the teaspoon, she deliberated one more time. She shouldn't be doing this. It was wrong to give someone pills without their consent or knowledge. She couldn't do it. Cinnamon jogged her hand, and the powder tumbled into Jim's mug of tea. She stirred it thoroughly, adding two spoons of sugar.

"Thanks," mumbled Jim. He was slumped on the settee watching a football match. "Just put it there," he said indicating the coffee table. "Arsenal are one nil down. Can't believe it. The ref is an idiot. He allowed a penalty when it was clearly offside." He groaned loudly as a player fell to the ground clutching his shin. "Did you see that?"

"I'm off to bed. See you in a while," Dawn said.

"That was a foul. Ref, are you blind or what?"

Dawn left him to it. He would be up to bed after the match and his tea. It was a good thing he liked a night time cup of tea. How else could she have slipped him the pills? He would come to bed after he had drunk that, football, or no football.

She worked out it should take about half an hour to work. Researching it, she found out it took longer if a large meal was eaten, so she ensured Jim only had a light supper of fish. He complained he was still hungry afterwards and polished off half a packet of crackers, along with an enormous lump of mature Cheddar. She hoped it didn't slow down the effects too much. She would have to wait and see.

She had a quick shower and sprayed herself with her favourite perfume she only used for special occasions. She abandoned her t-shirt and socks and slipped in between the cool sheets. Now, she just needed to get into the mood for a horny Jim. She thought about the conversation at the writers' group. She marvelled at how someone like Zee Zee Bagor could write about sex and such intimate details so easily. She hadn't read the books, of course. If Jim caught her reading something like that, he would have thought she had turned into a raving nympho and would have been merciless in his comments. Jim was a conservative chap. Dawn only knew the missionary position, although when they had been in the first throes of love, she mounted him one drunken night. He didn't mind but he didn't request they did it again. He was the sort of man who liked to be on top and always took the lead in sexual advances. She wondered if his knowledge of sex was as limited as her own when they met. For years, she thought he knew all about sex, and she wasn't his first conquest. But more recently, she had begun to suspect Jim was quite shy in bed and probably wasn't even that keen on sex. Certainly, he wasn't keen on any adventurous sex. She pondered idly about what it would be like to dominate a man who wanted her so badly he would cry out for her. For a brief while, she attempted to envisage herself astride Jim making him groan and squirm with pleasure. She could only picture her own wobbling backside bouncing up and down and so the image popped. Her thoughts went back to Cinnamon and what she might have done to her ex-husband once she found him. She still carried a lot of baggage as far as that man was concerned. She would have been very unforgiving having discovered he had let down another woman and worse still, a child,

She woke in a sweat. She was dreaming that Jim came into the bedroom. He pulled down his trousers and underwear, flung back the bedclothes and leapt on her, regardless of the fact that she was asleep. He fumbled about and entered her immediately, paying no heed to her protests. It had hurt. He jack-hammered into her incessantly, his face blotchy and red with effort. He was a man possessed. A large blue vein throbbed in his forehead and his unseeing eyes bulged. She tried to speak to him, but he kept pounding harder and harder. She was sore, and she was afraid of the unrecognisable face staring at her.

"Jim, please, stop or kiss me," she begged, hoping to bring some romance to the sex ... or something! Jim leant forward and licked her face from chin to eyebrow leaving the stench of stale cheese lingering. She tried to wriggle away from him, but he maintained his anguished rhythm, face contorted in concentration. She feared he would have a coronary, and part of her hoped he would so this misery would end. He began to chant in an ugly tone, "Yeah, babe… yeah, babe …" He had never called her babe before. He always used her name. This was not the man she knew.

Then she woke up. Christ, this was all her fault! She should never have put Viagra in his tea. It would have been a disaster. Realisation hit her at last. Viagra wouldn't make someone loving or romantic. Jim wouldn't want to caress her, hold her, or get her excited. He would have just wanted relief from a throbbing erection and probably want it several times. She shot out the bed and grabbed her old dressing gown hanging on the back of the bathroom door. She would hide in her office until the blue pill wore off.

She glanced at the digital display blinking brightly on the clock on her desk. It was 3.40am. Where was Jim? The wretched stuff should have kicked in hours ago … unless something dreadful had happened. She rushed down the stairs to the lounge. The television glowed in the corner of the room. A presenter was attempting to sell some miracle hard-skin remover on the shopping channel. She picked up the remote control and clicked off the set. Jim was fast asleep on the settee, head back, and with his mouth wide open. Cheese drool had stuck to his chin. On the coffee table stood the mug of tea, its contents untouched and cold. She picked it up and took it to the kitchen where she threw it down the sink. Returning to the lounge, she gently patted Jim on his knee. He mumbled, "Ref's a twit."

"Yes, I know. Come on sleepy head. Let's get you to bed."

Cinnamon shrugged her shoulders. You can't win them all, she thought.

"Quail. That's fourteen, on a double-word score which is twenty-eight and another eleven for 'za'."

"What does 'za' mean?"

"It's one of the six letters of the Arabic alphabet. Also it's an old solfeggio name for B flat, the seventh harmonic, so called by Tartini," replied Jack, writing down his score on the notepad.

"Are you suddenly speaking in a foreign language? I have no idea what any of that means. How come you know all this weird stuff?"

"Plenty of time on my hands to learn new things," he said and smirked.

"Come on, you're hiding something."

"Well, all right I confess. I joined Facebook some time ago, and you can play Scrabble there. I play a lot online. I was playing an American lady last week, and she used this word. I had to ask her what it meant, and she told me. I looked it up on Google too, in case I got the chance to use it against you."

"You old rascal. Facebook! What possessed you to join that?"

"Dan explained it to me. Said it'd be a good idea for me for those days when I can't get out and about. It means I still have someone to chat to. I mentioned it to the girls at dancing, and they are all on it now too. I have twenty-five friends. We chat about all sorts of things. It's ideal when you are alone. You can go online, and it's like sitting in a room with someone, except it takes me ages to type a message to anyone. I'm friends with Dan there too. He sends me funny jokes."

"So, you've got a computer now?"

"No, I won one of those tablet things in a crossword competition, and Dan gave me his old phone when he upgraded his last month. It has things called apps, so I can go onto Facebook on it. Dan set it up for me. He's a good chap."

"Wow! There are no flies on you, are there? You're more with it than me. So what else have you been getting up to that I might not know about?"

"No, that's all. Apart from the fact that I have been accepted for the next round of Britain's Got Talent next month, along with Molly Hampton. We do a very good raunchy dance act. I've been practising for months, and I've learned to do the splits, and with Molly being double-jointed, we should take the judges by surprise."

Dawn's jaw dropped. She was about to splutter her protestations when she noticed her father's twitching lips.

"You so-and-so. You're teasing me."

"Couldn't help myself. You are always so easy to tease. I couldn't resist. No, don't worry; I won't be on television, with or without Molly Hampton. I certainly can't do the splits. Some days, I can barely stand. I have enough to keep me busy though, and I do enjoy being with people."

Dawn sat back and looked at her father. He had aged, but he still possessed vivacity and humour. That was what had seen him through the last few years.

"Change of subject, I had a letter from Mary Gilbert this week."

"The lady you courted for a while, when I went off to university?"

"Yes, that's her. I'd hardly say we courted. She lost her husband and was distraught, and I was just coming to terms with losing your mother. It was more companionship than anything else. We certainly didn't indulge in any courting activities. We went out for a few meals together and dropped by each other's houses for coffee. She was what I needed to help me get on the path to humanity again. You were a fantastic help, but I needed to find my feet in the adult world again. I'd been a drain on you for long enough. Your mother left a huge gap in my life when she was taken from us. It was dreadful. I didn't feel complete anymore. Mary and I rediscovered life together. She was a kind woman. Anyhow, she wrote to tell me that she's getting married again."

"Goodness!"

"Yes, she's been with this chap, Frank, for about three years now, and they have decided to tie the knot. She's invited me to the wedding. I don't think I'll go, though. It's in Cambridge, and that's quite a way to travel. Besides, I don't know any of the family who'll be going. I'd be on my own there. Nice of her to think of me, though. I'm glad she's found someone who can make her happy again."

"That's quite something. She must be in her late seventies."

"Age is just a number. It's how you approach it that dictates if you actually are old or not. That and good health. I'd have preferred to have got old with someone. I'd have liked to have enjoyed adventures and hobbies with her. It would have been much more enjoyable to have shared all these experiences with her."

He looked wistful again. Dawn smiled at him. She knew he was talking about her mother. She thought for a moment about getting old with Jim. Somehow, she couldn't envisage it. She couldn't see them going to dance classes together or having fun. It was difficult enough being together now. The future suddenly looked grey and daunting.

"Come on," she said shaking herself out of her thoughts. "Let's see this new tablet you've got, and you can show me your apps. I can meet your friends at last even if it is just virtually. They don't put up saucy messages on your wall, do they?"

The room was buzzing with lively conversation when Dawn got to the class. Jason was sitting at a table for two nearest the door and motioned for her to join him. The room resembled a classroom with desks facing the front. Blake sprawled on a chair in front of a large desk facing his students. Today, he looked very stylish wearing a paisley waistcoat over a plain shirt with jeans. Dawn gave him a wave and he nodded back. She slipped into the chair next to Jason's.

Harold was becoming more vociferous. "So, I wondered, Blake, if using initials rather than full names could be linked to success. Take E.L. James ..."

At the table in front of theirs, Margaret sat back and groaned. "We're not going to talk about the success of erotic literature yet again, are we?" she voiced.

"No, hear me out," continued Harold, biro in hand. "E.L. James has enjoyed, as we all know, untold success. J.K. Rowling ..." He paused as if this were of major significance yet received no reaction other than bewilderment. He continued. "A.A. Milne, E.E. Cummings, E.M Forster, P.D. James, J.R.R. Tolkien."

"T.K. Maxx," said Jason idly. Dawn stifled a snigger.

"J.D. Salinger," Harold said, oblivious to the comment. "So, if we were to use our initials instead of our names when we send in a script to an agent or publisher, maybe that would help us gain better recognition," he finished with a flourish of his biro.

Blake was looking confounded.

"I might change my name, Harold Albert Witt to H.A. Witt."

"Just missing 'Leonard and Frederick', and he could be H.A.L.F. Witt," mumbled Jason. Margaret's shoulders shook with silent laughter, and Dawn suppressed another snigger.

Harold squirmed around in his chair. He had blue biro ink on his lips. "What do you think then, people?" he asked. "Colin, what's your middle name?"

"James."

"That's good. You'd be C.J. Thomas. Sounds professional. Geraldine?"

"Bearnice, although I still fail to see your argument. There are plenty of authors who have enjoyed success who have used their full names or just one name, like Stendhal."

"G.B. Honours!" said Harold writing out the name on his pad.

By now, Dawn was struggling hard not to snort. Craig had turned around and was making hand gestures that indicated Harold was batty, and even Blake had a twinkle in his eyes as he watched his class become a little unruly. Jason began pulling faces at her. She felt like she was back at school. She felt youthful, invigorated, and had a terrible desire to burst out laughing.

"Dawn," called Harold. "What's your middle name?"

Dawn kicked Jason who put on a pout and rubbed his leg. She tried to regain composure.

"I'll just stick to Dawn if you don't mind."

"Please yourself, Jason, what about you?"

"I think we've got the idea now. Thank you, Harold," interrupted Blake. "Whether you use your name, your initials or a nom de plume, I think that's a decision you only need to make once your manuscript is complete. That's enough free discussion today. Ah, Josie, you're here. Welcome dear. No, don't worry, you haven't missed anything important. Okay peeps, shall we get started? I'd like to talk about muscle verbs." Jason flexed a bicep at Dawn, who obligingly gave it a friendly squeeze, looked impressed and then settled down to listen to Blake.

"Fancy a cappuccino? To make up for trying to distract you," added Jason, as they packed away. "The coffee here is fine, but I could really do with a frothy coffee and some chocolate."

Dawn didn't have to rush away. She agreed and they left together.

"I hadn't thought about the way I use verbs to beef up my sentences before," she commented later as she and Jason sat in a coffee shop near the museum.

"Yes," agreed Jason. "I've learned a lot more than I thought I would when I signed up to this group. I half expected it to be full of bored old people but it's turned out to be a real surprise." He gave her a meaningful look. Dawn squirmed under those piercing dark eyes.

"There are some characters there; that is a fact. Poor old Harold. He tries so hard. Colin is like an aged schoolboy, and Geraldine—"

"Is clearly loaded and doesn't know what to do with her time," finished Jason. "Did you see her shoes? They were Christian Laboutin. Cost a fortune."

"How do you know about Laboutin shoes?"

Jason put on a camp voice, "Oh, sweetie, you should see my closet. I wear them for my drag act."

"Twit," she said.

"Real men know what women like," he explained. "Shoes, chocolate, chick lit, soppy films, men who like to listen." He sat back smugly.

"So, you're a real man, then?"

"Yes, I am one of a kind. The sad fact is that I like most of those things. I have a penchant for shoes and clothes. I love watching fashion shows too. How weird am I? Kick boxing and chick flicks ... a fiendish combination."

"You're certainly different from Jim," Dawn said and then wished she hadn't brought Jim into the conversation. She suddenly felt she shouldn't be enjoying herself in Jason's company.

"So, what's your middle name?" she asked trying to lighten the feeling that had made itself present in her chest.

"Same as Colin's. It's James, which would make me J.J. Jackson. All the Js. Is that likely to earn me even greater recognition?" he asked in a voice that mimicked Harold's perfectly. "What do you think, Dawn?"

"Idiot!"

"No, truthfully, I am Jason James. My mother had a thing about the letter J. So what's your middle name?"

"Dawn is my middle name. I don't use my first name. It doesn't suit me at all. I have never used it."

"Okay, what's your first name then? Egbert, Tiffany ... ?"

"Dawn," she replied. "I'm just Dawn."

"Just Dawn, you are a woman of charm and mystery. And, I love a good mystery," he concluded.

Tracking him down was proving to be more difficult than she thought. The unshaven private detective, dressed in a scruffy coat and strangely resembling the television character, Columbo, reeled off the list of places he had visited and efforts he had made thus far. Huddled in the corner of a pub, neither of them attracted attention from the few Friday-night revellers who trickled out of the place with their loud voices and laughs, off for a night on the town.

"He's either gone abroad or started a new career," he declared. "He's certainly not joined any new accountant firms. I've not given up yet though. Late last night, I was given a possible lead, and there's a slim chance he might be in Manchester. No one can stay invisible for long. I'll find him."

Cinnamon fiddled with the beer mat on the table. "Thanks, Joe. Let me know as soon as you find him. He really needs to answer some questions."

Joe drained his glass of Coca-Cola and crunched on the last of the ice cubes.

"I hope you don't mind me making a comment, Miss Knight," he said rubbing the stubble on his chin. "I don't want to know what this guy has done to make you hire me, but I can see it hurt you deeply. You have a harshness in your eyes when you mention his name that I don't come across very often. It was obviously something lousy. But you're a very attractive lady, when you aren't hiding out in giant Puffa jackets and wearing blooming awful glasses," he added, smiling shyly. "I just wanted to say that not all men are rotten bastards, you know. I see the way you glower at them. You've been giving that drunken fool at the bar a few icy glares. Let this bloke of yours go. Get him out of your system. You have a life to lead. Sorry, I said too much. I don't normally interfere. It just seems a shame, that's all."

Cinnamon managed a smile back. "Thanks, Joe. I know that. It just seems that all of those I meet are lousy, present company excepted, of course."

"Thanks, Mrs Joe will be pleased to know that. We're celebrating our thirtieth next week. I can't believe it ... thirty years of marriage, and she's stuck by me, even when I had my accident and had to leave the Force. She's been—what's the favourite saying these days— my rock? I'm just lucky, I guess. Righty-ho, must get off. She's cooking my favourite for dinner—steak and chips." He rubbed his stomach. "I'll find your man. I'd hate to be in his shoes when you confront him though."

Cinnamon gave Joe a warm smile. "Mrs Joe is lucky too."

"Okay, I'm out of here. Oh, and Miss Knight ..."

"Yes."

"Stop shooting daggers at Dick-brain over there. He's only a drunken fool."

"Don't worry, Joe, I'll behave. Enjoy your meal and say hello to

Mrs Joe for me."

They shook hands. For one moment, she thought Joe was going to give her a fatherly peck on the cheek. The man seemed to like her. He told her when they first met that she reminded him of his own daughter who had left for a new life in Australia. Maybe that was why he dispersed extra advice as well as doing his job. He even congratulated her on giving up cigarettes. Told her that she had done really well to go cold turkey like she had. The man was solid gold. She was glad to have found him. He had been a police officer for twenty years, then one day managed to be in the wrong place at the wrong time and was shot. He didn't talk about it at all, yet his face took on a haunted look if it was mentioned.

Joe shambled off. This profession suited him. He blended in well into backgrounds, much like she did. If asked to describe him, you wouldn't have been able to remember if he had grey hair, dark hair, or was bald. He needed no disguises because, like a chameleon, he could make himself invisible. Cinnamon removed her glasses to polish the lenses. Like Joe, she preferred to remain hidden. People were far more likely to recall a lady wearing a large bright Puffa jacket and purple-framed glasses, rather than her actual facial features. It was easy enough to stay below the radar if you tried. She had spent most of her life under it and now only surfaced when she felt like it.

Geoff would have to wait, but there were plenty of other cheating sods who deserved their comeuppance. She returned her cold stare to the Dick-brain. He was flirting outrageously and rather aggressively with the young barmaid. That wasn't too bad in itself, but not only was he was wearing a wedding ring, he had been telling his mates about the new baby his wife was expecting. Cinnamon watched as he leered at two women headed towards the toilet.

"Fancy a threesome?" he yelled at them, clinking his glass with his fellow drunken friends. The women scurried past. "Dykes!" he yelled after them.

"Come on, Kyle, we're off for a curry. You wanna join us?" asked one of his friends.

"Nah, I'll have one more, then try my luck here," he said nodding in the direction of the barmaid. "She's probably gagging for it, and I don't suppose I'll be getting any for a while once the sprog is born."

"I'd hate to be your missus," laughed one of the men.

"Yeah, well, what she doesn't know won't hurt her, eh?" he replied, tapping the side of her nose.

He threw back the remains of his glass. "Fill it up, sweetheart, and one for yourself. Just going for a Jimmy Riddle," he slurred.

"You've been watching too many episodes of The Sweeney, talking like that!" laughed one of his friends. The barmaid smiled at the man as he winked at her. He put one hand over hers as it reached for his glass and whispered something to her. She went pink and nodded. He winked and proceeded to weave his way to the far end of the bar in the direction of the toilets, passing Cinnamon's table. Cinnamon looked about, waited a few seconds, then rose unnoticed and followed him.

The man was whistling tunelessly, one hand was against the wall of the urinal as he attempted to steady himself. He swayed slightly trying to unzip his trousers with the other hand. Just as he started to urinate, Cinnamon appeared from nowhere and shoved him hard in the back.

"Oh crikey, sorry!" she said, hand in front of her mouth in feigned dismay. "I thought you were my boyfriend. You look just like him from the back. I came in to give him a, you know, surprise."

The man looked down in horror. A large wet urine stain spread down the front of his pale grey chinos. His soft leather shoes were also spattered.

"You clumsy cow ..." he began. Cinnamon didn't hang about to hear the rest of the sentence. She left, stopping only to remove her glasses and put her empty tonic water bottle on the bar where she spoke to the barmaid.

"There's some drunken guy out there who's pissed himself," she said indicating the toilets. "He tried to make a pass at me. What a total prat. I told him he was too drunk to get it up even if I wanted him too. Honestly, some men never grow out of nappies." She laughed in a sisterly fashion to the barmaid. "Judging by the horrible smell, that one probably wishes he was wearing one!"

The wind was howling. It was picking up leaves and hurled itself at the windows. Dawn's nerves were jangled. She hated the wind. She wanted to go to the gym, but she didn't dare ask if she could take the car out. Jim would have undoubtedly refused her request claiming that it was far too dangerous to drive, and he didn't want the car damaged by branches falling on it.

It had been a different matter when he worked. He drove a company car, and Dawn had sole possession of the Volvo. He didn't know or worry if she went out in the wind in those days. With just the one car, he claimed it as his own. Dawn almost needed to put in a request to use it. He was getting worse by the day. The day before, he had insisted he drove her to the shops to get the weekly shop for them and Jack. He made some comment about her lack of parking skills, which she felt was unjustified. She decided not to argue about it and let him take charge. In the absence of people to boss about at work, Dawn had become his scapegoat.

He not only drove but decided to also take charge of the shopping. Every time she put something in the trolley, he removed it, and replaced it with a cheaper brand. He wrinkled his nose at some of her choices and spent ages in front of the reduced cabinet, where he finally settled on a pack of fish and a ready-prepared salad. The fish was on its sell-by date, and when she challenged him about it, he shrugged, saying at least it would be easy for her to cook. In the end, she felt like sticking him the trolley, wheeling it to the nearest canal, and dumping him there in it.

She was getting jolly sick of being told what to do. The wretched man had even begun to follow her about the house and make comments about her housework. The day before, she caught him cleaning a window she had already cleaned. She demanded to know why he was taking over her duties, duties which she had performed for decades. He merely replied that the window was still smeary and he thought he would be helping.

Dawn wished he were still at work. Her life had been so much better when he hadn't been at home all the time. She had made a routine for herself. Each morning, she would ensure the house was hoovered and dusted, beds made, and any washing or necessary cleaning done. She would phone her dad for a chat mid-morning to make sure he was all right. After a light lunch, she would settle down with a book, magazine, or watch an afternoon television quiz show. She enjoyed nothing better than the chance to set up the ironing board, get on with the weekly iron, while simultaneously watching a film she had recorded the night before or borrowed from Dan. Dan shared her passion for animated and adventure films. She always watched films with him when he was younger. Now, she had to watch them alone. After a cup of afternoon tea, she would put the radio on, prepare dinner, and wait for the men in her life to come home and tell her what had happened in their worlds.

Now, it was impossible to do any of those things. The first time Jim saw she was watching afternoon television, he went mad, saying afternoon television was for losers. He banned it until after seven o'clock each day and told Dawn she could surely find something more entertaining or useful to do than waste her time in front of 'the box'.

Trips to salons or spending a day out shopping were also things of the past. Not that she went very often. Finances wouldn't stretch to those 'luxuries' and even if they did, she would have to ask to use the car, and that would set off a blazing row.

It wasn't just Jim who lost out when he was made redundant: Dawn lost out too. Her life was becoming increasingly like living in a prison. That was, until she discovered the writing group and, thanks to Cinnamon, her exercise classes. She loved going to those. She got such a buzz from them. Just as she was debating whether to ask Jim if she could borrow the car, a cheerful face appeared at the kitchen window. It was mostly hidden in a large hood, so only sparkling eyes shone out. It waved a brown package. Dawn motioned for it to come round to the door.

Leaves swirled around Viv. "Come in, before you get blown away," said Dawn feeling glad to see someone. "Thanks," puffed Viv. "I was going to put it in your letterbox, but it's been damaged in transit, so I thought I'd deliver it to you in person and apologise. It's nothing to do with me. It arrived at the depot like that. We put it in the plastic bag to keep the contents safe"

"I'm surprised you're out and about in this weather. It's the windiest I've seen it for a while."

"Nothing stops the Royal Mail," replied Viv proudly. She handed the brown box package to Dawn. "So, are you going to watch the DVD with Mr Ellis?"

"Crumbs, no. This is for me. It's to give me some practice with some moves that I can't seem to master easily." Dawn protested.

Viv gave a snort.

"It's an exercise DVD."

"Uh-huh," replied Viv. "None of my business what you get up to, or what you watch."

"It's an exercise DVD!"

"I'd like to see you try some of the moves on that DVD then."

"It's for pump-it-up classes. I'm taking them up next week, along with kick-boxing, and I don't want to be the novice in the class. The others have been doing it for a while, and I don't want to hold them up or go wrong and make a fool of myself."

Viv grinned like a Cheshire cat. "I love delivering to you. You make my day!" she said. "Better go. I have still got all of the estate to do yet. Hope the exercise DVD isn't damaged," she chortled. "Wouldn't want you to get behind in those moves."

Dawn shut the door. She was completely baffled by Viv's behaviour. She should have taken out the DVD and shown her. It was only an exercise DVD. The DVD was still in its cardboard container but had been put in a plastic see through bag. There was a note stuck on it from the sorting office apologising that her package had come apart and hoping Dawn had not lost any valuable contents.

Dawn turned the plastic bag over. The back of the cardboard box had ripped off and the DVD front cover was exposed. You could see the photograph on it quite clearly. The world stood still as Dawn looked at the DVD. She was positive she ordered *The Ministry of Sound, Pump it Up, Ultimate Dance Workout*. The DVD she held and the sorting office had repackaged for her showed a naked woman being groped from behind by a young man and was called *Pump it Up Me Harder*.

Dawn had received a letter from the National Savings people alerting her that a bond she had set up five years previously was about to mature. She needed either to renew it or encash it. She had invested £1000 and now it was worth a little bit more. Jim would no doubt tell her that in today's market it was worth less than the original sum, if you factored in inflation. He normally handled all their finances. He had a self-invested pension and a few holdings in stocks and shares. Nothing left the house without Jim knowing about it. He kept a tight rein on their expenditure, more so than ever since he'd lost his job.

They didn't have a fortune, but what they had was enough to help them get by. It was a good thing that they had been frugal over the years, or they would have been in a complete pickle by now. At least she still didn't have to take up a part-time job somewhere. At her age, she doubted she would get a job. Even a supermarket checkout job had so many applicants chasing after it that a middle-aged woman who had never worked in her life other than raise a child and look after a house would surely be overlooked.

This money was hers, though. She inherited it when an elderly aunt passed away. She didn't fritter it away at the time, but decided to put it into a small investment. The National Savings Certificate was in Jim's filing cabinet in his den, where he kept all the important papers. He was out, so she decided to root out the form herself and cash in the savings. It had been so stressful of late. Jim and she spent much of the time avoiding each other. When they were in the same room, they snapped and snarled at each other about ridiculous things. Jim had told her off the day before for not defrosting the freezer. A thick layer of ice had built up in it, and he was furious about it. Dawn was sure it was because he had left the door ajar but let him rant. He got crosser and crosser then marched off with a screwdriver, which he had stabbed repeatedly at the ice. Dawn had protested. He gave her a look colder than the ice in the freezer, and she left him to it. Of course, he had damaged the freezer, and he had gone out to find a replacement. He was fuming when she last saw him. He was also mad at her about the DVD she had bought. He made her send it back along with a stern letter saying they wanted a full refund and a copy of the DVD they had ordered for free as payment for embarrassment caused. It was a shame he couldn't see the funny side of it.

What they needed was a holiday. Jim had been dreadfully testy in recent weeks. Being unemployed zapped him of his confidence and was making him bad-tempered. They needed a break from it all. A holiday would help patch up things in the bedroom department too. It was amazing what sea and sun could do to make you feel well, and of course, romantic.

She had seen just the place for them. It was on one of the Canary Islands: Lanzarote. Lanzarote offered all sorts of marvels, but it was really the hotel that had decided it for her. The hotel Volcan was unlike any hotel she had seen. She admired the photographs of shimmering swimming pools surrounded by large black volcanic rocks and fabulous coloured birds of paradise flowers. Wooden bridges traversed the pools. The hotel was modelled on a typical

Lanzarote village with pretty white buildings tumbling down below a volcano. Gardens and romantic hidden courtyards were hidden among the 'streets'. Up a level, there were two further small swimming pools and near those areas, designed to resemble vineyards, allowed couples to lie together on sun beds. It offered everything a guest could want, including entertainment, a spa, boutiques and several restaurants, one being Japanese. The interior of the hotel was a delight. Reception was housed inside the volcano and tumbling from it was an internal waterfall. It was breathtaking. She ached to go there. It would be so romantic and exciting. It was just what they needed and, with this money, she could take them there.

She shoved open the door to his den. It was very neat in there. Jim's laptop lay on the desk. A small letter rack was behind it, and some files in a very tidy pile were positioned next to the laptop. Pens were placed side by side in a regimental line on top of the files. Pity he didn't keep the rest of the house as tidy, she remarked mentally, thinking of the kitchen which had boxes of screws strewn on the worktops. Her eye travelled along the bookcase next to the filing cabinet where Jim kept his finance and accountancy books, along with a couple of thrillers. He wasn't much of a reader. She doubted he had even opened the Clive Cussler thrillers. They had been Christmas presents from Dan.

She opened the filing cabinet searching for a file with her name on it. She couldn't help but notice the bank statements in the first file as she rustled through. They caught her eye. There seemed to be a lot of withdrawals. The account was in both their names, but Jim always kept the statements. He was an accountant, after all. She had no need to bother with them. Finances were his department. It seemed peculiar that there were cash withdrawals for £150, £300, and one for £500 the month before.

She found the form she was looking for at the back of the cabinet. She was about to pull it out when she heard Jim calling for her. He was back and no doubt was still in a bad mood. Without knowing why, she shoved the form back into the cabinet, shut the drawer, and made sure she had left no evidence of being in the room. Something niggled in her brain. Something told her that things weren't right.

Walking past Stowe Pool, en route to the writing group, Dawn noticed Jason sitting on a bench, notepad and pen in hand writing.

"Hi! Late again with your homework?" she asked.

Jason looked up and gave her a dazzling smile.

"Am I glad to see you? I could do with some help. Can I copy yours?" he joked.

He invited her to sit down on the bench.

"You too busy partying over the weekend to get the work done?" she joked.

Jason laughed. "I wish! No, I was busy training the youngsters. They had competition matches all weekend, and I just ran out of time."

"You train young boys and girls?"

"Yes," he admitted and blushed. "Don't laugh. It's my pet project. I set it up myself. I hold free classes for disadvantaged children. Or for those who feel bullied at school, that sort of thing."

"Well, that's very commendable," replied Dawn, warming to him even more. "What made you decide to do that?"

Jason put down his pad and ran a hand through his hair. "I don't normally talk about this, but well, let's say I was a bit of a runt in my day. I know, difficult to believe looking at me now. I grew up in a tough area. When I say tough, I mean really tough. You didn't want to go outside in the daytime let alone at night. When I was about eleven, I got mixed up with a bad lot. They were kids from my school. That is, they were kids who were supposed to go to my school but spent most of the time bunking off and causing trouble. It sounds so dumb now, but at the time I wanted to prove myself because I wasn't as big and strong as all of the others. I ended up doing really stupid things like smoking, trying to steal fags, and so on. I got out of hand. I caused my parents no end of worry. My dad was really scared for me and thought that if I continued to hang out with these guys, I'd end up in jail, so one day he took me to a martial-arts centre in Birmingham to learn self-defence. It worked. I loved it. The guy who taught me was a massive bloke, and from the off, I wanted to be like him so much that I did everything he said. I soon gained some self-respect and started training seriously. It kept me off the streets."

"I took up fighting too. The proper sort, not just brawling. It helped me release all that teenage frustration I had inside. I became passionate about it. I travelled to Thailand to train for weeks at a time. I was completely obsessed with it. It is more than just fighting. You learn a lot about yourself and learn a huge amount of self-control. Thailand is a wonderful country too. The people are incredible."

"Thai boxing helped me take charge of my life. I left that dark world behind. I've been addicted ever since. I haven't really had time for other things or people in my life because I have always been training or fighting. I've got quite a few awards, actually, if you want to come up and see them some time," he joked. "Last year, I hit forty. Don't look at me like that."

"You can't be forty. You look much younger," gasped Dawn.

He grinned back, "The boxing, focus on health, and good living keep me youthful. Oh and the regular shots of Botox," he continued.

Dawn laughed again.

"Anyway, to be serious for just a few more minutes, I decided I wanted to put something back into the community. I've had great life travelling and training and so on, but I missed out on a proper relationship and having a family. Maybe part of me didn't feel mature enough to settle down. Hitting forty made me realise I was too old to get hitched and have kids, so I decided that I wanted to help other boys or girls, who will be able to have opportunities and confidence they are lacking today. It's better than being just a dad. This way, you get to help lots of children."

He looked up again. His eyes were shining with enthusiasm. Dawn couldn't help but smile back at him.

"So, what happened to all your old friends?" she asked

"One is doing a six-year stretch for GBH, one lost his life to heroin last year, and the third disappeared. We have no idea what happened to him. There was a rumour he had been done in by a rival gang member. I was lucky. If I hadn't been steered in the right direction, I would've been like them."

"Do your parents still live at your old home?" she asked tentatively.

"Gosh, no! They moved to the South of France years ago. I nip over now and then to say hello, and grab some time out. Dad is into painting, and Mum enjoys the warmth and French markets. I don't go to Thailand nowadays. It's too far to travel, and well, I really am getting older. It's time for me to leave the fighting circuit and have a more normal life. The centre keeps me focussed now…that and my classes at the health club."

"Good for you. That's quite something," she said and resisted the urge to hug him. His determination, combined with an inner calm, was very attractive.

"And so, back to the homework. I didn't do it this week, but I have been trying out some ideas for my project. Can I trust you with them?" he asked.

"Of course you can. I promise not to steal them, or give them to the press."

"I've been working on a couple of ideas for a teenage novel. One that will give them a character to admire and maybe emulate. It's to go hand-in-hand with what I do. I thought I'd make my protagonist a Thai boxer who settles scores with bad guys. What do you reckon? Not too sissy, is it?"

"Not at all. If anyone can write convincingly about that subject, it's you. Put down good descriptions of Thailand, training, and fights, and you'll reel them in. Children need heroes and people to admire."

"Yes, I totally agree. I think adults do too."

He returned his pad to a rucksack sat on the floor beside him. "Come on, lovely lady. I guess it's time for us to go and learn how to become better writers. I do hope 'sir' won't make me stand in the corner, wearing a dunce's hat, for not doing my homework." He chuckled.

"You can have mine if he asks you. It's not very good, but we can't have you squirming about looking embarrassed."

"Dawn Ellis, you are a completely charming and kind person."

"Mr Jackson, I believe the same can be said of you."

The swans on the pool floated by exuding serenity. A small child was feeding bread to the ducks nearby and crowing with delight at their antics.

Jason and Dawn watched for a moment then made their way to the Samuel Johnson Museum chatting comfortably. Anyone looking at them would assume they had known each other for years.

"Hi! Come in," welcomed Dawn, hugging first her son and then the pretty dark-haired Phoebe. "It's been ages since you came round to eat with us."

"It's all these extra shifts Phoebs has been doing. When she isn't at the agency, she's behind the bar."

"Well, we want to get that deposit for a house, don't we? Preferably before we're fifty years old!"

Dan looked suitably humble and squeezed her arm affectionately. "Lovely to see you, Mum," he effused. "Not seen you for ages, not since—"

"Shh! He doesn't know about that," warned Dawn. She didn't want word to get out to Jim that she had been trying to hot wire a car. He would have gone ballistic. Dan tapped the side of his nose. "Mum's the word," he joked. "So where is the old grumpy g—oh, hi, Dad, there you are!"

They did a part hug, part pat, man-thing ritual that they always performed. Jim gave Phoebe a peck on the cheek.

"You look amazing, Dawn," gushed Phoebe. "Doesn't she, Dan? You've lost weight, and well, you look a lot younger."

"Oh, I started at the gym a few weeks ago. I've got a great trainer who puts me through my paces all right. They've worked magic, though. I can now hold my stomach in!"

Phoebe laughed politely. "No, it's more than that. You seem more youthful somehow."

Seeing a look flash across Jim's face, Dawn brushed away the comments airily and walked Phoebe into the kitchen.

"So, what have you been up to, apart from looking after my hopeless son and working all hours God sends?"

"Uh-hum! I am not useless. I cooked tea last night. And I cleaned the bathroom yesterday."

Dawn pretended to look astonished.

"He needs to mend his ways," said Phoebe. "Especially now—"

Dawn's antennae picked up. "Go on," she urged. Phoebe hugged Dan's arm and looked up with little girl eyes.

"Come on. We have to tell them now. I am bursting to tell them."

Dawn caught the glint from her finger.

"Big news. Phoebe and I have got engaged," announced Dan.

Phoebe waved her sparkling ring about in front of their faces.

Dawn let out a whoop. Jim took a while to realise what had been announced then shook Dan by the hand, mumbling congratulations. Dawn threw her arms around them both.

"Jim, there's some cava in the outside fridge, left over from last

Christmas. We should celebrate. Would you go and get it please? Come on," she said, grabbing Phoebe's hand to look at the ring. "Tell me all about it. Did he propose properly?"

Dan chuckled. "Oh yes. I did it by the book. Phoebe's father is a proper stickler when it comes to these things. He might be a farmer, but he's an old romantic at heart. He told me I couldn't propose to Phoebe until I had asked permission from him. He also wanted a herd of Jersey cows as a wedding dowry for her. I bought him a furry Milka cow and a pint of Gold Top. We went around last week, and I asked if I could marry his daughter. I told him I couldn't give him a herd of cows, but I promised to look after, protect, and love Phoebs with every fibre of my being. I almost reduced him to tears. He gave me his blessing. Then, I had to choose the right moment to propose." Jim lumbered off to find the cava.

"We've both had this week off to spend some time together. We never seem to see each other for long these days, and we were both owed a few days off. Phoebs knew I was going to propose to her, but she didn't know when. I took her to Alton Towers on Monday, and I was going to ask her to marry me at the top of the Oblivion ride, but we were both too busy screaming and had our eyes shut! Then, I thought I'd ask her when we went out for a drink at a wine bar in Sutton Coldfield. I was going to drop the ring in a glass of champagne, but I read about a girl who swallowed her ring when her fiancé did that too, so I got cold feet. I thought about making her breakfast in bed and putting the ring on the tray—that was a bit lame. So, yesterday we went for a meal at the Thai restaurant by the narrow boats at Barton under Needwood. I was about to do the deed when all the lights went out in the restaurant and I nearly dropped the flipping box with the ring in it. All the waiters burst into the restaurant, carrying a cake exploding with fireworks and sang happy birthday to the woman at the table next to ours. I looked a right idiot on one knee. I had to pretend I was doing up my shoelace. In the end, we went for a walk by the marina. It was one of those calm starry nights, and I asked her there and then, under the heavens."

"How sweet. Your dad asked me to marry him in the kitchen at his digs. Not quite as planned or as romantic as your proposal."

Jim crashed back into the kitchen at that moment, bottle of cava in one hand.

"Who's for a glass?"

He popped the cork, Dawn cheered. They clinked their filled glasses together. Dawn proposed toasts to the happy couple.

"When are you planning the actual wedding?"

"Oh, not for a good year or two. We really need to get a decent deposit down on a house, and weddings take some planning. Good thing Phoebs is an estate agent. At least she knows about mortgages and when a good bargain is about to come up for sale, or we'd never find a property in this market."

"A year gives me time to lose some more weight and find a suitable hat. Can't have the groom's mother letting down the side."

They chatted for an hour. They refused to join Dawn and Jim for dinner because they had to tell Jack the news.

"We promised we'd take him round some fish and chips tonight. We'll get him a can of Guinness too, so he can celebrate," said Dan, enveloping his mother in a bear-like squeeze. He glowed with happiness and pride. Dawn felt an ache for him. He was still her little boy, but she had to let him go now. This time she really had to let go. Phoebe would look after him. For the moment, she was happy that he was happy. Phoebe hugged her too, face flushed. "I'm very lucky. You brought him up well. He's so sensitive for such a big guy. Love him to bits."

Dawn's eyes filled a little, and she ushered them out of the door.

"Tell Granddad I'll pop round tomorrow to see him. I'll get him a newspaper too, so he needn't go out in the morning to buy one."

The happy couple departed, leaving the house strangely sad and empty. The vibrancy departed with them. Jim was washing up the glasses when Dawn walked back from seeing off Dan and Phoebe.

"They looked really happy, didn't they?" she remarked as she picked up the tea towel to dry the glasses.

"Leave them, they can drain," barked Jim.

Dawn recoiled at the brusque tone in his voice. She hung up the tea towel, opened the fridge door in search of food for dinner.

"Fancy some fish?"

"No, not really. I'm not very hungry. I might just go and sort out a few things in my office, then grab a shower and have an early night."

"Are you okay?"

"Yes, fine," came the curt reply.

"I thought you'd be happier, especially after hearing the good news."

"It's not that good, is it? He's only twenty-five years old."

"We were younger than that when we got married," commented Dawn and wished she hadn't. Jim's face said it all.

"He should be seizing new opportunities, not saddling himself with …" Jim paused. Dawn was waiting for the unsaid words, ready to leap up and shout at him. "Debt," he continued and went back to rinsing the glasses under the running water from the tap.

Dawn knew what he meant. He had almost voiced what he wanted to say. He really wanted to say 'liability' or 'a wife'. Saddened, she turned to leave him, hoping he would make things better and say something, anything that would show he cared about her, but behind her there was nothing. She was almost at the staircase when Jim coughed.

"I'm going out tomorrow. I'll be gone all day and all night. Trevor Baker from Chilternz has invited me to join him and a couple of ex-clients for a round of golf at the Belfry and a stay-over. We don't want to drive back if we've had a drink or two."

"That'll be nice. It'll be good for you to see Trevor again. What time are you going?"

"We're teeing off at eleven thirty. I'll leave here about ten, so there'll be some time to have a catch up chat before we play. I haven't played in so long, I might even try a few practice swings at the range first. I'll probably let everybody down. I'm well out of practice," he said. For a moment, he sounded more animated.

"You'll be fine. It might get you back into it. Then you'd have something to do with your spare time."

"Yeah, right, going off to play golf with other bored bastards."

Dawn gave up. He was determined to be a miserable old sod. Maybe a day with his old work colleague from Chilternz would cheer him up. Heavens knew he needed something. Still, at least she would have a whole day to do whatever she wanted and an entire evening to watch whatever she fancied on the television or have a bubble bath or drink an entire bottle of wine without him glowering at her. The thought made her tingle. She would write a chapter of her book in the morning then treat herself to some pampering, paint her nails, do her hair, and enjoy time alone.

"Pity you can't think of someone to invite over to keep you company," said Cinnamon with a smirk.

Dawn shooed her away.

It was quiet in the Belfry bar. Cinnamon was contemplating what to do with her evening, when a larger than life figure bustled through the door and ordered a large coke. The woman, dressed in a fluorescent pink Polo top and matching sun visor, along with the brightest blue and green check trousers ever seen, checked out the surroundings and headed in Cinnamon's direction.

"Mind if I join you, honey?" she asked, and before Cinnamon could object, she plonked down onto the chair beside her.

"Hi. I'm Mary-Beth. I'm from Florida. Here with my best buddy, Fran, who is at this moment trying to find something suitable to take home for her husband. She loves memorabilia. Got lots of those little china plates. We've just done eighteen holes of this mighty fine golf course. Isn't it a picture here? Do you play golf?"

Cinnamon hadn't even thought of a reply when her new friend began again. "My Bruce said I should come to the finest golf course while I was here in England. We were going to try at St Andrews, that's where your Prince William and Kate came from, isn't it? But it is too far to journey just for some golf. Some of the best matches have been played here and now we have too. We had our photo taken at all the holes to show the boys. They are going to be so jealous. Tomorrow, we're going to Stratford to see William Shakespeare. Ha! Not really see him, of course not, he's dead. Just to see the playhouse and where he lived and all. Do you know Stratford?"

Cinnamon's head began to ache. This woman was all energy and chat. Cinnamon wasn't used to such gregariousness. She was about to say she had to go when Mary-Beth let out a cry, "Oh, here she is! Come on over and meet this lovely girl. Isn't she a doll? What's your name, honey?"

"Cinnamon."

"Oh, isn't that the loveliest name? Sugar and spice. This is Cinnamon, Fran. Cinnamon, this is my very best friend in the whole world, Fran."

Fran who looked a lot like Mary-Beth gave a dazzling smile, nodded, and dropped down to join them.

"Geez there's some stuff in that shop. Wanted to buy it all. I got

Bud this. What do you think?"

She hauled out a ginormous shirt with the words "The Belfry" emblazoned on it and a matching baseball cap.

"Is that large enough for him? Might be a little tight. Still, he can show off those big biceps of his!" The women rocked about, hooting with laughter.

"So, are you on a tour of the UK?" ventured Cinnamon.

"Uh-huh. We're on a European tour. It's our wedding anniversary present."

"You're ... together?"

The women laughed out loudly again. Mary-Beth bashed Cinnamon on the arm in a friendly gesture.

"Oh, you Brits are so funny! Fran and I met at high school, and we've been friends ever since. We met our sweethearts in the same year, got married the same year, had children the same year, and live in the same street. Our sweethearts are best friends. Here, I have photos of them."

Mary Beth emptied the contents of her handbag onto the table. Lipstick and purse tumbled out among mints, receipts, coins, golf score cards, tees, gloves, mirror, and other paraphernalia. She found her iPhone and proceeded to search through the photographs on it, alighting on one and shoving it towards Cinnamon.

"That's Bruce," she said pointing to a large ruddy-faced man with some stubble, "And that is Fran's husband and his best buddy, Bud!" She pointed at the other man, who looked identical to the first except he had less stubble. They were grinning at the camera and holding a large fish between them.

"We've been married for thirty-five years this week, so we thought we'd give them an anniversary present. We've come to Europe and they are having the time of their lives without us. They are in a cabin in the middle of nowhere, drinking beer and fishing. It's the perfect celebration," declared Mary-Beth and roared with laughter once more.

"Don't they mind you coming all the way over here on your own?"

"Haha! No. I'm a black belt in Karate, and Fran here has Old Holler."

"Old Holler?"

"She wanted to bring Old Faithful, but we thought that might be a bit too dangerous. It's made out of wood, and if she smashed it into anyone's knees, she'd sure as heck break them. She's awesome with a baseball bat. Bud let her bring Old Holler. It's made out of light rubber, but if Fran whacks you with it—"

"You'll holler!" they choroused and fell about laughing yet again.

"My Brucie also gave me these," said Mary-Beth, ferreting about in her bag once more. She pulled out a large pair of handcuffs. "These were his cuffs. He didn't hand them back in when he retired. We've had some fun with these in the past," she joked, waving them about and making Fran honk.

"So, if any of those frisky I-talians want to pinch our butts, we'll be ready for them," added Fran, nudging Mary-Beth.

"Italy?"

"Yes, we're here for three more days, then on Monday we are off to Gay Paree, France. We might try out as cancan girls there. Do you think we have the legs for it?" Fran rolled up her trouser legs to reveal meaty calves. "We used to be cheerleaders in our heyday, so I bet we could match those French girls with their moves. Bud suggested we try out at the Folies Bergère, but I told him if I danced topless, I'd flatten the entire front row of the audience and give myself black eyes!"

"Down to Monaco after that, to break the bank at the Casino. I hear it's not as good as Vegas, but they have some fancy food there. I want to try out some of those escargots. I want to take some home for Brucie. Might find a couple of millionaires down there in Monte Carlo too, then we'll leave the boys and stay in France?" They indulged in more nudging and smirking.

"Next, we go to Venice. We are dying to be serenaded in a gondola. Then we go on to Florence, so Fran can pose with that nude sculpture of David by Michelangelo and pretend he's her toy boy. Then we stay in Rome. Fran wants to meet the Pope. After that, Prague ... and then we fly back to the States."

"That's quite an adventure. Is this the first time you've been to Europe?"

"Yes and we are just loving it. We might have to do this again next year!"

"Okay, honey, we have to go. We're having dinner in Sam's Bar and then an early night because we're off to Stratford first thing. I still haven't got used to the time difference. I might try and phone Brucie and tell him about our golf match. Hope to see you again before we leave, Cinnamon. Such a nice name. It really suits you."

They clambered up from the chairs, shook hands with Cinnamon and headed off. "Hasn't she got a lovely figure?"

"You could look like that if you gave up the Coca Cola and the fried chicken."

"No way. My Brucie likes something he can grab hold of."

The voices and cackling gradually faded into the distance. Cinnamon ordered another mineral water and fiddled about with something on the table. She had decided what to do with her evening.

It was dark in the Bel Air, the nightclub belonging to the Belfry. Loud, frantic music reverberated as flashing lights danced in time with the bass. A few bodies thrashed about on the dance floor. The whole air was filled with the musty scent of sweat. One young man extracted himself from a group of what were obviously businessmen. It was rep night and these guys were reps out on the pull.

They had spent all evening attempting to chat up the women there. Several beers later, they had almost given up and were now dancing drunkenly in a final attempt to attract attention from two females, who were in almost as bad a state, and who kept giggling while gawping at them. The man weaved around the bleached blonde women and winked at them. One nudged the other, who shook her head as the man passed them. He wasn't her sort. The man stopped at the bar to order some water. He had a meeting at nine am in Sheffield, and he really needed to sober up a bit. There was very little talent to be found that night. He needed to get some sleep. Luckily, he was booked in at the hotel next door. He would just have the water and then clear off for the night. Looking back at his colleagues, he could see the blondes approaching them. Looked like they would score. He wouldn't be missed.

He downed the water and placed the glass on the counter, getting out his wallet to pay. It was then he noticed two dark mischievous eyes staring at him. The woman staring boldly at him was mesmerising. It wasn't that she was spectacularly beautiful; it was her confidence and magnetism that held him spellbound for a moment. She looked him straight in the eyes and purred. Yes, it sounded like a purr, at him. She gazed at him as if she knew him. He felt a little uneasy.

Smiling slightly, he regained his composure and held out her hand,

"Hi, I'm James. I know that this sounds like a corny chat-up line, but do I know you?"

"No, but I hope you'd like to get to know me."

James struggled not to gulp. Was this rather sexy woman propositioning him?

"I'm not a hooker, before you ask. I'm just someone, who if she likes something enough, gets it. I'm in room 503 if you would like a nightcap or ... me."

She smiled at him, and he felt a tightening in his groin. Was she for real? Cinnamon leant forward and brushed her warm lips against his cheek. Her perfume with heady notes enveloped him. She pressed the key card for her room into his hand.

"Don't be long. We don't want to waste any time, do we?"

James watched Cinnamon slink off to the exit. Her tight trousers clung to her sculpted figure. Boy she looked tasty. It took less than thirty seconds for him to make up his mind. Bugger Sheffield! Hot totty was rare and getting rarer to find. He threw a ten-pound note on the bar and hastened after Cinnamon.

She moved like a tigress. She covered the area between the Bel Air and the hotel effortlessly. James had trouble keeping up with her. He really shouldn't have had those vodka shots after all that beer. He was getting a bit too old for all this 'Boys Out' stuff. He had a fiancée back home. He should calm down and behave more responsibly. He promised himself he wouldn't do this again, but once the lads had suggested a night out and grab a bit of fun, he couldn't refuse. He just wasn't the faithful sort. He loved his missus, but well, she wouldn't need to know about these dalliances, and he had promised to take her out shopping at the weekend for some new clothes for their holiday to Marbella the following month. Once he got married, he wouldn't do this again. It wasn't as if they were actually married after all, was it?

He reached room 503 and fumbled for the key card. He grabbed the doorframe to steady himself. Those Vodka and Red Bull chasers had been stronger than he thought. He breathed into his hand and tried to smell his breath. He grabbed the doorframe again and attempted to insert the key card into the slot. The red light at the side of the door flickered red. Damn! He pulled the card back out and tried again, missing the slot twice more. He peered closely at the slot and willed his hand to stop shaking. The key card went in, and the green light flickered on. Bingo! He was in.

The room was in complete darkness. That woman was incredible. Had she managed to get her kit off already and was waiting for him? He fumbled about with his shoes, pulling them off and letting them thump to the floor as he writhed about trying to pull off his socks. He unbuttoned his jeans. His eyes were just getting used to the dark now, and he could make out the shape of the bed. Funny she hadn't said anything to him. What an incredible creature she was. He could imagine the fun they would have.

"Are you ready for me?" he murmured. "Oh yes, I'm ready all right," came the reply as the bedside light switched on. A large woman with night cream smeared on her face, wearing an enormous nightshirt, swung at him with a baseball bat, while another, equally well-proportioned woman, screeched "Yee-ha!" in his ears and cuffed his hands behind him. Waiting outside the door, Cinnamon smiled at the screams and shouts. It sounded as if Fran was a great batswoman, and Mary-Beth more than able to control a man. It had been very fortuitous that Mary-Beth had left her room key card behind on the table when she had emptied her bag. All it had then taken was a discreet enquiry at reception, where Reme, a friendly cheerful receptionist, had informed her that her American aunties were in Room 503. That would teach the little cheat. She had overheard him at the nightclub telling his pervy friends that his fiancée would be best kept in the dark about the boys' nights out. Maybe that would be the last time he would try that game. How she detested infidelity.

It was a bright but cold day when Dawn stomped down to the bus shelter. She was fed up. Blasted Jim had gone out and taken the car. She protested when he said he was going out.

"But, what about the writing group? We've got a meeting today. You know we always meet every other Friday."

"It's only a silly group of people with aspirations that will never be fulfilled," he replied cruelly. He caught sight of Dawn's face. "If it means that much to you, catch a bus. I think the whole thing is just a waste of time, though." With that, he left. He didn't turn back to wave at her as he marched with determination to the car on the driveway, nor did he look back as he left, wheels spinning. Dawn was shell-shocked. Jim was becoming intolerable. He never used to be so cruel.

"You never used to dress like that to go out," whispered Cinnamon. Dawn smoothed down her black dress. She had been so pleased with her appearance ten minutes earlier. She had added some simple beads to the dress and thought she looked ten years younger. Some light make-up completed the picture. She felt good about herself for the first time in a long time when she had come downstairs. That was until Jim suddenly decided he was going out, and needed the car more urgently than she did and before he had been so negative about the writing group.

The more she thought about it, the angrier she became. She didn't ask for a lot in her life. When he was working, she had spent all her time at home ensuring meals were ready for him when he came in from a busy day, listening to him complain about ungrateful clients and making sure that she was the prop holding them all up. She was always the one to support Dan's football matches, go to his plays, help him with his homework, then cook a three-course meal for Jim and make sure a bottle of his favourite beer was chilling in the fridge each night. It wasn't much to ask that he be pleased she had an interest and was trying to do something slightly adventurous.

She decided that instead of sitting at home waiting for him to come home, she would go to the class. He was right; there was a bus that went to Lichfield. It would mean quite a walk to the bus stop, but what the heck? She would do it just to spite him.

It took a good forty minutes to get to the bus stop. Determination made the time pass quickly. Before long, she was stood next to an elderly lady at the bus shelter.

"You can never tell when it's going to come," said the lady as Dawn looked at her watch. "Last week, I waited a whole hour, and then I found out it had broken down at Barton Under Needwood and wasn't coming," she continued.

Dawn's spirits dropped. She looked at her watch again. When she looked up, a Mercedes sports car had pulled up next to the shelter. The nearside window dropped down. Jason was behind the wheel.

"What's a nice girl like you doing in a place like this?" he asked. "Wanna lift? I'm going your way."

Dawn jumped up, heart thumping, and opened the door. The old lady nodded at her.

"Pity there isn't room for three," she said. "Much nicer than the bus. And the driver's better looking."

Dawn laughed. "Hope the bus comes soon," she said.

Door shut, they moved away from the shelter, only to pull in again a few metres down the road near a post box. Jason said. "Do you fancy a bit of sunshine?"

"Yes, it's a nice day."

With that, he lifted a handle near the gear stick. The roof began to descend automatically.

"Oh wow! I feel like a superstar."

"You look like one too," said Jason, casting an approving eye over her outfit.

Dawn was about to protest when a red van drew up in front of them. Viv clambered out and meandered up to the car. She leant over the passenger's door and beamed at Dawn.

"So, who's this, then?" she asked. "Have you cast a spell on Mr Ellis and turned him into a handsome prince?"

"Hi," said Jason smoothly. "I'm Dawn's toy boy, Jason."

Dawn's jaw dropped. Viv took Jason's extended hand and held onto a fraction longer than she should, eyes gleaming. "I'm Viv. Nice to meet you. Well, Jason, if ever you get fed up with Dawn, I'm always available after duty."

"Might take you up on that, Viv. I love women in uniform."

Viv gave a genuine smile. "I'll make sure I carry my coat and hat around, then, just on the off chance."

She gave Dawn a delighted smile and raised an eyebrow at her. "You are turning out to be much more interesting than I first thought. Nice dress by the way. You look great. Bye both. Those letters won't take themselves to the sorting office." With that she strode off to the box, rattling a bunch of keys to unlock it. "Shall I bring my keys with me Jason?" she shouted as he revved the car.

"Of course, Viv, and don't forget wear your hat!"

The car leapt forward down the road with a throaty gurgle.

"You don't think she thought you were serious, do you?" asked Dawn still reeling from the conversation.

"Well, so what if she does? I don't care. It's not as if you are a minger, is it? You'd make a great Mrs Robinson. I always had a thing about older women. I used to play that song, Summer (The First Time) by Bobby Goldsboro all the time when I was a kid—it was one of my parent's records. I'd have loved to have been taken down to seaside and have an older woman make a man of me." He laughed again. "Sorry, Dawn. I can't help myself some days. Besides, you are very attractive, so let's give the local people something to gossip about, eh?"

Cinnamon purred in Dawn's ear. "A compliment! That makes a nice change, doesn't it?"

Dawn sat back and let the breeze blow past her head. It was invigorating.

"How come you've not got your car?" asked Jason.

"Jim took it. Told me to catch a bus."

"Not very chivalrous. Couldn't he drop you off?"

"No. I don't know where he was going, anyway. It might not have been my way. How come you are in this gorgeous car? I didn't know you had a Mercedes convertible."

"It's not mine. My car is in the garage getting a service. This is Agniezska's little toy. She doesn't take it out much, so she let me borrow it to give it a spin."

"Wow! She has taste, and obviously some money to afford one of these."

"Nah, she got it on one of those PCPs. It's a kind of loan where you pay a certain amount a month. She is a complete petrolhead and preferred to have a car she could ill afford rather than a mortgage. Must be something to do with growing up in a village with only tractors and donkeys as transport."

"That's some life. Has she been in the UK long?"

"Came over about five years ago. I met her in London. We worked together at the same gym and moved up here at the same time. We'd both had enough of city life. Have you done that exercise Blake gave us last lesson?" he asked, changing the subject as he joined the dual carriageway at speed and moved out into the outside lane to overtake a line of lorries. The wind carried some of his words away. She had wanted to find out if he and Agniezska had been or were lovers. She didn't dare pry any further. He clearly didn't want to talk about it anymore.

"Yes, did you?"

"I had a go at it, but I couldn't get my head around 'green' stories. Trust Harold to choose a difficult subject. Why couldn't he have chosen flesh-eating, sex-starved zombies or killer Kung Fu women from planet Zed?"

Conversation became more difficult as they whistled down the road towards Lichfield. The wind noise made it impossible to speak without shouting, so Jason put on a CD. Soon, 1970s music pumped through the speakers. Dawn gave him a quizzical look. He grinned back, shrugged his shoulders, and mouthed, "I like it." Dawn sat back and enjoyed the combination of sun on her face, wind in her hair and a good-looking man by her side. Stuff Jim. The writing club was just what she needed.

"So, how did we all get on with extra special homework? Today is our special award day. I'm looking forward to hearing your entries. Thanks to Harold for flagging up the idea of having this exciting competition. It's a pity he isn't here today to hear the stories. Pity too that Paige has decided to leave us. I understand from her email she has given up writing, and is embarking on a career in the media. I am sure she'll do very well." Blake paused for a moment to shake the image of Paige's large breasts from his mind. "So, without further ado, let's begin with the first entry for the Green Award. All entries must be something to do with ecology. As always, I'll ask who wants to go first." Blake paused again and looked about the room. The desks had been positioned in a square formation so there was nowhere to hide. It was just a question of who would break the ice first and dive into the cold sea. Dawn thought it was always terrifying to read out work to people. Someone would be sure to make a criticism, and after Jim's comments about writing, she was lacking in confidence more than usual. Others must have felt the same as they all eyeballed each other, willing someone to step up to the mark. Even Craig looked less cocky than normal.

"Okay, I'll choose randomly then," said Blake. "Can't say fairer than drawing a name out of the hat." Blake scribbled the names on small torn up scraps of paper. Jason squirmed. He hadn't completed the task and looked at Dawn with big eyes. She grinned evilly and shook her head. No, she wouldn't lend him her effort. He put out his bottom lip and pretended to sulk.

"Dawn!" said Blake and looked at her. Dawn gulped. Jason gave her a friendly nudge with his knee. She gulped again.

"Erm, this isn't terribly good. I'm sure there are much better efforts," she began.

"Nonsense, Dawn. We're here to improve our writing. How can we improve if we don't let anyone help us? Come along now. Don't be shy. I've read some of your work, and it was very good," coaxed Blake.

Jason nodded supportively. She took a deep breath.

"It's called The Gardener's Apprentice," she began .

The female whale and her offspring swam contentedly beside each other in the tranquillity of the vast ocean. The mother whale, the size of which cannot even be imagined, was the chief gardener of the ocean, and as the oldest female in this sea, it was her duty to pass all her knowledge onto her precious son to take over from her when the time was right. They had been swimming together for many, many months in the silent waters, checking the various gardens and allotments that were vital to the ocean. Periodically, they would hear a soulful cry of a fellow whale thousands of nautical miles away, also tending plants and gardens, and she would answer in her mournful song telling them where they had travelled and what they had seen.

"My son," she murmured lovingly, "all that is around you is precious. Even if you can't see it amidst the gloom, you must learn that we are here to protect it and allow it to flourish. It is our duty to nurture our plants and to help them become the beautiful precious gifts that they are." Her son acknowledged his wise mother and kept his eyes open for the small allotment they were to maintain this trip. It was far away from where they lived.

"Plants need light and love," explained his mother, smoothly gliding through the stillness. "We need to make sure they have all that they need and are not being attacked by parasites which choose to feed upon them." Her son listened attentively, eager to learn from her, as he was not yet old enough or large enough to take over from his mother, the protector of the Ocean.

On and on they swam, seeing nothing but tiny particles of broken plant that flew towards them. Her son, still youthful but also immensely large, was playful, and in their travels would attempt to join other strange creatures that swam alone or in groups, as and when he met them. Occasionally, he would try to chase and dart after the flashing, shining streaking objects that flew overhead on a trajectory to some deeper point in the never-ending darkness. His mother knew exactly where to go, led by a keen sense of direction.

The son was beginning to wonder how much further they should travel when he realised that he could see more clearly, and in the distance he saw a shimmer of light.

"Mother!" he gasped. "I can see brightness. The allotment must be ahead, and we shall find your plants."

"Ah yes, my son, it has been so long since I planted them, before you were born, that I have almost forgotten where they are. I wonder how they have grown. This is a very nice area, full of light and hope. Look around, and you will see that the conditions are just right for nurturing."

They headed towards the shimmer, which, in turn, expanded to an infusion of light, bringing with it warmth. The gloom evaporated completely, and light filled the space in front of them. The light produced warmth, and the young whale felt the temperature change, as he swam closer. The smaller whale blinked at the change and as his eyes became accustomed to the sudden brightness and the rays of light that pierced the darkness, he saw nine spherical plants.

"Oh Mother!" he exclaimed. "The plants. They are there, and they are huge." They moved closer to inspect the plants. "Oh no! I'm afraid that some of them have not had enough light and have not grown much," he said pointing to the smaller plants positioned further away from the bright light. "But this one," he pointed towards the third plant, "this one is a beautiful iridescent plant. It is almost green-blue in colour. It is the most breathtaking plant I have ever seen!" He floated, transfixed by the glorious colours of the living, breathing plant which appeared to be enveloped in strands of soft white cotton.

"Oh my dear son!" replied the mother whale sadly. "I am afraid this one is not what you may think. This one has been attacked by parasites." She turned the plant around to check it. "Look carefully through the magnifying glass. You will see how they have bred in the millions and have grouped themselves all over the plant, harvesting the goodness from it without replenishing it, and draining it of its energy." The son examined the plant in horror. She continued, "Some of the creatures that live symbiotically on the plant have attempted to regenerate leaves and stems, but they are insufficient in number, and the parasitic creatures have taken too much sap from the plant to allow it to heal itself. We have left it too late to help this poor plant," continued his mother. "Look how there are huge patches in it where the greedy parasites have sucked the life out of it and eaten through its glorious green foliage. Smell how it emits a poisonous aroma. This is a plant which is dying."

The plant was very large, but it had, indeed, been brutally ravaged in places. Its natural green protection had been removed. Parasites used it to provide for themselves, building larger and larger colonies, which then led to more raping of the plant. The plant's sap, its lifeblood, had become a dirty brown colour instead of being clear. It had been polluted by the parasites, fouling it in many ways. The parasites had weakened this marvel of nature, and although it had tried to repair itself, it was now in too poor a state. Weakened by the constant demands on it, it would not last much longer. Even as the whales watched, they could see small explosions and revolting gases seeping from the gaping wounds covering the plant.

After examining it as carefully as they could, the mother shook her huge head sadly and confirmed that the plant was beyond their skills.

"What about the others?" asked her son.

"The first two plants have had too much light and heat and cannot flourish. Maybe in time when the brightness lessens, they will begin to germinate again. Others are too far away from the light, and now, I fear they may never germinate, but the fourth one, next to the poor sick plant, looks promising. If we use it to replace the sick one, it should stand a good chance. It has a healthy colour and may even become more beautiful than this one."

Heartened, the smaller whale waited for his mother to show him how to remove the plant correctly, so none of the parasites spilled onto the neighbouring plant. She had done this before several times. A diseased plant was not unusual to her. She would dispose of it so it did not contaminate her beautiful ocean garden.

"Don't be sad my son." There are many other plants like this, some far more stunning. When we finish here, I shall take you to another of our allotments, and then you will see them for yourself."

Her son was placated and waited, for this was the important part.

He watched and learned as his mother opened her huge mouth. It became wider and wider until finally it was large enough for her to consume the entire plant, which slid into her vast stomach, where it would no longer pollute her precious ocean.

The two whales repaired their allotment and replaced the vacant spot with its neighbouring plant. It began to improve in colour almost immediately.

"Mother?" queried the young whale. "Is it true we have names for all our allotments and plants?"

"Yes, son."

"What did you call this allotment?"

"This one was called The Solar System. It is part of a larger garden known as The Milky Way."

"And the little sick plant?"

"That, my son, was one I had hope for. I planted it in the best spot I could. That was called Earth."

Dawn put down her pad and looked at the faces watching her.

"Well written," said Craig immediately.

"What a beautiful, tender, insightful story," added Margaret.

The compliments continued to flow. Dawn flushed with embarrassment and then pride. Blake raised his hands and applauded her.

"Well, you are hard act to follow," he said. "It'll be difficult for whoever is next. Let's draw another name ... Craig!"

Jason leaned over and whispered into her ear. "That was amazing—like you."

She drifted into the house. Her face glowed with pride. Jim was in his den. She knocked on the door and he growled 'Wait a minute,' at her. She waited patiently until Jim's head appeared. "Yes?" he said, needling her immediately. There was no need for such a surly tone.

"I'm home," she began.

"I can see that," he replied unkindly.

"Well, I wanted to show you something."

Jim sighed, as if she were preventing him from doing something very important. "What do you want to show me?"

"This!" she yelped triumphantly and handed over a certificate.

"The Green Award. Awarded to Dawn Ellis. Best Short Story," he read. He handed it back. "Well done," he said with no enthusiasm in his voice.

Dawn's hackles rose. "Is that it?"

"What? I said 'well done'. What do you want me say? 'Oh that is incredible. How marvellous!' It's hardly a Pulitzer Prize, is it? It's just some homemade certificate that I could produce on a computer. It is only a silly little contest. How many entered? Hundreds? No, I bet only about ten people, tops. Did you win a prize or any money along with that?" he asked pointing at the paper certificate.

"No, of course not, but it means something to me. It shows that people like my writing."

"It shows that a bunch of bored housewives, who probably think The Only Way is Essex is great, enjoyed your story. I bet the competition wasn't much."

"There were some very good entries as it happens. I was proud to have my story chosen above the others. What is the matter with you? You are being horrible. You're always so grumpy these days? All you do is complain and bicker. Thanks for taking the shine off my success and for making me feel miserable. Are you trying to get me to feel like you do? After all the years of just being a boring old housewife, I finally do something that is a little different, something I turn out to be good at, and you are just a miserable giant squib. You never used to be so snappy."

"And you never used to be so argumentative or such a shrew. I said 'well done' and all I have had since I said it, is abuse from you. You're a right harpy. Now, clear off. If you can't be civil, then just shut up and leave me alone!"

He shut the door firmly. Dawn stood open mouthed. This wasn't at all what she expected. She turned on her heels and went upstairs clutching her certificate, close to tears. She stared at it. All that pride she had felt evaporated. How come she now felt so unhappy? Tears rolled down her cheeks.

"You're being silly," said Cinnamon, draping herself across the table. "Remember what I told you. Be very careful whom you give your love to. Remember, whoever has your heart also has the power to hurt or destroy you. You need to toughen up a little. Words

117

shouldn't do this to you. He doesn't have the right to treat you like that or talk to you like that. Ignore him. It's only jealousy making him spiteful. Get on with some more writing, or go for a long walk. Either will help you through this."

"Thanks," replied Dawn. "You're right. I get too emotional about spats like that. I suppose it's because I'm not used to arguing all the time. Maybe it's my age too. I could be getting hormonal."

Cinnamon snorted. "I think he's the one getting hormonal, not you. He could do with a hobby to keep him occupied. Give him time, and he'll sort himself out."

Dawn nodded, wiped her eyes and running nose. She would go out for a walk and give Jim time to calm down. She was about to leave when she got a text. It was a photograph of a small cute dog sitting in a large silver trophy. The message below read :

Congratulations on winning the best story award. Will you still talk to me when you're famous? Jas x

Cinnamon raised her eyebrows. "I bet that text has made you feel heaps better than my words of advice."

"Yes, a little kindness goes a long way."

"Kindness? I think he's flirting with you. That whole thing about Mrs Robinson and what about Summer (The First Time)? You need to be careful, my girl."

"Cinnamon, your imagination runs away with you some days."

"No, it isn't my imagination that does all the work. Tread carefully. You don't want to start anything you can't finish. Don't you dare reply to that text message."

Dawn thought about it for a few minutes then sent a text back.

Thanks . Love the trophy. I'll put it on the mantelpiece with all my others. I won't forget you when I'm famous. I never forget my friends.

Cinnamon groaned and left her to it.

Downstairs, Jim stood staring out of the window. He was feeling some remorse for his harsh words. Dawn didn't deserve that sort of treatment. The problem was that he just couldn't control himself. Words spilled out of his mouth before he could stop them. It was the frustration of it all. He felt so trapped. He never expected to find himself stuck at home. Dawn was a good woman but being in the same house all the time was impossible. This was the worst scenario possible. He knew he should try to be nicer. He should try and control his anger and his dark moods. He dreaded each day. They were all the same. The repetition was driving him insane and then there was the other problem.

He sighed and rubbed his head absent-mindedly. None of this was Dawn's fault. She deserved an apology..

He stood for a moment longer. She would be busy on a writing project or something. He would leave it for now. Dawn would come round and forgive his temper. He would try harder. He could not be sure though that it would be enough.

Dawn looked in the bedroom mirror. Her heart was heavy. Cinnamon looked back. "Look, ignore the old sod. He's still in a strop because you have found something you are passionate about, and he ... well, he's bored!"

"I don't think I'm cut out for this writing. Jim's probably right. It's just fantasy. I was a lot happier when I baked cakes for Jim and—"

"No, you weren't," said Cinnamon softly. "You did it because you thought you had to. You believed you had to play the role of the perfect wife who makes sure that the laundry is done on a Monday, shopping on a Tuesday, Wednesday, clean all the house, iron all Jim's shirts ... You know what I mean. You've only been living half a life all this time."

"No, it was a full life while I had Dan."

"Okay, I agree. It was more rewarding when you had Dan. Think about it, though, how much of your life has been fun?"

"We had some fun times."

"Funny, I don't remember too many fun times. Jim was usually up to his eyeballs in work. He was never as interested in Dan as you thought he would be. He didn't use to take him out to the park or play football in the backyard with him, did he?"

"He was maybe frightened of getting too close, especially after we lost Elisabeth. It hurt him too. I think in some ways, because I was so depressed about it all, I may not have realised the effect it had on him. He changed after that, too."

"Come on, Dawn, you're no dummy. What if Jim only married you because you were pregnant with Elisabeth and then felt trapped afterwards? You wouldn't be the first couple to have raced into a relationship then regretted it for years after."

"He could have left me at any time, if that were the case. Why did he stick by me?"

"Felt sorry for you? Got so involved with work? It was convenient to have you at home? Didn't have the guts to tell you because you were a broken human being for so long that he might have tipped you over the edge by leaving you?" said Cinnamon, her voice rising. "It doesn't matter what or why. The fact is that all is not right now. Do you want to hang about and get hurt every time he ignores you or says something cruel? Or do you want to start standing on your own two feet? You've made huge steps forward since you started this writing. You have taken hold of your physical shape and mentally, you are much more challenged. You look better, for goodness sake."

"You spent all your young life looking after Jack, then you spent years looking after Jim, then finally, you spent the last twenty-four years running around and looking after Dan. Can you see who is missing out of that little family group? Yes, you. Up until now, you haven't done anything for yourself. So yes, your writing might flounder. You may never get a publisher or an agent. So what? At least you are writing a book. How many people can say they have written a book?"

"You may not win prizes or become a best-selling author, but you are doing something you enjoy. You have won in other ways because of it. You look much better than you did and are probably a lot healthier. You are stimulated and look happier. You have even made friends thanks to it, and I mean friends, not just women acquaintances whose kids happen to be in the same class as yours."

"Figure it out, Dawn. I shouldn't have to spell it out ... why do you think I am here?"

With those final words Cinnamon disappeared, leaving Dawn open-mouthed at this revelation.

Crikey. Cinnamon was right. Dawn had created her because deep down she wanted to be, in some way, like Cinnamon. She yearned to be a strong, independent woman who had no need of anyone. One who set her own rules.

Jim was wrong. Her writing wasn't pointless. Her award at the writing class the day before had proven that. There was genuine enthusiasm when she read out her story. Blake had praised her efforts. Geraldine gave her a thumbs-up. Colin smiled at her, and Jason ... well, Jason had squeezed her hand and told her she was amazing.

The thought of Jason thrilled but also saddened her. She couldn't possibly contemplate a relationship with him, even if he offered her that chance. It seemed he might be leading up to something. He had sent her two more texts since the one with the cute dog on it. He also told her he was looking forward to their next session at the gym. She felt warmth creep up her neck at the prospect of seeing him again.

However, she shouldn't encourage him. . She believed in the sanctity of marriage. Jack believed in it too. She owed it to him to stick by her man. She would have to put up with Jim's moods and hope that they lifted. She had married him "for better or worse," and she owed him loyalty at the very least.

Wiping tears from her eyes, Dawn caught her breath again. Jason was demonstrating his ability to mimic characters and accents. His latest performance involved acting out some of the funniest lines in the film *Despicable Me*. He was currently pretending to be evil Gru talking to the minions. His facial expressions had Dawn in hysterics. She shook her head for him to stop. He bowed his head and grinned.

"So, you enjoyed it then?"

"It was hilarious. Thank you so much for lending it to me. I laughed so much throughout it that I nearly woke up Jim."

Dawn handed back the copy of the DVD Jason had loaned her.

"I don't know why I seem to enjoy these children's films as much as I do. I suppose it's because they are so cleverly animated. It's more than that though. They have simple, wholesome messages," she said wistfully. "It reminds me of when times were less complicated," she added. "Oh dear, now I sound like an old woman. Next I'll be talking about the 'Good Old Days' and saying that the internet is the work of the devil."

Jason laughed and nudged her leg with his own. "No, I know what you mean. There is so much violence these days, not just on television and in films but with computer games. It is just nice to sit back and laugh at something that is clearly not for children. It is far too amusing. Mom, someday, I'm going to go to the moon," he quoted.

"I'm afraid you're too late son. NASA isn't sending the monkeys," Dawn joined in, laughing with him.

"So, was that your favourite animated film?"

"I loved it, and I thought the minions were adorable. I really want to see the second one too, but for the moment Up remains my favourite, along with Toy Story, Madagascar, Kung Fu Panda ..." she reeled off counting on her fingers.

"Squirrel!" shouted Jason, and they both laughed again.

"Better change the subject. We're attracting too much attention," whispered Jason leaning forward and winking. Two ladies at a nearby table were giving them disapproving looks. They had already been guffawing loudly at Dawn's story about Viv delivering the raunchy DVD. Jason had asked innocently if he should borrow it, perhaps, earning him a punch on the arm.

"What did you think of Geraldine's story the other week?" asked Dawn.

"I thought it was pretty good. She's grown in confidence, hasn't she? I like her. She seems a bit aloof, but I think that's because she's quite wealthy and she's not used to hanging out with poor people like me. Craig was chatting her up today. He wants to sell her a new car. He's got an old Jag he thinks would be perfect for her. I didn't like to tell him that she bought a brand new top-of-the-range Range Rover Evoque last week. She told me all about it. In fact she asked me what I thought, and I told her it was very Footballer's Wives."

"What did she say to that?"

"Excellent. I like to convey an impression of style."

"She's outrageous!"

"No, she's just individual. She doesn't conform to the norm. I'd love to know more about her past life. I heard from Dotty that Geraldine was married to some billionaire lord. She left him a few years ago, but took away a huge amount of money as a divorce settlement. Now that is one lady you would want as a Sugar Mummy!"

Dawn looked aghast.

Catching the look on her face, he told her, "No, not me. I'm not in the market. I am not motivated by money. I prefer my women to be challenges."

"Like Agniezska," said Cinnamon loudly, making Dawn almost jump. Cinnamon was giving her a beady eye. "Isn't it time you went home and stopped canoodling with a young dark-haired sexy man in a tearoom. Someone who knows you could come by any minute, and then Jim will find out. Go on, scoot. Make an excuse. Look at your watch and tell him ..."

Dawn shushed her. Jason was looking a little nervous. She hadn't spoken out loud had she?

He coughed to clear his throat. "Erm! I know this is a little unorthodox but you wouldn't come with me to the cinema on Sunday to see Monsters Inc in 3D, would you?" His eyes pleaded, and he shuffled slightly in his chair. "It's one of my absolute favourite films and I would love to see it in 3D. The trouble is it's a matinee performance, which means the cinema will be full of children and parents. You can imagine what they'll think about a grown man sitting about on his own. I'll buy popcorn. Go on, Dawn. It'll be loads of fun. You haven't seen the film before and in 3D it'll be even better. You can pretend I'm your simpleton nephew or something. I can act the part." He then did a passable Forrest Gump impression which reduced her to tears of laughter.

"Pleeeeease," he wheedled. "If you say no, I'll sit here and hold my breath until I faint."

"Okay. Which cinema? I'll meet you there. What time do you want to meet?"

Jason looked delighted. "Tamworth, Sunday, 11:20am. Shall we meet at 11 sharp in the foyer?"

"Now, I have to go. I promised I'd drop by and see Jack before I went home. Thanks for the coffee and the DVD."

"You are more than welcome. And thank you for agreeing to go to the cinema with me."

"It's not a date, you know. I'm only going because I couldn't bear to see you hold your breath. You've manipulated me into this."

"Yes, but you loved it, didn't you? Besides, you'll really enjoy the film, and when was the last time you went to the cinema to enjoy a film on the big screen?"

"A while ago. See you Sunday. Must dash."

Cinnamon was waiting for her as she rushed off to get to her car and visit Jack. She was already late. She hadn't intended taking up Jason's offer of coffee, but when he invited her, her mouth answered for her, while her brain shouted no. Cinnamon was not happy with her.

"Well, I see you did well sticking to your decision to discourage the man. What about infidelity and standing by your man? Only a few days ago, you were going to stick by Jim. Now you're making cow eyes at young Lothario just because he lent you a DVD. Worse still, you've arranged to go out with him. You are about to play with fire, and you know what will happen. This is how it starts, you know. You get to know someone. You have a few things in common. You laugh at the same things. You fancy each other. He'll pull a move on you on Sunday. You just know he will. You are walking right into this and you know what will happen. Be aware of the consequences Dawn. Go home, make tea for your husband, and send Jason a text saying you can't meet him. Nip it in the bud, now!"

It was windy and cold, and Cinnamon was feeling particularly cross. Joe couldn't find out where Geoff was and, until he did, she felt she was in limbo. She spent years getting the blasted man out of her system, and now the wound had healed, it had been reopened first by The Rat, and then thanks to her encounter with Jessica. She needed closure. Proper closure this time.

She stomped off to the gym where she intended to work off her anger. Nothing like excessive effort and sweat to make one feel better. She was a member of the Belfry Health Club, which in turn was part of the Belfry Hotel. It boasted a decent gym, a good size pool with Jacuzzis, and an ice and fire sauna experience. Often, the hotel guests would use the facilities there. That suited Cinnamon because it meant that there was a variety of people working out or attending classes, and not the same old regulars. It afforded her the anonymity she craved. She wasn't into striking up relationships and conversations with fellow gym bunnies.

The changing room was empty. She changed, grabbed a bottle of ice cold water and her weight lifting gloves from her bag, and slung it, along with her clothes, into a locker. A woman entered the changing room as she was leaving and smiled at her. Cinnamon merely nodded back at her, eager to get started on working off some of the tension she felt. A few minutes later, she was pounding along on a treadmill, earphones on, listening to the new running album she had downloaded. She was oblivious to the other people in there.

She needed to find a raison d'être. She couldn't spend the rest of her life just reading, training and attempting to right wrongs. She was too old and under qualified to find employment. Besides, she didn't need the money and she found communicating with people almost impossible. She had spent too long locked in her own world. Damn it! She had come full circle and was once again the shy girl she had been, before she met Geoff. She growled aloud. The man in the corner lifting weights looked up at her and watched her for a while. A slim woman in her thirties finished her session and left the gym. All that could be heard was the loud repetitive sound of her running shoes slapping onto the treadmill as she thundered along, lost in thought.

Cinnamon brooded some more about what she was going to do after she found Geoff and what she intended to do to the cheating, useless no-hoper, once Joe found him. Gradually, small beads of perspiration appeared on her forehead. She ran steadily to the beat of the songs on her iPod, her pace unrelenting. Sometime later, she slowed the pace down. The gym had thinned out now. In one corner, an instructor was showing a man in his late sixties how to use the equipment. The only other person, apart from her, was another man, suntanned and fit, who wore a t-shirt with a large black rhino on it.

She stretched for a while to limber up then donned her weight-lifting gloves. She was about to pick up some dumb-bells to work her triceps and biceps, when she glanced in the mirror which ran around the gym. Reflected in it, she could see the Rhino guy lying under a heavily loaded barbell. He had lifted it but now it had slipped and was threatening to crush his trachea. He was gasping, face contorted with effort trying to prevent the barbell from crushing him. She galloped over to him in four easy strides, put her hands under the barbell and lifted it away from him, putting it back on the stand. The guy, red faced, rubbed his throat.

"Oh geez, that was close. I knew I shouldn't have come here after a heavy day of travelling." He tried to sit up. Cinnamon extended her hand and helped to pull him into a sitting position.

"You okay?"

"I think you saved my life. You must be my guardian angel. Wow, what a lucky bloke I am to have such a beautiful and strong guardian angel."

The man turned turquoise eyes onto her approvingly.

"Thank you. I mean that. If you hadn't been there and noticed me, I don't know what would have happened. I feel such a dolt."

His accent gave away he was from foreign parts. Cinnamon couldn't place it. It was almost Dutch, or maybe Australian.

"Not a problem. When muscles fatigue, they can easily just go on you. You should have had a spotter with you, though. You shouldn't have tried to lift that amount of weight without someone to watch you. That's quite a heavy load."

"I normally manage that when I train. I underestimated how tired I would be. I flew in from Jo'burg this morning. I'm Marcus, Marcus Erikson," he said and extended a large brown hand. "And if you would do me the honour of accepting a drink with me, by way of thanks, you'll make me a very happy—happier—man. I heard you should always be polite and courteous to guardian angels." His smile spread to the corners of his eyes and exuded warmth. It was a genuine smile. Cinnamon thawed and accepted his hand, which consumed hers completely. She agreed to have a drink with him at the bar in the hotel.

They met up later at the Belfry Bar. Marcus was waiting on a bar stool. He was now dressed in a white shirt and dark jeans. The shirt enhanced his suntanned face in which bright eyes sparkled as Cinnamon approached.

"My guardian angel," he said, leaping from his stool and pulling out the one next to him, for her. "Unless you'd rather sit somewhere else?" he asked, indicating a table and sofa nearby.

"Here's fine, thanks," replied Cinnamon slipping onto the stool.

"So, what can I get you? As far as I'm concerned, you are welcome to a magnum of champagne after your heroic efforts. I'm guessing though, judging by your physique, the way you were working out and your clear eyes, that you are not much of a drinker."

"Well observed. An orange juice please. I'm not a big fan of drink. I only drink now and then," she added.

He rattled a large glass of coke at her. "Me neither. I prefer to keep a clear head and a healthy liver, although I clearly don't care about my teeth drinking this stuff," he laughed revealing perfect white teeth. "Listen, I have to explain that I am not usually as dumb as I look," he said. "Thank you again for rescuing me. I thought my time had come when I lost control of that barbell. I was out of sight in the corner, and I couldn't lift the wretched thing. My arms failed me," he said prodding a healthy-sized bicep. "Must be old age catching up with me," he joked.

"Hardly. You're no geriatric."

"Ah, time is catching up with me. Soon I won't be able to lift a dumb-bell without falling over. Anyhow, I'd like thank you again, and cheers!"

They clinked glasses and fell into an easy conversation. Marcus's clipped lazy accent married nicely with his strong large frame. He chatted freely and candidly. Cinnamon found herself enjoying his company. He was relaxing to be with, and as he told her stories about the game reserve in South Africa where he worked, she felt the tension she normally carried around with her departing. Time passed quickly, and two drinks later, he invited her to join him for dinner at the hotel restaurant Sam's Bar. Cinnamon decided to take him up on it. After all, it was only dinner. The conversation continued as they waited for their main course.

"So I haven't asked you … what brings you all the way from sunny South Africa to wet and windy Birmingham?"

"Love. No. Not me. My best friend, Pete, from back home, decided to fall in love with a Brit. She lives and works at the same game reserve as him. They're both rangers too. They're going to live in South Africa, but she wanted to have the wedding here in the UK, so all her family, including a frail auntie who can no longer travel, can be at the wedding. I had to come along because I'm the best man. The wedding's the day after tomorrow at some village near Lichfield. Her family comes from there. It has a weird name, Yox Hill or something like that."

"Yoxall," corrected Cinnamon. "I live there."

"Wow! What are the chances of that?"

Cinnamon didn't know the family, but she knew the church—St Peter's Church.

"It's quaint," she told him when asked.

"I'm not over-familiar with churches," he said. "Or marriage. I hope I don't stuff up, make a wrong turning, and end up in the font, or lose the ring, or worse still, lose the groom. Listen, we're going for a meal tomorrow night at the pub opposite the church. I don't suppose you'd like to join us, would you? Please say you'll come. If you don't, I'll feel like a giant gooseberry. Us single guys cramp people's style, and those two might even try and fix me up with a date for a laugh. I hear the chief bridesmaid is a horror. Pete says she has a tattoo the size of Kilimanjaro on her backside!"

Cinnamon laughed. "So, you've never taken the plunge and got married?"

"No, it's a long story, one that isn't suitable for discussion over dinner," he said as the waiter turned up with two plates of spaghetti carbonara for them. Once he had left, Marcus continued, "Circumstances have dictated the way my life has gone. My job as a ranger never allows me time to get properly involved with anyone. I've had girlfriends," he laughed. "I'm not a complete monk, but they just didn't work out. I'm a bit particular. I prefer the company of wild animals. You know where you are with them. Give them space and respect them, and in return, they leave you alone to admire their grace, beauty, and strength. You know, you kind of remind me of a wild animal, a beautiful wild cat. I thought that when I first saw you. You're aloof, with a hint of danger about you." He looked up at her, and she felt a small flutter in her stomach.

"I know where I am with wildlife. Nature never disappoints."

Cinnamon sipped her glass of water thoughtfully. She might just take him up on his offer. What had she got to lose?

This was wrong. She should never have agreed to this. Cinnamon was cross with her. What did she think she was playing at?

"It's only a film," she hissed at Cinnamon.

Cinnamon glared back at her and refused to comment.

Jason was waiting for her in the foyer as they had agreed. She took in his tall bearing. His good looks, combined with the brown leather jacket he was wearing, made him look a little like a movie star. She half expected him to have a motorbike propped up outside and carry her off on it like Tom Cruise in Mission Impossible. She took a breath. Cinnamon wasn't around to tell her to forget it. She opened the glass door to the foyer. Jason caught sight of her, and his face lit up.

"Glad you made it," he said.

For a second, she thought he was about to kiss her on the cheek, instead he took her arm and marched her over to the sweet stall.

"I couldn't have come here on my own. People might have thought I was some weirdo, or worse still, a pervert," he commented. The girl behind the sweet counter looked up from the till and batted her eyelashes at Jason. He didn't notice.

"Come on, what do you want? We can't go to a children's movie and not have some sweets and popcorn. What about midget gems, or hey, what about these?" He picked up a scoop and poured in some pink shrimps. It didn't stop there. Before long, he had a large bag of all types of sweet, including several long strawberry laces.

"It's been years since I ate any of this stuff. I'll probably get all hyper now, and you'll have to tie me down." He followed this with a pause accompanied by a thoughtful look. Dawn blushed. The girl at the counter almost drooled into the sweet bag, as Jason gave her a dazzling smile and paid for his booty.

From there, he rushed over to the popcorn counter.

"Are you insane? We'll put on about a stone if we eat all that."

"We'll work it off tomorrow. I have an evil high-impact routine planned. Eat up. You'll need that energy," he grinned.

"I can't believe I agreed to come and see *Monsters Inc 3D* with you."

"Isn't it great to feel young again? I used to come to the cinema every week when I was a kid. I've always had a love of films. I'm not bizarre. I like adult films too. Hey, *Les Miserables* is showing here. Don't suppose you'd like to see that another time, would you?"

Dawn sighed. She could think of nothing better than coming out with a good-looking man and watching a superb film together, then enjoying a nice meal, over which they could discuss all the highs and lows of the film. Jim had never been a filmgoer. He didn't have the patience to watch films even on television. He didn't like television much either and only watched football, or some sport, or the occasional documentary. Oh, to live with someone as excited and enchanted by films as she was! Fortunately, she didn't have the opportunity to reply, as they joined a queue of excited children and some tired-looking parents for the film. The film usher clipped their tickets and told them to make their way to screen four. Children pushed by them to get the best seats at the front.

It was quite dark as they entered the screen. Lights illuminated the rows, but it took a while for the eyes to adjust. Dawn couldn't see clearly at all. Jason took her by the hand and led her to a row right at the back, choosing the middle seats.

"Best position for the film, and you won't have to keep getting up and down when the children want to go to the toilet."

"You've done this before."

"Not for a very long time, but I remember trying to watch X-Men and having to move all the time because some kid kept getting up and going to buy hot dogs or drinks. He can't have seen much of the film, and I bet he got through loads of money. Can I offer you some cherry lips?"

Dawn sniggered and rustled through the bag, dragging out a sweet. It was a large jelly snake.

"Glad you aren't squeamish," he chuckled, as she bit its head off.

They donned the 3D glasses Jason had purchased with the tickets and sat back to enjoy the film. Periodically, they rocked with laughter. Jason ensured she was kept well supplied with popcorn and sweets. It was perfect. They were two adults enjoying some childish pleasure, forgetting the real world for an hour and a half. The film was over far too soon. The credits rolled and they stood up to go. They squeezed out into the line of children and adults leaving the screen. As they erupted into the hall, Dawn turned to look behind. As she did so, she caught sight of a figure she recognised. It was Viv.

"Jason!" she whispered urgently, eyes wide with panic. "Viv is behind us. She'll see us." Jason took charge of the situation and, grabbing her hand again, raced her off to screen five, opposite the door they had exited. They slipped in. It was dark. No one was there. Jason peered out. "We'll wait here until she's gone."

Dawn was shaking. It was ridiculous. She hadn't done anything wrong. If Viv saw them together, she would draw the wrong conclusions and Dawn couldn't have Jim finding out about this. She told him she was visiting Jack. She had never lied to him before. What was it they said about a lie? It gets bigger and bigger. That must be what they meant by that statement. If Jim found out, she would try to concoct another lie and so on.

She was so busy worrying, she didn't realise Jason was now standing in front of her. Warmth exuded from his body which was almost touching hers. Her senses kicked in, and she was suddenly acutely aware of him. She breathed in the citrus fragrance he wore. He let out a soft groan and pressed his body to hers. Her body melted into his, willing him to embrace her. He found her lips and grazed them gently with his own. She tasted cherries. His lips pressed harder. Her own lips responded, parting eagerly to greet him. His arms were either side of her, pinning her to the wall. His body moulded against hers. Hearts thudded in unison. She was aware of the burning currents which flowed up and down her body. She wanted more. The desire was urgent, desperate. She could feel him hardening too, his desire mounting to match her own.

Cinnamon screamed in her ear to stop. Suddenly, Dawn woke up to what she was doing. She pushed against Jason's chest. She pushed harder still until his lips left hers.

"No, I can't. I mustn't," she said.

Jason ran his fingers down the side of her face, leaving a burning trail behind. She shivered.

"I can't … do … this," she said more firmly.

"Dawn, if you only knew what you do to me," he whispered back. He stood back. Cold air flowed between them. "I'm sorry. I shouldn't have. I couldn't help myself."

"It's okay. I was to blame too. Must have been all those sweets and the E numbers," she joked. They both knew it wasn't that.

"Is it okay if we wait a couple of more minutes? I can't go outside like this," he said. She knew what he meant. "Don't want to frighten the children."

They laughed again, but it had the tinny sound of false laughter. The atmosphere had changed, and although they chatted for a couple of minutes about the merits of 3D films, both realised there had been a shift in their relationship.

Guilt flooded every pore as she walked into the kitchen, hung the car keys on the hook, and turned on the kettle. She shouldn't have gone. It had ended the way Cinnamon predicted. Her relationship with Jason had changed. It would be difficult to have that easy-going friendship they had been enjoying. She had a training session with him in the morning. She thought about cancelling it.

"Don't be such a baby. You both knew it was wrong. He's not a child, even if he does like animated films. He knows you are married. Be grown up about it. Go to your session. It'll be fine. He got carried away, that's all. Heaven knows why, given you are quite a bit older than he is, but he'll get over it." Cinnamon's voice filled her head, almost drowning out Jim's.

"I said, did you remember to ask Jack about borrowing his spirit level?"

Dawn dragged herself back to reality. "No, sorry. I forgot. I'll ask him next time."

"Dear Lord, it wasn't that difficult to remember, was it? I don't ask you to do much, and you can't even remember to do a simple thing like that. I'll phone him."

"No, don't do that. I'll sort it out. It was my mistake," replied Dawn, heart beating rapidly. It was so easy to get caught out. "He said something about going out, so he probably won't be there," she lied.

"Honestly!" continued Jim, his face becoming blotchy. "You are hopeless these days. You walk around in a daze. Are you going through the change or something? It's like living with a zombie some days."

Dawn rose to the bait. "No, I am not. How dare you. You're always picking on me these days. It's all because you haven't got a job anymore, while I have an interest that gets me out and about. You've changed ever since you gave up work, James Ellis."

Jim snorted. "An interest," he sneered. "You exercise and play at writing a novel that'll amount to nothing. It's not going to bring in money. It's not going to help pay off the mortgage still on this property, is it? No, only my savings and the effort I made over the years, is going to help us survive. I am fed up of being the one to support everyone. I am the one who has carried this family for years, and now, when I need someone to understand what is happening, to help me for a change, I get snapped at, ignored, or treated like some old useless twit. You've changed, Dawn. You're the one who has changed, and I don't like the person you've become."

Jim stomped off, slamming the door and headed to the garage. She was mortified. She was angry. How dare he speak to her like that. She had looked after him for decades. She didn't need hissy fits from a man going through some sort of male menopause. This was dreadful. She needed to make sure things settled down again. It was becoming ridiculous. She phoned her father, asked if she could borrow the spirit level, and had a brief chat with him.

"You sound odd, Dawn. Is everything okay?"

Dawn hesitated a second. "Yes, fine. Jim's struggling with things at the moment. Look, Dad, I know this goes against everything you believe in, but if Jim asks, could you please tell him I was with you this morning?"

"Dawn, I'm not keen on lies. You know my take on them."

"Please Dad. I wouldn't ask but Jim is, well, going through a tough patch. He doesn't need to know where I was today."

"I'm still not keen. Let's hope he doesn't ask me." Silence fell, then he said, "But I'll do it if he asks. You are my daughter, after all."

She thanked him. Relief coursed through her veins. At least she now had an alibi. It was awful being devious and lying. It ended up hurting too many people.

She went upstairs to change into her jeans. Sadness had replaced anxiety. She and Jim were at a crossroads, and she knew she had to do whatever was necessary to patch things up. His words stung. Her writing was important, yet she could understand some of his argument. She hadn't contributed to their savings. Although she had never spent money recklessly, she had never been taken any responsibility either. Her mind wandered to the National Savings Certificate in the filing cabinet. She would cash it in and book that trip to Lanzarote for the two of them. It would help heal the wounds they had inflicted on each other recently.

It would be nice to go away on a romantic trip. The thought led her to think of Jason. Part of her had really wanted to respond to Jason. For a moment, she was transported to a place she had never visited before. Every atom of her being had vibrated in anticipation and sense abandoned her. She knew what it would be like to make love to Jason and be made love to. She could tell in that kiss, by his soft groan, by the heat that rose instantly when they touched. It would be perfect.

She couldn't let it happen, but she could experience it in a different way. She set off for her laptop and wrote.

"I'm so pleased you agreed to come long tonight." Marcus raised his glass of orange juice and clinked it against Cinnamon's. They had enjoyed a meal at the Golden Cup with Marcus's friends and another couple aged about thirty-five. Cinnamon had fitted in perfectly, even though she was not used to being in company.

Dressed in a bright red, figure-hugging woollen dress, the pub had fallen silent when she walked in. There was no doubt that every male in the bar had noticed her. Marcus had taken her arm protectively. The men at the bar dropped their eyes and gone back to watching the giant television screen in the bar and cheering their football teams.

The six of them had been ushered into the dining room where they had enjoyed a traditional pub meal. The men had all opted for steak, while the women had chosen gammon or fish.

Ellie was the bride-to-be. She was petite with freckles and a healthy tan from the African sun. She took to Cinnamon immediately, insisting she sit near her. The conversation was lively and fascinating. Marcus and Pete were hilarious. They had some very funny stories about life in the bush, from chasing aardvarks and getting stuck in a termite hill to monkeys stealing from guest's rooms or getting into the bush pilot's aeroplanes. Life was certainly colourful for some. Pete and Marcus oozed a confidence, unlike the arrogant attitude she saw in the men she had known over the last few years. They were warmer. She felt comfortable in their company. Ellie's too. The other couple, Sarah and Chris, were from the village. They were Ellie's friends from her schooldays. They had visited her and Pete in South Africa a couple of times and were obviously very pleased to be part of the celebration, but were quiet by comparison to the South Africans, who exuded energy and enthusiasm. Pete and Marcus held court. It transpired that Marcus was quite a photographer, as well as a ranger, having won some prestigious awards for his photographs of animals and birds in the bush. He was modest about his achievements, even though Ellie praised his efforts in front of him.

"Some of his shots have appeared in the national press, haven't they, Marcus?"

Marcus put a finger up to his lips. "Ellie, you'll make me big-headed."

A local couple recognised Chris and Sarah and stopped to speak to them.

"Come on, Cinnamon, time for us girls to have a quick chat about the men," said Ellie and rose to go to the ladies.

"You behave yourself, Ellie. I know that look," said Pete wagging his finger.

"Me, behave? No chance. Come on, Cinnamon."

She put her hand out and pulled Cinnamon up. "I'm only going to have a girly gossip and fill her in on what you two are really like after the guests go to bed. Which one was it that wore the lion-skin rug and tried to frighten the cook?"

They left the table and went to the toilet where Ellie refreshed her lipstick and spoke to Cinnamon. "I'm so happy Marcus has met you. He's not been this relaxed with a woman for, well, since I don't know when. He obviously likes you. You can tell by the way his eyes shine when he looks at you. And, boy, does he keep looking at you."

"He's a nice man."

"Yes, he is. But he's also reserved. Yes, I know. He doesn't seem reserved. This is most unusual behaviour for him. He only ever lets his hair down with people he has known for years. I've known him ten years, and Pete, well, he's known him a very long time. I don't know what will happen between you two, but I can feel electric currents whizzing past my ears every time he turns that hundred-watt smile on you. He's not as tough as he looks. Be careful with him. He's had it very rough."

"Go on."

"He won't want me to tell you this. However, I'm a good judge of character, and I think you should know. Marcus might not realise what is happening, but I can also see that he is falling for you. And, I think you, might be having some rather strong feelings for him."

Cinnamon was about to protest.

"No, don't say anything. I am very astute, and I speak my mind. Life is too short to shilly-shally about. I've also had a little too much wine, and I'm drunk on love and excitement about tomorrow, so that makes me want to blab a little."

"Marcus had a dreadful experience when he was younger. His mother and father ran a very successful guest lodge on a large estate. They used to take their guests to visit the Battlefields in Kwa Zulu Natal. Marcus wanted to be a ranger in the bush, but it was decided that he was to join the family business. He went to college to study history in order to become a guide for his parent's guests. While he was there he met Serene. They fell for each other big time, and after a while, she moved to the guest house to be part of the family. Marcus doted on her. When he found out she was expecting their child, he was so proud. Pete went round that night and joined in the celebrations. They were planning to get married the following month."

Ellie stopped and pretended to check her reflection in the mirror. It took a moment for her to continue.

"Marcus had to go to Johannesburg to get the main jeep repaired. They needed it for a large party of important guests who were arriving. The parts they needed hadn't been flown in as expected because bad weather had suddenly sprung up, and the plane bringing the parts had been grounded until the weather passed through."

"Some parts of South Africa are very rough. It is dangerous there. We are used to it, and we always take necessary precautions. However, that night, while he was gone, intruders broke into the estate. They managed to kill the two patrol guards, poisoned all the guard dogs, and made it to the main house, where they threatened his parents. His father, who was South African born and bred, and tough as tough could be, stood in front of Marcus's mother to protect her and told them to clear off or he'd shoot them, then waved his gun at them. The intruders also had guns and shot him first. They then ransacked the house, knifed his mother, who bled to death beside the body of her husband, and killed Marcus's fiancée. The authorities never found the men. They weren't local people, and some said that they were crazed on drugs. The whole community mourned for a long time."

Ellie stopped to regain her composure again. "It stills upsets me to think of it, even though I didn't know Marcus then. Imagine how that must have affected Marcus? He sold the estate, travelled about aimlessly for a long while, then became a ranger. He moved to Kruger Park and has been there ever since. He lives for his work. He is happiest when he can sit quietly hidden in a jeep taking photographs of the animals. He is such a loner. He's never ever been like this with any other woman. I see him regularly, and he has had girlfriends but is always so standoffish with them. They all love his stature and good looks and want to control him, but I think his heart became frozen after that dreadful experience."

"I wouldn't tell you any of this, except tonight I have seen a side of him I have never seen before. When he told Pete he had met you yesterday and asked if you could come along tonight, I noticed something I have not ever seen in his eyes before … a sparkle, an energy, even. If it is meant to be and he really does like you, then tread carefully, Cinnamon, because if you hurt him, you'll have me and Pete to deal with. Marcus is like our brother, and we love him dearly. However, something says you won't hurt him."

Cinnamon was thoughtful when they returned to the table. The rest of the evening flew by. Sarah, Chris, Ellie, and Pete decided to leave. Pete had to bed down at Chris and Sarah's for the night, so as not to bring bad luck to the marriage. Ellie was going home to her mother and father's house. They said goodbye to Marcus and Cinnamon who had been invited to the ceremony too. She had refused to go to the wedding, claiming it was for friends and family, but accepted an invite to the buffet and dancing at Swinfin Hall later that day. Ellie hugged her fiercely as she left.

"See you tomorrow. Watch out for the bouquet. I'll be throwing it at Swinfin Hall."

Marcus sat for a while longer with her. It was getting late, and only a few stragglers remained in the bar next door.

"I had a terrific night. Thanks again for coming along. You look stunning. I didn't say anything before, but you took my breath away when I saw you earlier. How the heck have you managed to stay single?"

"I haven't always been single," confessed Cinnamon. "I was married once. He dumped me for a younger woman. I don't normally discuss that part of my life. I don't seem to have found anyone since. I haven't tried. Bruised ego. Broken heart. That sort of thing."

Marcus placed one large warm hand under her chin and cupped it gently. Looking deep into her eyes he said, "The fool. Who could do that to you? You're more like a wild animal than I thought yesterday. You don't trust anyone, do you? You can trust me."

Silence settled between them, and for a moment nothing else existed in the pub. Both were unaware of the landlord cashing up, or the voice of a man saying goodbye, as he staggered out into the cool evening.

"I'd like to walk you home, if I might," said Marcus. "No lady should be out on her own at this time of night."

"I am quite capable of walking home, Mr Erikson," she replied, smiling at him.

"I am sure you are, but I'd like to, all the same."

They walked side-by-side down the deserted road to her house, saying nothing, enjoying each other being there.

Turning off onto the lane, away from the street lights, it became very dark quite quickly. Marcus walked closer to her side. "Ah, see you need a ranger to protect you from the wildlife down here," joked Marcus. A rustling followed his statement, and a large rabbit hopped out into their path where it stood under a shaft of moonlight, nose twitching. "Aaargh! Save me, guardian angel, from this hideous, wild creature," he yelped. "Watch out, it might be one of those vicious killer rabbits," he shouted. Cinnamon thumped him playfully on his arm. He turned to protest, looked at her instead, and then pulled her towards him, enveloping her in his strong arms. He kissed the top of her head then looking into her eyes, bowed his head until their lips touched. Cinnamon was rooted to the spot. Her body responded to his own as if each were magnetically attracted to each other. The kiss was tender but then became deep, passionate. Her lips felt bruised, yet she yearned for more. An eternity passed where only they existed. They were perfect for each other. At last they parted, breathless, but eyes aglow with life and desire.

"You can come back to mine. You can stay," urged Cinnamon.

Sadness replaced the glow. Marcus slumped. "Cinnamon, I can't. I can't treat you badly. I can't just use you then fly back to South Africa in a few days and pretend nothing has happened. You're too special for that. It wouldn't be gentlemanly. I want to," he groaned. "God, how I want to. You have no idea how much I want to, but I don't want to sully the beauty of what we have. I live thousands of miles away. It wouldn't be right."

He held her at arm's length. Pain played across his features. "I spoiled it. I should have just hung out. I shouldn't have crossed the line. I'm sorry," he said.

"Don't be sorry," she replied huskily. "You've just done something magical."

A chink of light fell across the bed from the window where the curtains had not been drawn properly. She breathed a long sigh of contentment. Next to her, a shape stirred.

"Morning! Fancy a cup of tea?"

The shape moved under the sheets, and a large, suntanned, muscular arm snaked out, grabbing her around the waist.

"No, I want you."

This was the fourth time they had made love. It was definitely making love, not just torrid animal sex. Cinnamon had never experienced such sensual pleasure or tenderness. This man knew how to make her feel desired. He made sure she was completely spent before he allowed himself to explode inside her, crying out her name. He held her in an embrace after the event, talking late into the night and caressing her. The urge would become too much to bear again, and they explored each other's bodies again, until both reached heights of passion never before experienced.

"Haven't you got a groom to collect?"

"Do you think they'd miss me?" he asked, turning towards her and kissing her nose.

"No, but Pete might need that ring you're supposed to be guarding."

He sighed. It was a sigh more of contentment than frustration. "I'd better go. I have to get dressed up like some sort of penguin too. At least I'll look genuinely happy at the ceremony. I doubt I'll be able to remove this grin for the next month."

She smiled back. "Look, I know you were worried about going this far and then leaving me, but I can assure you, I wouldn't have swapped last night for anything. If that was the only time we ever had together and I never saw you again, I wouldn't change it. It was worth it."

"It's a good thing you are as determined as you are. I'd have never come back here if you hadn't ravaged me in the lane!"

"Ravaged, ha!" she laughed. "I only kissed you and asked you to reconsider."

"No, the way you kissed me, I was definitely being ravaged. Ravaged by a sleek beautiful wildcat. I suppose I'd better get up. Can't leave the groom in a panic. I'll come by straight after the ceremony, and we'll go to the reception together as planned. You sure you want to go? We could just spend the afternoon here, and I could show you—" with that he began kissing her throat and neck, descending to her breasts. She pushed him away reluctantly.

"Enough. It's Pete and Ellie's day. Off you go. I'll have a bath and wait for you. Sure you can face driving down with me? I don't exactly go at snail's pace. I might frighten you."

"As if! I drive jeeps about all day through the undergrowth, dodging rhinos. I don't see how a girl driving a car on a road in the UK can scare me. I'm a tough South African, remember. I'll see you later. I'll be thinking about you during the ceremony."

They kissed one last time, and then Cinnamon pulled the bed sheets off him and pushed him out of bed.

"Grab a shower if you like. I'll make you some tea, or would you prefer coffee?"

"No chance. You fancy taking a shower with me, and forgetting the coffee?" he asked.

She looked down at his muscular torso. Her eyes strayed down his body. She smirked. It was obvious he wanted her. She flung back the covers from her own body, sashayed up to him and, slapping him on the backside, raced him to the shower .

"Cripes! Look out!" yelled Marcus as Cinnamon was about to race past a large truck, only to have an elderly gent in a Honda Jazz pull out in front of her. She dropped speed immediately and held back. The Black Maserati growled in annoyance. As soon as the Honda had overtaken the lorry, she stepped on the accelerator, hurtling past the Honda driver who remained oblivious to the presence of the menacing car.

"Jeez, this is worse than the bush!" he said, feigning fear.

Cinnamon smiled. "Don't worry, little scared ranger. You have your guardian angel to take care of you."

"An angel driving a demonic car. No, not demonic. It's more 'stealthy', like a fighter jet on wheels. It suits you."

"It's nice to drive."

"It's like its owner ... dark, mysterious and powerful."

"I bought it because it reminded me of a panther, as it happens. It seemed to be beckoning me when I saw it."

"Yeah, I get that. Not much scope for cars like this where I live," he began, then fell silent.

Cinnamon knew what he was thinking. He would be gone in a couple of days, and they didn't have long together.

"Carpe diem, Marcus. Let's enjoy today."

She wound the car up. The exhaust burbled throatily, and they sped down the road towards the hotel and the reception. They would not have much time together, but Cinnamon was going to ensure they had the best time together. They both deserved it.

The cafe at the Stay Fit Health Club was empty apart from Dawn and Jason. Dawn had fancied an orange juice after her training session with Jason. She had just sat down when Jason appeared.

"Ah! Great minds," he joked and plonked himself down at her table.

Conversation revolved around the training. Jason invited her to join the timetabled kick-boxing class.

"You'll be able to keep up with the regulars now, and it'll give you a chance to practise with different people."

"I like practising with you," she blurted out. "Oh, I mean, I feel more confident with you. I'm not sure I'd feel that confident in a class of young, fit things what with me being old enough to be their mother," she burbled, getting increasingly embarrassed.

"Dawn," said Jason, softly placing a warm hand on top of hers and causing electric shocks to tingle through her fingers and up her arm. "You are not old nor should you feel under-confident. You have transformed in a few short weeks, and you are without doubt, my all-time favourite pupil."

Dawn flushed. Jason left his hand on top of hers. She was far too aware of the sensation it was creating. The flush deepened. Neither had discussed the episode at the cinema. Jason had treated her as he always did. He had been friendly and professional.

"Like the new outfit, by the way. Those combat trousers suit you."

"Thanks. I got them in a sale at TK Maxx. They were only a fiver."

"Wow! That's amazing! I'll have to get down there and see if they have any stuff for men. Love that shop. I always end up buying lots more than I intended. It's a weakness. I think in another life I was a woman. I'm particularly bad about shoes or trainers. I got these last week," he said, lifting up his leg to show off a smart, red and black Adidas trainer. "I shouldn't have bought them. I have about twenty other pairs in my cupboard."

"You are just like a woman. Every time I go into a shoe shop, I get palpitations and want to try on everything," she remarked. "I bought three pairs of boots last year, just because they were reduced by seventy-five per cent in the sale."

"Looks like we have a few more things than we thought in common," Jason said, his eyes resting a little longer on hers than they should have. An electric jolt raced through her body. Jason was flirting with her. That was bad. She was too old for this. Worse still, she liked it.

They held each other's gaze. For one crazy moment, she thought he was going to lean forward and kiss her again. Time slowed. She wouldn't have stopped him. She remembered too clearly how his lips had felt at the cinema. Seconds which seemed like minutes passed, and the atmosphere fizzed.

The spell was broken by the arrival of Agniezska, dressed in a fluorescent yellow halter top and white combat trousers. Her stomach muscles were visible. Damn, thought Dawn, the woman had the flattest stomach in the universe. Dawn automatically sucked in her less muscled tummy. She greeted Agniezska, who flopped down beside Jason. She clearly wanted to speak to him. Dawn couldn't be sure, but she thought she detected a look of annoyance on Jason's face.

She finished her juice, made her excuses, and departed. She was about to leave the building when she remembered she had left her gym bag in the café. When she returned, she could see Jason and Agniezska were deep in conversation, heads huddled together as if they were a couple. She was reminded of the first time she saw them. They shared a familiarity and intimacy that only couples or relatives share. She tiptoed behind them hoping to grab her bag, undetected. They were whispering conspiratorially. Agniezska was rubbing Jason's hand.

"No, it's okay. Don't be cross. We can hide it. In lock-up. With others."

"Agniezska, I told you something sporty and subtle that we could pass off as your own. With your wages, even with a PCP loan, you couldn't possibly convince people you could afford an Aston Martin, for goodness sake!"

"But Jas," she whined, "I hav always vanted Aston Martin. Iz so sexy…"

"It'll be impossible to hide it, even using the lock-up. Someone will soon figure out we have it."

Jason suddenly stopped talking. Agniezska looked up and saw Dawn dragging her bag out from under the table by the door where she had left it and scowled. Jason turned a full beam smile onto her. "Hey, thought you had gone," he said.

"Forgot this," she replied, pointing at her bag which was then free of the table leg. "I'd forget my head if it wasn't screwed on," she continued and groaned inwardly at her naff remark. Originality wasn't her strong point when she was under stress.

"Catch you at the class on Friday," called Jason. "I'm taking an extra class here tonight, so I might need to copy your homework, yet again, this week," he joked.

"Ha, of course. Bye!"

Dawn beetled out for the second time, stopping only when she reached the car. Her brain was working at full power. She opened the car door, threw her bag into the back, slumped into the driver's seat, and sat, staring into space. She couldn't make any sense of what she had just overheard. Cinnamon tapped her on the shoulder.

"Hustlers," she said. "We saw it on that programme, Hustlers, remember? Daft chump puts up his car for sale on the internet. Beautiful girl answers his advert and asks if she can take it for a test drive on her own. Says she is a bit nervous of driving with male strangers. Bats eyelids, and offers to leave the keys to her own Porsche or Mercedes as collateral. The twerp gives her the keys and off she goes. She drives off chump's car and takes it back to the lock-up and her boyfriend, who is also a conman. Later, when she doesn't return, the chump checks out the car she's left behind, which turns out to be a hire car. What have you stumbled on here, Dawn?"

Cinnamon let Dawn digest the facts. She got there in the end. "Crikey, Jason and Agniezska are hustlers," she said aloud. She started the Volvo, heart heavy. She would have to tread extra carefully with Jason. He was trying to hoodwink her. All this romance wasn't for real. He was planning some move on her.

"And tonight's winners are..." The presenter built up the suspense as the nervous ice-skating contestants waited to see who had made it through to the next show. Her viewing was interrupted by the sound of the back door opening. She couldn't help herself.

"Where have you been?"

Jim gave her a cold stare. "Out."

"Is that all you're going to say? I've been worried about you. You didn't say you were going out. You might have told me. Anything could have happened to you. You might even have been involved in an accident for all I knew."

"I don't want an argument. I'm tired. I'm going to bed."

He trudged towards the stairs. Dawn turned her attention back to the television and stared at two contestants hugging each other with unseeing eyes. She scrunched the chair cushion up between her hands and then punched it hard. This was all wrong. She couldn't comprehend what was happening to them.

They were never 'lovey dovey', but they had enjoyed a reasonable relationship before now. She hated being such a nag. She had never been a nag before now. She went over the relationship in her mind.

When Jim worked, they managed a civil and fairly happy marriage. Yes, Jim was focussed on his work, and often went into his den at night to work on clients' accounts, but by and large, they had some time for each other, didn't they? She examined the facts. It maybe wasn't as perfect as she imagined. If she were honest, they had lived separate lives to a large extent. The whole upset with Elisabeth certainly changed them as people. Dawn was the first to admit she had been difficult to live with for some time after the loss of their child. But then, later, she was happy looking after Dan, the house, and content in her own little world of reading, crossword puzzles, soap operas. She used to visit friends, from time to time. Not that she had many friends. She was more comfortable with her own company or visiting her father. All the women she knew seemed to be mothers of Dan's friends. She met from time to time in coffee houses and chatted about what their children had been up to at school. She had always had difficulty in mixing with others. It must have been the result of having spent so much time alone as a teenager. It wasn't so much that she was shy, it was more that she wasn't able to relax in their company or talk easily about the same things. It might have been better if she had joined a book club. At least she would have had something in common with people there. She was definitely a square peg in a round hole when it came to socialising.

Life had been okay. The trouble definitely begun after Jim had lost his job. Up until then, he had even been attentive at times. Just before he was made redundant, he had even taken to coming home with flowers for her or small gifts. He had become miserable almost overnight. But surely that wouldn't have been enough to make him so distant and cold with her. What had she done other than go to the gym and start writing? Surely, he should have been proud that she made an effort. He couldn't be jealous, could he?

She went over this time and time again. It needed to be resolved.

She would fix it.

She went into his den and switched on the light. She pulled out the drawer to the filing cabinet and collected the form. She needed a black pen to sign it. Jim would have one. The pens weren't on the top as they had been last time she entered the office. She opened the top drawer and rustled through it looking for a pen. Her hand brushed across a mobile phone. That was odd. She thought Jim had handed in his phone when he had left work. Closer inspection revealed it to be a more modern mobile, not at all like the old Nokia phone he used to have. Jim wouldn't have had a mobile phone. He complained enough about the cost of the one they shared. Dawn usually carried it about in case of emergencies and Jim used it when he wanted to call his stockbroker. Other than that, they both used the house phone.

Dawn looked at it again, then curiosity got the better of her. She turned it on. It lit up. It was active. She had an ominous feeling. She didn't dare look at the list of contacts.

"Do it," said Cinnamon.

She looked at the list. There was only one number in the phone. Against it was no name, only the letter S. Dawn's hand began to shake. She knew what this meant. She marched upstairs and threw the phone onto the bed.

"I know you're not asleep. What's this?"

Jim made a fuss about being woken up.

"God, what now?" he snapped. He looked at the mobile. "Well? What do you want me to say? It's a phone."

"Bravo! There is no need to be sarcastic with me. I'm not the one with a mysterious mobile phone in my office drawer. What's going on?"

Jim's temper flared, and he launched an attack of his own. "Since when do you have the right to go through my private drawers? I wouldn't go through your desk."

"Since I went looking for a pen to sign some papers so we could go away together and fix this mess that used to be called a marriage. You shouldn't have secrets from each other in a good marriage," she yelled, tears of frustration beginning to flow down her face.

Jim was unrelenting. "No good ever comes of snooping. And while you are on about 'good marriages' whatever happened to trust? If you trusted me, you wouldn't be carrying on like a total cow."

Dawn took a deep breath then in a quiet voice asked, "Why do you have a mobile that I know nothing about?"

"I don't know. It probably got swept up among my things I collected from the office when I got booted out. It's not mine. It belongs to one of my ex-colleagues. I've never used it. It probably doesn't even work," replied Jim, his eyes steely cold. "So, are you going to apologise now?"

"Sorry," snapped Dawn.

Jim snatched up the phone and slammed it on his bedside cabinet. He turned over in bed and ignored her as she left.

She may have said the words, but she wasn't at all sorry. What she was sorry about, however, was that her husband of twenty-odd years was lying to her. It was his phone all right. The battery life of a phone isn't very long. The phone would not have fired up unless it had been charged. It was Jim's phone, and he was lying to her.

It had been a tough decision, but she decided to go to the writer's group meeting that morning. She needed to take her mind off what she had discovered.

Jim might have protested his innocence, but she knew better. She had taken a note of the phone number stored on the mobile. She called the number on the mobile she and Jim shared. She dialled 141 in front of the number to protect her identity. It rang twice before it was picked up. A female voice answered, "Good morning, Susan Parkinson speaking." Dawn had wanted to ask her how she knew Jim but her courage failed, and she pressed the 'end call' button.

She made sure she arrived late to the class. As it happened, Geraldine had cornered Jason, and they were discussing something when she entered. The desks were set up like school desks again. Blake hadn't appeared yet, so the members were chatting.

Dawn asked Margaret if she could sit next to her.

"Certainly, pull up a chair," replied Margaret. "Nice day today, isn't it? Makes a change after all that rain we've had recently."

Dawn smiled politely. She glanced up at Jason and Geraldine. Geraldine was handing over something to him. Her antennae pricked up, and she strained to overhear their conversation.

"Good taste … very classy …" Jason said.

"Please do ... worth ..."

"You can trust me," Jason replied, giving her a friendly pat on the top of her arm. He slipped the small box into his jacket pocket. Turning around, he noticed Dawn and gave a small wave then pulled a sad face at her because she wasn't sitting near him. She made an effort to smile back at him, but inside she was a mess. Her mind was working in overdrive. Jason had just taken what looked like a ring box from Geraldine. What was the woman thinking? Now that she knew he was a conman, she reckoned he was going to do Geraldine out of whatever was in the box. Hadn't he told her that the woman was loaded? They both knew it. That would explain why he was here. He wasn't interested in writing at all. All that rubbish about heroes for children. He was here to con people and cheat old ladies out of their money.

Dawn's anger mounted. She could do nothing without proof, and she certainly didn't want to confront Jason. He would deny it. Look how easily Jim had denied that the mobile she had discovered wasn't his.

Blake came in with effusive apologies for being late. He threw his coat on the back of the 'teacher's chair' and began the class immediately.

"We have spent a lot of time talking about the accuracy of what we write. If we write about someone having a heart attack, we need to ensure we have all the facts. A novel isn't like some sort of television drama where a man is attached to a defibrillator having suffered a heart attack, gets a jolt, and wakes up saying, "Thanks, Doc, I feel great now." There were a few chuckles.

"I want to discuss murder today. This is clearly a subject close to my own heart. It is important that if you are going to kill off a character, you need to do it with accuracy or indeed choose some outrageous method. If you were going to murder a character what method would you employ?"

Margaret beside her said, "Broken egg shells."

"Go on Margaret."

"I'd make my character eat broken egg shells. I heard they block the gut and can kill you."

"I think you'd have to give your poor victim a lot of eggs," said Craig. "Wouldn't the stomach acid react with the shells? Besides, they're pretty crunchy, those shells. What had you planned feeding your victim?"

"A McDonald's Happy Meal," replied Margaret with a wicked smile. "Someone should pay for the way they have made people obese. I thought I might create a character who poisons a fictitious executive of a make-believe company like McDonald's, in my story about corporations and the way they ruin lives."

"I don't think they can be blamed for the obesity epidemic. People don't have to eat McDonald's food. People just consume too much," Harold volunteered.

The group rumbled on about overeating, trying to work out how they could best poison a victim. Dawn switched off. Her mind was elsewhere. It jumped between the mobile phone, and Jason making off with some of Geraldine's jewellery. She paid no attention to Blake.

They broke for a coffee break. Jason made a beeline for her, but she had anticipated that and had already engaged Craig in conversation. Jason got caught by Colin. She excused herself from Craig and managed to get Geraldine on her own.

"Hi Geraldine,"

"Hello, dear."

"I hope you don't think I'm being nosey, but you handed over something to Jason earlier."

Geraldine looked at her sharply. "Well, you are being nosey. That was between Jason and me. I know you two are close. No, don't protest. I've noticed the way you always sit together. It's obvious you are involved with him, yet I have never discussed my suspicions with anyone here. What goes on between you is not my business. I would appreciate it if you afforded me the same privacy. What he and I discuss is between us," she reiterated.

Dawn felt humbled. She felt more than that. She felt chastised. She had been an idiot thinking she could have a friendship with Jason. She shouldn't have encouraged it. Jason was an attractive man. If Geraldine had picked up on it, then it must have been apparent to everyone here that she had thrown herself at him.

They must have all thought she was a tart. A stupid, old tart who should have known better. She decided to leave them to it. She couldn't think straight. She didn't want to speak to Jason either. He was just out to make her look a fool. He and Agniezska had probably already enjoyed a jolly good laugh at her expense. What a pair they were. She packed away her book, told Blake she felt ill, and left the room. What Jason did was none of her business, and if Geraldine didn't want her to help her out, then she wouldn't. She had other bigger problems to deal with.

She had just passed the bank when she heard someone shouting for her. It was Jason.

"Dawn! Hold up! What's wrong?"

Tears welled in her eyes. She couldn't hold on to her emotions much longer.

"Everything," was the response.

Jason had concern etched all over his face. "Come and sit by the pond for a while. You need to talk," he urged.

"No, I don't need to talk. I need to be left alone to sort out the mess I am in. Go back to the class, Jason. Go and do whatever it is you've planned. Leave me alone."

She threw off his hand that he had put on her shoulder and made her way back to the car. Tears blurred her vision. Worse was the unbearable pain she felt in her heart. Who could she trust? Certainly not Jason, but Jim, she should have been able to trust him, and now she didn't.

Marcus had gone. He didn't want to leave, yet they both understood that what they had could only be temporary. As she drove back home, Cinnamon attempted to replace her feelings into an imaginary box and lock them deep within herself. It was a tactic she had learned years before. Each box could not be opened, once she locked it away. It had served her well in the past. This time though, it was much more difficult.

Marcus promised to write. He even suggested trying to Skype each other. He invited her to visit him in South Africa. She said she would think about it. She wasn't sure it would be ideal to have an on-off relationship with someone so far away. It was unlikely they would see each other again.

The pain she felt as they drew apart for the last time was nothing compared to the unbearable raw hurt she had experienced before in her life. It was what they called a bittersweet pain. At least this time, she knew he would leave, and was prepared for it. This time there was no anger, only sadness. It had been her choice to embark on a brief, if not passionate, love affair. He had been everything she could have hoped for. He had restored her faith in men. He had not duped, lied, or used her. He was open with her from the start.

Marcus had come into her life at the right time. She needed to get out of the destructive rut she found herself in. There would be no further one-woman crusades to right wrongs of straying males. She would find something more productive to do with her time. She might take up art again. She had a flair for painting, and she could use her creativity to produce some canvasses. She had used her anger in the past as therapy and painted bold, swirling canvasses like the one that hung in her lounge. Now, she quite fancied painting some colourful portraits of wild animals. She would buy a wildlife book and get some inspiration from the photographs in it. A weight had been lifted from her shoulders. The world did not seem as formidable as it had always done. She felt different. Unable to put a finger on what felt different exactly, she decided that her heart had probably defrosted slightly.

She considered dropping by to visit Ellie and Pete later that day, before they also went back to South Africa. They had been very generous in letting her join their celebrations, and she wanted to thank them again. It was thanks to them she had been able to get to know Marcus. It was thanks to them and to fate. For once, fate played a positive role in her life.

She thought again about Marcus. She recalled his parting words as he walked through the gate to the departures lounge. "You really are my guardian angel. You not only saved my life, but you have saved me from myself. I might be able to finally start living now." She felt much the same. They really were very alike in some ways.

They had spent every minute together since the wedding reception. There was little time for sleep. Secrets had been shared. Feelings unleashed. Marcus talked about the terrible loss he experienced as a younger man, and how until he had met Cinnamon, he had been unable to consider a relationship with another woman after Serene. He blamed himself for not being there on that fateful day. He should never have left his family overnight. They all knew it was dangerous at times, and his father had been getting older. He had let down not only his parents, but his fiancée and, of course, his unborn child. He had carried that guilt around for far too many years. Cinnamon also poured out her life story. She shared the pain of losing her babies and being unable to have children again. She disclosed how she had run wild in recent years and tried to right wrongs committed by other men. Marcus didn't mind. He wasn't put off by her wanton behaviour. He understood that she had been lost. He stroked her hair. "Poor baby," was all he had said, and kissed her with a warmth and tenderness that made her want to cry. Love-making replaced talking. Eyes looked into eyes. Hands trembled and explored. Desires were spent and two souls cradled each other, understanding the emptiness which had transformed them into the people they had become.

At last, two broken hearts had found some comfort and ease. Now, she felt unburdened—cleansed almost. Cinnamon considered the possibilities of a new start. That was, until the phone rang.

"Ms Knight. Sorry to trouble you. I've found him at last. Do you want the address?"

Cinnamon's face hardened in an instant.

"Yes please, Joe, I'd like that very much."

She gunned the Maserati. She still had one last piece of unfinished business before she could move on.

As soon as she got home, she swept past Jim, who was staring out of the kitchen window, and shut herself away in her office. Putting her head into her hands, she wept soundly. The pain rose from somewhere deep inside and erupted into her chest. She thought she would die of misery. The last time she cried like this was when she lost Elisabeth. That memory made it worse. She was losing someone again. It wasn't fair. What had she done to lose all the people she loved most? The sobs got louder and louder. Her whole body throbbed with misery. She was unable to control the tears which splodged onto her desk and puddled. She heard a door slam. Jim was leaving her. He wasn't going to comfort her or tell her that everything would be all right. This time it wasn't going to be. This was the beginning of the end. The car started up and pulled off the drive. A wail came from somewhere deep within, and she heard a strangled cry as it erupted from her mouth. She had lost all control.

Day was turning into dusk when the final hiccupping sobs abated. She had cried out all the hurt and frustration. Now she was left with no emotion other than intense anger. Cinnamon cursed and growled in the same room, prowling about like a caged tiger.

Eventually, some form of sanity kicked back in. Along with the sanity came lucidity. She started up the laptop and pulled up Cinnamon's story. What had Blake said about ensuring facts were correct? When she wrote the chapter about Cinnamon using Mary-Beth and Fran's room key card, she neglected to check that the Belfry actually used key cards. If they used proper keys, then she would have to change the wording. She found the hotel number and got through to reception.

"Good evening. I know this sounds ridiculous, but I'm writing a novel, and I have mentioned your hotel a couple of times. In one of the scenes, I mention you have key cards. You do have key cards and not just normal keys, don't you?"

"Yes, we do."

"That's a relief. Thank you. Oh, whilst I'm here, could you give me one of your real room numbers. I have just used a random room number, and it struck me that you might start your rooms at 200 or something rather than zero."

"What sort of room did you have in mind?" asked the receptionist.

"A double room," replied Dawn. "Actually, I have some special friends who stayed down there a few weeks ago. I'm using their names in the book too. It would be nice for them if I used the room they stayed in. It'll give it all a real, authentic flavour. They were celebrating an anniversary when they stayed with you, you see. This mention will bring it all back for them. Would it be possible to have their room number?"

The receptionist wasn't happy to give out information of a personal nature, however, Dawn used all her charm, and since the clients were not currently at the hotel, the receptionist gave her the information that she needed. She confirmed Dawn's suspicions. Mr and Mrs Ellis had used room 503 not just on that occasion, but twice more since then.

Her hands trembled as she put the phone down. It was beginning to fall into place. She knew why there had been larger than normal withdrawals on their bank account, why Jim had a mobile phone that was linked to Susan Parkinson's number, and most important of all, why he had been such a miserable grouch since he had retired.

It had all been there under her nose. She had been too occupied with her writing, and Jason to see what was now patently obvious.

What should she do now? What would Cinnamon do?

"Kill him," hissed Cinnamon. "He's a cheating louse. Face up to him. Find out how long this affair has been going on and then hit him over the head with a frying pan. He deserves it."

"I can't do that. There isn't anywhere I could bury the body. I need a better solution. Anyhow, if I was going to kill him I wouldn't want to get caught."

"Do you remember that episode in Desperate Housewives?" asked Cinnamon. "The episode where Carlos kills Gabby's stepfather? Then the women bury him in the woods?"

"Yes," said Dawn. "I remember it, but that was just a television drama. This is real life. In real life, sane people don't murder their spouses. Although, I have to admit that at the moment I feel neither sane nor real. I can't see how it could even be possible."

"Oh, it is possible. You just need to be strong. You need to let Cinnamon help you out with this. Take a break and let me sort it out."

"Where's the car?"

"I took a taxi. I needed to see someone ... I needed ... I don't know what I needed," she said and shook her head sadly.

Jack ushered into the lounge. She dropped into the large comfortable chair and looked at the television. Jack was watching Mastermind.

"Am I interrupting?" she asked.

"Never," he replied and switched the television off with a flick of a button on the control. "It must be important for you to come round on an evening without letting me know. Do you want to talk, or have a cup of tea first?"

"Talk please. I don't know what to do, Dad. Jim is having an affair. I'm 99% certain he's having an affair, and I just don't know what to do about it. The whole thing is a complete mess. You see, I'm to blame. I can't have tried hard enough. I was always busy with Dan when he was little, and recently, I have been more interested in my own world than Jim's. I haven't been there to support him when he needed me. I guess being made redundant hit him badly, and instead of being understanding about it all, I let him flounder about. Someone else helped him instead."

Dawn told Jack everything she had pieced together.

"The one thing you haven't done, is ask him about it. You haven't actually asked him if he is having an affair. He might have a reasonable explanation for it all."

"Dad, I know you believe completely in the sanctity of marriage and sticking by your chosen one, but I think the evidence speaks for itself. Besides, Jim has really changed. He looks at me so coldly these days. I feel like I have let him down, Dan down, and you down. If only I weren't so weak ..." her eyes filled and she dabbed angrily at the tears to stop them falling.

Jack cleared his throat. "I'm going to share something with you now. Something I have kept to myself for more years than I care to remember."

Dawn looked up. Jack was gazing at the photograph of her mother, and his eyes were also becoming glossy with tears.

"Many years ago when you were a small girl, I had what you might call ... an indiscretion."

Dawn gasped. "No, not you, you adored Mum."

"I am as ashamed of myself today as I was then. I was arrogant and had youth on my side. Your mother was wonderful. I genuinely loved her and you. I don't know how or why the affair began. I was happy enough with life. I had a good job, a super family. I should have been satisfied with that. Francine was her name. She worked in the front office. I used to share a few words with her as I checked in and out of the bank, nothing more. One day, she and I bumped into each other at the park where I always ate my lunch. We got chatting. Next thing, we were meeting daily for our lunch. We had a lot in common. She was a pretty thing too. She wasn't flirtatious, but she made it quite clear that she liked me. I was flattered. I wish I could fathom out why I got involved with her. We both attended the Christmas party for the bank employees in London. I had a couple of glasses of wine. I was relaxed. I'd just found out that I had received a handsome annual bonus, and I was in good spirits. She and I ended up ... you don't need to know the details. Suffice it to say, I was unfaithful to your mother. Worse still, I remained unfaithful for another month until I came to my senses and called it off with Francine."

"I had to tell your mother. She was, well, you can imagine. You can understand that feeling now. I'm telling you this because your mother didn't throw pots and pans at my head, like I expected she would or should. She didn't scream or shout at me. She forgave me," Jack's voice cracked. He found his handkerchief and blew his nose. Eyes red, he continued.

"I didn't deserve such selflessness. I knew then that I had chosen the right woman for me. She was the only person for me. She never brought it up again. She never made me suffer for it. She only demanded that I never stray again. I asked her why she wasn't furious with me. She said she was, but she understood that things like that happened and was glad I had the courage to tell her about it. She told me it didn't matter as much as she thought it would, because she knew I loved her. Besides, I had given her the greatest gift a man could give a woman—a child. She put her arms around me ..." Jack faltered. "And ... told me that she loved me. That that love would see us through. It did. I wish my love had been strong enough to have seen her through her illness," Jack's face crumpled. Tears ran down the crevices of his face. "You see, that's why I could never find anyone to replace her. She was so strong. She was much stronger than me. You're your mother's daughter. If you love Jim enough, you'll forgive him. Think about what you want to do before you confront him. I wish I could turn back the clock, you know. If I could, I would never, ever have hurt your mother."

Dawn left her chair to kneel down in front of her father. She wiped his tears and hugged him tightly. Daughter and father cried until both felt better.

Cinnamon watched from a distance. Jack may have had his thoughts, but she knew she was stronger. She would be the one to dole out the punishment and forgiveness wasn't high on her agenda.

The Maserati ate the motorway. It took her no time at all to reach the outskirts of Manchester. It was payback time. Geoff had mistreated her and Jessica. She didn't care much about Jessica, but she did care about the child, Charlie, who was stuck in the middle of all this. What man could neglect his boy? She thought up all the ways she could hurt him for this last treacherous act. She would make him suffer for all the pain he had caused her, Jessica, and Charlie.

A large plastic bag was now in a small cool box in the boot of the car. The man had it coming. She would soon be able to put this particular part of her life to rest in more ways than one.

She screeched the car into a parking space near the address she had been given, and checking she looked good, she smoothed down her short, bright red skirt.

The apartment block needed a coat of paint. The lift had graffiti scribbled on the walls. The whole place smacked of neglect. She found the flat she was looking for and rang the doorbell. Geoff opened the door. His eyes opened wide in surprise.

"Oh, my God. Cinnamon? What are you doing here?" he blurted. "Sorry, I'm forgetting my manners. Come in. Wow! You look incredible."

"Hello, Geoff. I heard from a friend that you were here. I thought I'd come and say hello and see how you are," she purred.

Geoff was overwhelmed. "Come in. Sorry about the mess. Do you want a drink or anything?"

The flat was untidy. A television was on in the corner of the room tuned into a sports channel. It was as Joe had described. The man was down on his luck.

"A glass of wine would be nice. You look good too."

Geoff blushed and out a hand over his thinning hair.

"Not as good as you do. Sit down."

He disappeared into the kitchen to return almost immediately with two generous glasses of wine. He sat opposite her on a chair, while she sat seductively posed on the settee.

"I often wondered how it would be if we met up again," said Geoff after a while, fortified by the glass of wine. "I expected you to be really annoyed with me. No, more than annoyed with me. I handled it all wrong. I have thought about it time and time again. I should have phoned you or …"

He ran his hand through his hair again and gave a small shrug.

"I grew up," said Cinnamon and took a sip of wine which wet her lips. She licked it off suggestively.

Geoff squirmed in his chair.

"So, what have you been up to all these years?" she asked. "You still single?"

"Yep. I stuffed up again. Jessica and I parted a while back. I don't know why I took off with her. She wasn't really my type. I have tried to fathom out what happened and I owe you some sort of explanation. It was down to weakness on my part. I wasn't the right guy for you or her. There were a multitude of factors. Hell, I was under a heck of a lot of stress at work. I hated that job, by the way. Really hated it. Anyway, let's just say I wasn't myself at the time and I didn't think through any of my actions. Jess was there and I thought I could start again. Things hadn't been fantastic between you and me. I needed to get out. You know, a fresh start... thought it would turn me into a new man. Anyway, I know now it was cruel of me to leave you like I did," said Geoff staring at Cinnamon's long legs in her high-heeled sandals.

"It's water under the bridge. Things like that happen. I'm older and wiser," she said taking another sip and setting the glass down on the table in front of her.

"Aren't you mad at me?"

"I was. I was so angry I couldn't function. But look at me now. Do I look angry?"

"No, you don't. You look ... fabulous."

Cinnamon seemed pleased by his compliment. She appeared to ponder for a moment then in a hesitant tone asked, "This may seem odd, especially with what we've been through, but why don't we go out for a meal, for old time's sake?"

Geoff coughed a dry nervous cough. "Erm, yes. I suppose we could, but erm, finances aren't too fluid the moment ..."

"Not to worry. I have a better idea. Why don't I nip out to the shops and get some food, then cook it here. It would mean we could have a drink and ... catch up," she added, crossing her legs again, and giving Geoff an appreciative look.

"Okay. Yeah. That should be fine. Are you sure? I'll pay half of course."

"Right, that's settled. I'll come back after I've got some shopping. You can get the place ready. We have some catching up to do."

Geoff swigged his glass of wine and stood up. "Lovely, smashing. I'll just tidy up a bit before you come back."

Cinnamon joined him. In her heels she was slightly taller than him. She moved towards him and bent slightly, kissing him on the cheek.

"That'd be lovely. See you soon," she murmured. She departed, leaving Geoff astonished. Was he about to be reunited with his ex? An ex who had transformed from a frumpy old hag into a stunning vixen? His luck was changing. He rushed off to the bathroom for a quick shower. Who knew what might happen this evening.

Cinnamon strode back to the car. Slimy toad, she thought. His eyes were practically hanging out of his head. What a predictable prat he was. This would be so easy. She sat in her car to clear her mind and ensure her plan was fool proof. No one had seen her arrive at the apartment, and no one would be able to say what had happened. She had done her research. She had been waiting for this moment ever since she had spoken to Jessica.

In the cool box were some vegetables and two quail. The meal would be simple but deadly. The quail had been living in a cage hidden in Cinnamon's garden for a while. She had been feeding them a mixture of birdseed and hemlock seed as part of their diet. She discovered that quail often ate hemlock seeds and were immune to the poisonous seed. Hemlock caused a gradual weakening of the muscles and intense pain as the muscles deteriorate and die. Although sight might be lost, the mind remains clear until death occurs. It can take several hours for a man to die. Eating the quail would paralyze Geoff and ultimately kill him. It would be a torturous way to go, but didn't he deserve that?

Cinnamon killed her quail that morning, plucked them, and stored them in the cool box. The perfect murder was about to take place. She listened to the radio for a while, thinking through her plan. When the programme ended, she checked her make-up, collected the bag, and made her way back to the flat.

The smell of roast quail filled the kitchen. Dawn had prepared the table. The centrepiece consisted of three large, fat red candles. Silver confetti sparkled on the tablecloth. A bottle of Rioja stood on the worktop, waiting to be consumed. Dawn was dressed in her black dress, hair freshly washed, lips painted a soft pink colour. Music played softly in the background: a Carpenters CD.

The sound of the car pulling up on the drive alerted her to Jim's presence. She poured the wine, plastered a smile on her face, and waited for him to enter.

"What's this?" he asked, looking surprised.

"Thought I'd treat us to a nice meal. We haven't had any time for each other recently, and I have been distracted with one thing and another. I thought this would give us the chance to talk and enjoy each other's company."

She handed Jim a glass of wine. He took a sip, nodded appreciatively. "Nice," he said. Then he cocked his head to one side. "This is about something else though, isn't it? I know you, and you're up to something. You don't normally cook. In fact you don't normally spend time in the same room as me these days, so what is the real agenda here?"

This wasn't how Dawn had wanted to play it. She was cross that Jim had seen through the show. Worse, he had made her feel less forgiving or amenable.

"Okay, we need to talk. We need to be honest," she replied. "I know about Susan."

Jim put down his glass, sat on the kitchen stool, and let out a heavy sigh.

"I knew we'd end up having this conversation. I had a feeling you would find out. I should have come clean after you found the phone. Yes, I have been seeing Susan. I have been seeing her for a while. In fact, I have been seeing her since before I was kicked out of my job."

Dawn grabbed the kitchen top to stop herself falling. This was much worse than she had expected. The fight drained out of her. She felt the floor evaporating. "Hang on," urged Cinnamon. "Be strong."

"In fact, I have just been with Susan, and we have had a serious talk. I'm sorry, Dawn, I didn't want this to happen. You deserve better …"

"Look, I have to tell you that whatever you have done, we can get through this. We have been together for two decades. We know each other inside out. We can get over this. I won't blame you. I'll pretend it didn't happen," she said, her voice breaking as she spoke.

Jim looked at her tenderly. "Dawn, we have been together for years but we both know that we haven't been in love for years. We are just used to each other. It was comfortable. We got by. You're a good woman, and I don't want to hurt you, but surely you can see how trapped I have begun to feel. Since I have been at home, it's been obvious we can't stay together. It was all right when I was out of the house most of the day but this, well, this has highlighted the problems. I'm very fond of you. We have shared so much together.

We have been together a long time, probably too long now. We should have talked about this a long time ago."

"Susan is leaving her husband, and we're going to start a life together. I won't leave you in the mire, though. I owe you my support, and you'll get that. After all, you have looked after the family for years. We'll come to an amicable agreement about the house and the few savings we have left. I won't see you without."

Dawn's shoulders began to rock. The crying was soundless. Tears rolled down her face.

"No, Jim, there must be some other way."

"I've spent months thinking about this Dawn. It isn't just something recent. I have honestly thought this through. It was never going to be easy, but you'll see, it will be the right decision. You can do your writing and have your own life. I've been pretty horrible to you recently. I haven't meant to be. I couldn't help myself. I've regretted a lot of what I've said to you, and I'm sorry. I've reached a crossroads in my life, and I need to think about me now. I need to change my life before it's too late. I need to do something that will make me feel alive again. Hanging about here, treading a path that is well-worn is not going to work for me. You have Dan and Phoebe. You are still young for goodness sake. And, now that you look so good after that exercise, you won't be short of men."

"Don't you dare tell me what I'll have or not have. You have no idea what I feel."

"No, I don't. I am truly sorry, Dawn. I really didn't want it to come to this, but I need some variety. I need to spice up my life before I get too old. Before long, I'll be sixty, for goodness sake. I don't want to spend my life fixing mowers and doing DIY. I want to try new experiences before it's too late."

"What are you going to do that is so different?"

"Susan and I are going to volunteer in one of those underdeveloped countries. She's a qualified nurse. We're going to try and experience something quite different. I'm going to get out of the house tonight. Give you a chance to … you know?"

Dawn nodded numbly. She had no more questions. She had no more arguments. She had nothing left. She was empty and alone.

"I think I can understand that. It hurts. Lord, it hurts but I can understand. I need some time to think about it all, though. I need to digest all this. I don't want to part on bad terms. Will you stay for some dinner before you leave? I prepared it all especially, and it would be a shame to throw it away. We'll have a last meal together, and I promise not to be a cow. Let's part on a positive note. I'm cooking quail. I thought they sounded exotic. Stay for one last meal?"

Jim nodded, picked up the wine bottle, and poured out two glasses.

Her head throbbed. The music resonating through her body made the pain worse, still she kept pace with the other six women in the class. Dawn joined the kick-boxing class rather than have a personal training session with Jason. She needed to release some of this pain that threatened to consume her. Last to enter the studio, Jason was surprised to see her when he turned around to start the class. Agniezska was already at the front of the class, looking at her reflection and psyching herself up. He didn't have time to acknowledge her, other than a fleeting smile and a nod of his head before he began the warm up.

The women knew the routine by heart. Like a synchronised band of Amazon warriors, they followed his every move in time to the music. Dawn kept up with them. The routine was the same one Jason had shown her. The more she focussed on the movements, the better her head felt.

By the end of the routine, Dawn's heart was pumping. Adrenaline was circulating, and now she felt ready to unleash some of the anger inside. Cinnamon took over as she smashed her gloves into the punch bag being supported by a tall brunette who didn't dare speak or encourage her. A fury took hold of her. She hit the bag with every ounce of energy she had. When she finished thumping it, she began launching kicks at it. The woman couldn't hold the bag any longer. Agniezska came to control it instead.

"You are stronger than you look," she said as Cinnamon round-kicked and grunted. No matter how much she kicked and punched, she felt little release.

The women padded up and began practising moves on each other. Agniezska chose to be her partner and together they kicked and twisted like whirling dervishes. Some of the other women stopped to watch the pair. They were graceful but deadly. Some of the strikes were dangerously close to causing bodily harm.

Jason ended the session and brought the group back for a cool down. Cinnamon was now panting hard, and as the women marched about and brought down their heart rates, she went, leaving an exhausted Dawn behind.

Jason went to the back of the studio to turn off the music. Agniezska came up to Dawn. "You are different I think today, no?"

"No, Agniezska. I am the same person I have always been. I just haven't always let that person out."

Agniezska nodded in comprehension.

"You did well. I think you are very strong woman. I like you."

Dawn didn't feel the same about Agniezska. She grabbed her water bottle and headed for the door.

"Dawn, don't go. I need to talk to you," called Jason.

"Sorry, Jason. I don't have time," she replied and fled before he could say more.

She showered and changed into a bathing costume. She felt like taking advantage of the sauna to ease her sore muscles. She never knew they could work so hard. The sauna was adjacent to the changing rooms, near the large indoor swimming pool. She slipped in. It was empty. She put her towel out onto the wooden slats and relaxed onto it. Warmth seeped into her body, relaxing her. At last, her head stopped hurting. She was just contemplating what to do with the rest of her day, when the door opened, and a figure slipped in to join her.

"Don't go," said a voice. "I really need to talk to you."

Dawn opened one eye. Jason was standing in the sauna, dressed in his training kit.

"I haven't anything to say. It's best we don't see each other anymore."

"Well, I have a lot to say, and I'm not going until I've said it, even if I keel over in this heat first. I don't know what I've done wrong, but if I've scared you off by being too forward, I'm really sorry. I know I shouldn't have made any moves on you. You're a married woman, and I knew that all along. I knew that I couldn't have you, but some foolish part of me wanted to at least try. I've fancied you since I first saw you at the writing group. I couldn't get you out of my mind, and when you became my pupil here, well, that made it worse. Have you any idea how hard it was to train with you, to watch you as you tackled those moves with determination, to touch you? You got under my skin. Then when we kept finding things in common, I got carried away. You are exactly the sort of woman I have always wanted to meet. There is something hidden behind that façade that excites me. I know there is much more to you than you let on. You are my dream woman. At my age, I should have known better, but I couldn't help myself. And part of me sensed that all was not well in your marriage, so I wanted to test it and see if I stood a chance."

"I know now I went too far. I am truly sorry. I behaved like a love-struck schoolboy, but you had an effect on me that no one has ever had before," he continued. Sweat trickled down his forehead, and he looked flushed.

"Not even Agniezska?" she said.

"Agniezska? Agniezska is a friend. I've known her for a long time. She's just a friend."

Dawn huffed unconvinced.

"Dawn, I am telling the truth. Agniezska isn't my girlfriend. She's more like my sister."

Dawn snorted.

"Look, Agniezska is married already. Well, that's not quite true. She's going through a messy divorce. It's been going on for a while. She was with a brute of a man. He used to beat her. I met her in London. She worked on reception at the gym where I worked. We used to chat, and one day, she came in with a horrendous black eye. She was an emotional mess and confessed that the guy was using her as a punch bag. She showed me other bruises, vivid blues and blacks. It was dreadful. I couldn't believe someone could hurt her. She was such a sweet thing. She wouldn't leave him to start with. It was only after she was knocked out one evening and ended up in hospital with broken ribs and a smashed front tooth that I managed to convince her to leave him. I was about to leave the gym anyway to start my new job up here. I cajoled her into coming with me. She lived at my flat and started a course in physical training. She loved it. It made her feel stronger. That's why she's so obsessed with exercise now and takes extra classes. She never wants to be weak or bullied again. She never wants to be a similar situation again. She's still recovering from it all. She has nightmares some nights. I can hear her crying in the room opposite, but she is getting much better. She's come a long way from the subservient woman I knew in London. If you'd seen her then, you'd have thought it was a different woman altogether."

He stopped and sat heavily. He was sweating profusely now. "I felt responsible for Agniezska for ages. Her husband tried to get her to return at first. He came to my flat where she was hiding. I wouldn't let him get to her. I look at her, and I am reminded of how I used to be. She's like one of those children I train. She just needed someone to help her."

Dawn pushed herself up on her elbows. "Okay, let's get out of here, and I'll hear you out," she said.

"Thanks goodness for that. I thought I was going to faint. I'd look a right idiot if I swooned at your feet."

Dawn smiled in spite of herself. They left the sauna.

"I'll meet you in fifteen minutes in the cafe," she told him.

"Thanks. I'll just go and stand under a freezing shower until then. I think I'm in danger of melting," he responded.

They sat with a mineral water each, and Jason took up his story. "So, Agniezska and I have been friends for a while. I know she looks incredibly tough, but she isn't. Most of it is still a front. She's getting stronger though."

Dawn played with her glass for a while. Silence descended on them. A couple who had been sat at another table finished their drinks and left. There was no one else around.

"I want to believe you, Jason, but I have to confess I heard you talking to Agniezska the other day. I wasn't eavesdropping. I came back to get my bag. You two were in such a deep conversation that I didn't want to interrupt. When I came to collect the bag, I heard all about the Aston Martin."

Jason nodded. "I suspected you might have heard that. I told Agniezska I thought you might have heard her. Okay, this is a really big secret. I am about to trust you with something huge."

He waited a moment and looked directly at her. His eyes were wide and honest. Dawn began to doubt her fears. Jason seemed too genuine to be lying to her. The story about Agniezska seemed plausible. Agniezska was definitely not interested in anything but exercise. It added up. His eyes pleaded. He swallowed.

"Go on," said Dawn. "I won't tell anyone."

"You can't. You absolutely cannot." He coughed nervously and looked about to make sure no one could hear him then leaned forwards to talk in lowered tones. "Agniezska is Zee Zee Bagor, author of Hot and Lusty, the novel that is taking the world by storm." Dawn's face registered complete astonishment.

"She wrote Hot and Lusty just after we moved up here. It helped her get over some of her issues. Heaven knows where she got some of the ideas for it. I never asked. Some things are best left unknown. I did the edits on it and helped her with the English. She's not very fluent at times, as you might have noticed. I uploaded the whole thing to Amazon for her. We thought it would just make a few sales, enough to tide her over while she was taking her qualifications to be an exercise instructor. It didn't sell many copies to start with, then suddenly, one of those important women's blogs wrote about it, and before we knew where we were, she was getting fat royalty cheques from Amazon. Next, we got approached by one of the big publishers who wanted to take it on. Well, it was a no-brainer. We insisted on complete anonymity, of course, until she is divorced. The whole team at the publishing house know who she is and has promised to keep it quiet until we decide to announce it. It wasn't intentional, but it has helped sales of the book rocket. I went through the legalities of the contract with her. She has signed an agreement to write two more books in the same vein."

"But why is she still an exercise instructor? She must be rich enough to buy a castle in Scotland or move abroad? It doesn't add up."

"The ex. He is still being difficult about the divorce. Agniezska has filed on grounds of assault now, and we are sure she'll get her divorce papers soon. We don't want him to know that she is incredibly wealthy until after the event. He'll want at least half of it. Best to wait until it has all been finalised. He was a dreadful bully, Dawn. You have no idea how beastly he was. I wanted to punch his lights out, but Agniezska was too scared that he'd come after her and take it out on her. It was best we both left when we did. It was better that he thought we had run off together. Like all bullies, he doesn't want to square up to someone his own size. He hasn't come after her since we moved. If he knew about the money, he'd turn up for sure, screaming for his share and terrifying her."

Dawn nodded numbly. It was starting to make sense. She had got it terribly wrong. She still had one niggling doubt that Jason was telling the truth, though, in spite of his innocent face.

"What about Geraldine?"

"What about Geraldine?" he replied.

"I saw you together. She gave you something, a ring or some jewellery. Why would she do that?"

Jason's face reddened. "You weren't supposed to see that. It was silly really."

"I still would like an explanation. I need to be sure about some things, and I need to trust you completely."

"You mean this box, don't you?" he asked pulling out a small blue box.

"Yes, that looks like it."

"Open it."

Dawn took the box and opened the lid. Inside were two small emerald earrings. They sparkled as she stared at them.

"It was madness, I know, but I bought them for you."

"Me?"

"Before he passed away, Geraldine's husband used to be a successful jeweller in the Jewellery Quarter in Birmingham. Geraldine saw me outside the jewellery shop in Lichfield after one of the classes. She told me that whatever I was looking for would be expensive there, and should I need anything, she still had many of her husband's contacts. She's a very astute lady. I think she knew they were for you, but she didn't make any comment. She couldn't have been more helpful. I gave her an idea of what I wanted to get. She chose these for me. I couldn't have bettered her exquisite taste. I paid her for them, of course. I have the receipt if you don't like them. I wanted to get you something special. I thought they would be an ideal prize for winning the 'Green Story' Award. You were so happy when you won that, your eyes sparkled with happiness, just like emeralds, and these earrings seemed appropriate. I thought you could wear them, and they would remind you that you can do this. You too can be a successful author. They are a sort of lucky charm." Jason finished and looked up at her again. "I was stupid though. I shouldn't have bought a married woman a gift like this. It'll be sure to make your husband jealous."

"No, it won't. I don't have a husband anymore," she replied fingering the stunning earrings and lifting them up to her ears.

Cinnamon relaxed against the back of the settee. The food was almost ready. Geoff was on his third glass of wine and was talking about how glad he was that she had decided to come back into his life.

Cinnamon checked her watch. Only thirty minutes to go. She wasn't sure how much longer she could continue with this ridiculous charade. So far, Geoff had thanked her several times and then fawned about her trying to help while she prepared the meal. She sent him to the lounge to get him out of her hair, suggesting he just relax while she sorted everything. It would soon be over. She was looking forward to watching him twist in agony.

He was about to change the music on the CD player when they heard a knock at the door. Geoff answered. There was a whoosh and a joyful shout of "Daddy!" Cinnamon froze. Geoff came into the room carrying a beautiful toddler, whom Cinnamon recognised. It was Charlie, Jessica's son. Jessica followed. She gave Cinnamon a look of shock but managed to regain her composure immediately.

"Look who's here, Jess," said Geoff, face shining with pride and happiness. "Cinnamon has come to visit. Cinnamon, I know this is a bit of a shock, but this little Munchkin is Charlie. Charlie say hello to "Auntie Cinnamon."

Charlie beamed at her. "Hello Sinnymum," he managed. Cinnamon softened in an instance.

"Hello, Charlie."

"Sorry to interrupt, but Charlie left Mr Snuggles here last night, and you know he can't get to sleep without him," interjected Jessica. "We'll just collect him and leave you to it."

"Righty-ho!" said Geoff. "Come on, Champ, let's go and find Mr Snuggles and leave these beautiful ladies to talk."

"Bootiful," agreed Charlie and squealed with joy as his father picked him up and put him on his shoulders. They made off to the bedroom.

"I don't know why you're here, but I hope it isn't to make trouble," hissed Jessica.

"I'm here for reasons of my own. I take it you haven't told him about our meeting," replied Cinnamon exuding calm.

"No, he has enough to deal with."

"I thought he'd run off and left you."

"He did but it wasn't his fault. He'd been under a whole load of pressure at work and the pills the doctor gave him made him worse. He had a breakdown. He and I have spoken since he came back. He's explained why he ran off. I don't think either of us realised how vulnerable he was. It seems that we all got to him and made him feel inferior. There's much more to it than that, and he is still having counselling, but Charlie is helping. He feels such a failure, Cinnamon. First you with all your wealth and vitality and then me with my high demands and focus on my career, we pushed him over the edge. He hated his job all along, and when others got promoted over him, it made him feel useless. He left me because he thought he'd be a dreadful example to Charlie. He realises now that he'll always be perfect to Charlie. They are great together. Don't be hard on him, Cinnamon. He's not bad. He just wasn't as perfect as either you or I had thought."

The door to the bedroom burst open. Geoff was pretending to be a growling monster, and Charlie was laughing and squealing again. Mr Snuggles, a large soft toy rabbit, was being dragged along by his ear.

"Mummy, Daddy monster!" he laughed. Geoff caught him and tickled him. Both fell about laughing.

"Come on Charlie, time to leave Daddy. You can see him soon. He's taking you to the zoo, isn't he?"

"Zoo. Aminals," replied Charlie smiling and nodding.

"See you Wednesday, Geoff," she said kindly. "Bye Cinnamon, nice to see you again. You really do look fabulous."

"Bye, Daddy. Bye Bye, Sinnymum."

"Bye, Jessica. Bye, Charlie," replied Cinnamon.

Charlie hugged his father goodbye at the door before skipping off to the lift with his rabbit cradled in his arms.

"Isn't he something?" said Geoff as he came back into the room. "I hope it wasn't too much of a shock. Especially with, you know … what happened to us."

"It's fine," she replied smiling. "He's adorable, and I am genuinely happy for you."

"Thanks, Cinnamon. You coming here today has really helped

me. I owe you an explanation about why I left you. I feel I can turn a corner now I've seen you again. I've not been too well," he began.

"No explanations are needed," she insisted.

"I need to tell you though, Cinnamon. You deserve to know. They sat for a while longer, and he poured out the whole story, part of which she had gleaned from Jessica. When he finished, she went over to where he was sitting, his face wet with tears. She kissed him gently on the forehead. She went to the kitchen to get the food from the oven while he poured another glass of wine. She removed the tray containing the quail from the oven. They were cooked to perfection. She tipped them into the metal kitchen bin and returned almost immediately.

"I'm afraid dinner is overcooked. Why don't we phone up and have a Chinese instead?" she announced.

Dawn sat in the kitchen. She had been sitting there for an hour, unable to get motivated to do anything. She had spoken at length with Jim again the night before, when he collected the last of his belongings. .It's funny, Dawn thought. In only a few days we've managed to end a relationship that's lasted over twenty years.

Dawn had thought marriage was for a lifetime. It wasn't. Once she was over the shock of Jim's affair, she sat quietly and analysed the situation. It was true to say that neither of them had been happy for a considerable time. They coexisted rather than enjoyed living together. If Jim had still been employed, they would no doubt have carried on in their own worlds and put up with each other. As it was, the shock of losing his job and being at home twenty-four hours a day with a woman he really didn't know too well had been the wake-up call Jim needed. That, along with the fact that he needed to do something significant with his life, before it was too late.

She understood that. They had both been treading water, and she wondered idly if many couples get into a similar rut. They get so used to being a couple that it is easier to stick it out than break up and maybe cause grief and anger. The fear of the unknown sometimes kept people together, when being brave might have yielded a better future for both.

Deep within her heart she had known they were unhappy. Part of her knew that not all had been well in her marriage for a long time.

Her writing had been produced by her own subconscious fears. She hadn't wanted to recognise she was being rejected, fearful of the outcome, yet when it happened, she had been surprisingly numb about it. Cinnamon had prepared her well.

Dan had taken it well. He had been surprisingly grown up. He wished his father good luck with his project and asked if he would stay in touch on Skype so he could see how they were getting along. He went to the pub with Phoebe to meet the new woman in Jim's life too. He had been supportive of both his parents and made sure Dawn was not upset or lonely. He even invited her around to his house for her dinner. That had made her laugh.

The crazy thing was that she didn't feel upset—empty perhaps and definitely saddened that she and Jim had parted but not upset or angry. If she were totally honest about it, she was relieved. There could be no more arguments or tension. There would be no more tears or tearing at each other's throats. It was better to be "friends" than trapped together in a relationship that was unravelling.

Jack had been supportive too. He had listened to her explanation. Although he too was sad to hear of the spilt, he praised her.

"I knew you had a lot of your mother in you. You have been incredibly strong. Not many would have been as generous, or able to let go like you. I am so proud of you," he said and hugged her fiercely.

The old family house was up for sale. Dawn couldn't decide if she would stay in the area, but given that she knew nowhere else where she would feel comfortable and she still had family here, it was likely she would use her share of the proceeds of the sale to buy something modern in the vicinity.

The radio was playing Abba's The Winner Takes It All. She felt a lump rise in her throat as she listened to the lyrics. She would not cry. As she fought back the urge to sob, she heard a light knocking at the door.

She opened it and found Viv on the doorstep.

"Hi. I'm off duty in a minute, but I wanted to deliver this to you. I saved you until last today because I wanted to say how sorry I was to hear about you and Mr Ellis."

Dawn felt a flood of affection for this woman who had taken time to come and see her.

"You're off duty? Then come in and save me from my misery.

Would you like a cup of tea?"

Viv came in and put placed the letter on the top for her.

"Coffee, please. I need some caffeine to see me through the afternoon. I've been up since four this morning. Such a shame," she said again. "I hope you'll stay in the area and won't leave us. I don't know what I'd do if I didn't have my weekly entertainment thanks to you," said Viv, making herself at home.

"I have to explain some of the strange things you have come across. I am not mad or weird or a sex maniac," added Dawn.

Viv's face lit up. "I know. It's been such a laugh though to see you squirm and try and explain yourself."

"What do you mean, you know?" said Dawn, turning to look at Viv's twinkling eyes.

"Well, I've known from the off that you've been writing a book about a sagababe who gets up to all sorts of crazy things, including some naughty sex with a young man."

Dawn poured the water into the cups, added milk and brought them over to the table.

"Sugar?"

"No thanks."

"How did you know about the book?"

"Well, apart from the fact that my aunt is one of your dad's dancing partners, and he is always talking about you."

"Who's your aunt?" interrupted Dawn.

"Laura Marks. She's a right card. I think she tried to convince your dad go away on a dirty weekend with her to Blackpool," chuckled Viv.

Dawn spluttered her coffee. "That was your aunt? Dad was flattered, but I don't think she'd have got him there, not unless she knocked him out with Rhohypnol and then drove him there."

"Knowing her, she might think about trying that next time."

The women laughed again. Dawn could feel the knots in her shoulders loosening.

"So, carry on. Please tell me more. Was it just Jack who let the cat out of the bag? I don't think I gave him too many saucy details about what I was writing."

"No. I found out from my godson. He's been bragging about helping a—what did he call you—cougar out with some hotwiring techniques. I think he had secrets hopes that you would contact him again and ask for help with other interesting projects."

Dawn sat back and shook her head in disbelief. "So MJ…"

"…is my godson," finished Viv. "Once he told me about a woman wanting to learn how to steal a car, my interest was piqued," finished Viv. "You haven't disappointed yet. It's been huge fun. So, have you finished the book yet?"

"Nearly. I'm not sure how to end it. I've been waiting for the right vibes. It keeps trying to write itself. With the stress of the last few days, I put it on the back burner."

"I'll be sure to get my copy when it comes out. It sounds like it's going to be exactly what I need after I finish my shifts."

Viv emptied her cup. "Lovely. That should recharge the batteries. So, will you be okay? If ever you want to talk, I'm only at the other end of the village. Drop by any time, as long as it's in the afternoon or evening. "

Dawn was touched. It was comforting to know that people cared. She suddenly felt she could get through it all far more easily than she anticipated.

"If you fancy a girl's night out, I'm always available too," added Viv. "That is, unless your delicious toy boy is still on the scene."

"No. He isn't, and as you well know, he was not my toy boy. He was kidding."

"Guessed so. You looked too horrified for it to be true. Pity. He was rather tasty," said Viv giving a cheeky wink. "Better get off. Don't forget. I'm not far away. I mean it. Oh yes, your letter," she added picking it up. "Looks like someone has booked a holiday," she chuckled pointing out the travel agent stamp at the bottom of the envelope. Going somewhere nice?"

"Lanzarote. I thought a couple of weeks away would do me good. Put things into perspective, you know."

"Yes. It'll do you good. Enjoy it. Hey, maybe you'll get some inspiration to finish your book."

"That's the idea. I can't focus here anymore. I need to move on."

"Life gets a bit dull sometimes, doesn't it? You need to add some variety, spice it up a bit. Catch you again soon. Thanks for the coffee."

Dawn saw her to the door and waved her off.

"That was what she needed, some spice in her life."

"It just leaves me to say, that I wish you all the greatest of luck. It has been a huge pleasure to work with you. I hope you have learned some useful tips. I look forward to seeing some of your names on the Booker prize list in the future," said Blake grandly and took a bow as the class applauded.

They gathered round one last time to chatter and drink coffee. Dotty had made a large sponge cake. On the top was a large iced book. The book was one of Blake's.

"What exciting news about Blake and Dotty, eh?" said Craig sidling up to swipe a custard cream.

"Who'd have thought they'd be corroborating on a book called *Recipe for Murder*. Super idea though, has a murder story interwoven by recipes. Love it. Wonder if I can get him to corroborate on *Vehicles for Villains*. Now there's a thought," he chuckled.

"You deserve congratulating too. A little bird told me that you got an article accepted by a motoring magazine," Dawn responded.

Craig coloured. "Pretty chuffed about that. I hope it leads to more work. I'd love to do some regular articles. My dream would be to be a presenter on a car programme, but first things first. I don't want to be a car salesman all my life."

"You should always have dreams and goals," interrupted Colin.

"Sorry to hear about your mother," Dawn offered.

"Well, she was eighty-nine, so she had a good innings," said Colin.

Colin moved off. "He's changed, hasn't he? He seems more relaxed," observed Craig. "He was asking me about buying an old MG. Said he fancied joining an old classic car club and possibly attending a rally. He'll be wanting to have a go at the Mille Miglia next! Seems a rather macho hobby for Colin."

"We all change," remarked Dawn.

Geraldine sidled up gracefully. She was wearing a trilby which suited her. "I have to dash off, dear. First, I wanted to wish you well and say I am delighted you like the, you know whats. You have my card if you need them cleaned or the stones checked. Let me know. I'll be away for a few weeks now. I'm off to my villa in Tuscany. I have some ideas for a new book. I thought I'd use the time to get them down. Nothing like warmth, sunshine, and a glass of Chianti to help the creative juices. I hope you'll stay in touch. It's been super meeting you." Geraldine gave Dawn a warm embrace then moved on to say her farewells to the others.

Margaret was next to leave. She had to collect her grandchildren from the nursery. She hugged Dawn too. "Sad isn't it? I've got used to these classes. It's a little like the end of term. I feel like I'm losing classmates who are all going off to do exciting things with their lives. I hope to bump into you again. Don't forget you can find me on Facebook or Twitter. I'll be about somewhere in cyberspace."

One by one, they finished their coffees, said their goodbyes and left the Samuel Johnson Museum for the last time.

Jason and Dawn were the last to go. They ambled to Stowe Pool to watch the ducks.

"I thought Agniezska was incredible on television this morning."

"She did really well, didn't she? She handled all the questions very confidently. I think her accent makes her seem even more exotic. It can only lead to more sales of Hot and Lusty. There is even some talk that they are going to turn it into a movie," replied Jason, throwing some cake crumbs to the ducks that had swum up to them.

"Is that Dotty's cake?"

"Yeah. I always save them some cake. I like to feed them. There's something majestic about swans. Serene aren't they? They're always together," he said pointing out two swans making their way towards him. "I don't think I've ever seen them apart."

"So, Agniezska is free at last. Is she going to stay with you?"

"No. She's buying some mansion up in Cheshire or somewhere. She saw it in one of those glossy magazines. Is enormoos. It hass ten bedrooms, Beeg fireplaces an large Aga in keetchen," He said, imitating Agniezska perfectly. "It's got stables too," he continued. "She's thinking of taking up horse riding. I think she'll be happy there. She loves the countryside. She'll be able to write the next two books in peace. She mentioned she might invite some of her family over to stay."

"What about you? You'll miss her."

Jason snorted. "No, I won't miss her. She's a lovely person, but like all relatives, you have enough of them after a while. I'll visit her when she gets settled. She needs me to go through the next book before she hands it over to the publishers. Anyway, she's been incredible generous. She's given over a huge amount of her royalties to me for editing her book and uploading it. I could buy my own mansion now.

He threw the last cake crumbs. "I'll miss this class. It was good fun. I first came along to get tips to help Agniezska really, but she doesn't need my help now. It gave me some ideas for my own stories, though. I shall have to work out what to do next. I'll try and get the stories written and, of course, work on my centre. I might even set up another now I have some decent money. What about you, got any plans?"

She shook her head. "I'm in limbo at the moment. There is an offer on the house, so I need to make sure it goes through then decide what I'll do. Jim is leaving for Uganda in a week. He and Susan are going to do some volunteer work for a while and then hope to get proper positions abroad, helping people who are living in poverty. It seems such an adventurous decision, yet neither is fazed by it. In fact, they are both very excited about it."

"Well, we're all different. I hope it gives them what they need. Personally, I think Jim is bonkers. Not for going to Uganda but for neglecting you."

"It happens. I'm not the only single middle-aged woman on the planet."

"There you go, talking dirty again. You know I am attracted to older women," he said and nudged her gently. "I realise it's a tough time for you at the moment, but don't forget, I'm here if you need me. I'm not going anywhere, and well, you know how I feel."

Dawn nodded and pulled her coat around her tighter. "I do. Thanks. Thanks for understanding. Thanks for … everything," she replied.

The swans, realising there was no more cake, swam off together nuzzling each other as they returned to the far side of the small lake. Jason placed an arm around her shoulders and held her against him. She could feel the ache inside him. She wanted to make it better. She wanted to say the right thing, but she couldn't. She wasn't ready. She wasn't sure if she would ever be ready.

A final hug and they parted. Jason stayed behind, a wistful figure watching the swans. She made her way to the car park. Her emotions were jumbled. She needed to get away. She needed space. No, she didn't know what she needed. Resting her head on the steering wheel, she tried to untangle her thoughts. She couldn't. She groaned loudly, thumped her head against the wheel in frustration, and begged Cinnamon for help.

Cinnamon had been feeling unwell for some time. She felt surprisingly weak and unable to exercise as usual, and she'd been sick several times, day and night, without warning.

Since visiting Geoff, meeting Charlie and discovering the reasons behind the failed marriage, her life had become more settled. She'd enrolled for evening classes in art and had started a large canvas of a lioness prowling in some long grasses. The animal was partly camouflaged, but its muscular shoulders and the sheer power within was obvious, even to an untrained eye.

She was now sitting in the surgery, waiting to see one of the locums. A mother and toddler sat opposite. The mother was reading a story to the child who sat passively on her knee absorbed in a world of teddy bears enjoying a party.

She glanced at a text on her phone. It was from Joe, the detective. She had visited him and his wife twice since the episode with Geoff. Joe was delighted that she had come to terms with the whole affair. He joked with her and said if ever he needed to set up a honey-trap, he would call her. Joe and his wife Gina, had become part of her life. They were like a surrogate aunt and uncle. She felt comfortable with them.

Cinnamon was still unsure of where her life was going. She was a middle-aged woman, and in theory, the whole world was her oyster. She spent so long being angry and hurt that she couldn't decide what to do next. She thought about applying to be a nursery teacher at the local school. At least it would be fulfilling.

Geoff phoned her since after she visited him. He was about to start a new job. It was nothing to do with accountancy. He was going to work on a new locally-backed scheme helping people who had suffered breakdowns. He felt it was a worthy cause. It would help him feel useful.

Jessica sent her a picture that Charlie had drawn. It was of a tiger he had seen at the zoo. Cinnamon put it up on her fridge door.

The doctor had received her test results back. He gave her the news. Cinnamon stared at him, asked him to repeat the words then put her head in her hands and for the first time in many years, wept.

Returning to her house, she knew what she was going to do. She lifted a box in which she had collected the letters Marcus had sent her. He had written every day since he had returned to South Africa. She phoned the travel agents and booked a flight to Johannesburg, First Class. She then emailed Marcus. He would be so pleased. He asked her repeatedly to go over. He needed her by his side. He knew he could never feel such love for anyone else.

Up until that day, she had chosen to ignore his pleas. She had nothing to give him. She was just a woman without direction. Marcus deserved better. But things had suddenly changed. Cinnamon was ready to join him, eager to see him again. She now had something to offer him. She had something, or rather someone, they could share and love together. She stroked her stomach and whispered to the tiny being inside her. She knew it would make it. This time would be fine. The doctor confirmed she was in excellent health and that, in spite of her age, she should have no problems. She would make sure she followed all advice. Nothing would go wrong. She knew that this baby would grow to be strong and a survivor. Cinnamon was finally complete.

Her novel was completed. Her heroine had found love. She deserved some happiness, mused Dawn, who now stood on a large black lava rock facing out to sea. According to the signpost near her, she was only 146 kilometres from Africa. She could almost sense it in the distance. She could imagine the look of contentment that would now be on Cinnamon's face as she descended the small bush aeroplane's steps to fall into the arms of Marcus, who would be waiting for her, eager to see her, kissing her repeatedly, tears of happiness brimming from his eyes to soak his handsome, tanned face. It was a veritable 'happy ever after'. That sort of ending belonged to romantic stories.

The light which had dazzled the island all day, was now fading. The land was bathed in a soft warm glow. One of the last ferries of the day was making its way from Fuerteventura leaving a white foamy trail as it approached. The island was preparing for the evening. A pink hue was developing in the sky heralding a magnificent sunset.

A gentle breeze had blown up and taken away the heat of the day. It was ideal for a jog back to the hotel.

Dawn ran rhythmically along the walkway towards the dark volcano that was in fact the hotel, towering above the white buildings of a fishing village that was the Marina Rubicon. She reached the marina, taking in the expensive yachts that were moored there. Gradually, she slowed her pace until she reached the back entrance to the hotel. The sun worshippers had vacated the swimming pool area. Sun beds were neatly tidied away for the next day. The pool resembled a large rock pool with large volcanic rocks placed around it and a fountain spurting in the middle. The hotel appeared deserted. Its guests would no doubt be getting ready for dinner or drinks. An impressive conservatory restaurant jetted out above the swimming pool. A beautiful sooty black cat with almond eyes was curled up under a palm tree next to it. The cat stretched lazily when it saw her, rolled on its back and meowed. She bent to stroke it. It reminded her of a contented Cinnamon.

She climbed the steps past the restaurant and a further pool surrounded by palm trees and exotic flowers to enter the hotel. The scene inside did not disappoint. A waterfall cascaded from the top floor to this point, passing through tropical plants before appearing to descend to the pools outside. She crossed a wooden bridge, enjoying the beauty of the plants and the calm trickle of the pale blue water. She mounted the stairs, passed reception and entered the chapel that resembled a church filled with candles, Gregorian music, and cool stone walls. It exuded a welcome coolness contrasting pleasantly to the warmth outside. It was an exact replica of the famous church at Teguise, Nuestra Señora de Guadalupe, which she had visited the day before. It was all so impressive, yes that was the appropriate word, she thought.

A lift ride away she had reached her room, the Tao Suite. The room was located in the 'adults only' area. She had to pinch herself every time she opened the outer door to it. The door opened into a private courtyard and patio, hidden from all other guests. Wooden decking stretched out from the patio, and in the middle, on a raised wooden platform, stood a Balinese bed with a sumptuous mattress. Here, she could drink in the views from every direction while sprawling comfortably. To one side, she could admire the islands of Lobos and Fuerteventura as well as the Castillo de los Coloradas, sitting majestically on black volcanic sand, while listening to the crescendo of waves as they crashed melodically against the dark rocks below. From the other, she could enjoy the view of the entire Marina Rubicon and the length of Playa Blanca overlooked by the mountain, Montana Roja.

She opened the door to her suite and entered the lounge. The air conditioning was most agreeable. She kicked off her trainers allowing her feet enjoy the cool of the tiled floor. The room, painted in citron and cream was opulent and burst with life. Saffron yellow curtains interspersed with beige hung from wide windows and the room was bathed in Mediterranean hues. She turned on the stereo and browsed through the selection of music, putting aside Handel and Schubert in favour of Mozart's *Symphony number 40 in sol menor KV550.*

Room service had left champagne chilling in a wine bucket. She idly opened the bottle and poured a glass. She sipped at it as she stared at the Montana Roja from the window lost in her thoughts. Earlier in the day, it had glowed the deep terracotta red earning it its name.

She stepped from the lounge to the bedroom decorated in the same shades of green, yellow and cream, and placed her watch beside the inviting four poster bed, adorned with silk cushions. Stripping off her clothes, she padded into the bathroom where she ran water into the Jacuzzi bath, large enough for two. Adding a handful of rose bath salts to the water, peace enveloped her. The music filled the room and sliding into the perfumed water, she let out a long sigh of contentment. The suite was aptly named the Tao Suite. Tao meant 'path' or 'enlightenment' in Chinese and, by coming here she had indeed found her new path. This was the gateway to her future. Since arriving here, she had made several important decisions about what she was going to do with her life. Somehow, the enchantment of the surroundings together with the flavour of the exotic that this hotel offered, had remedied her anxieties. She was now a new woman. Like Cinnamon, she was in control of her future. Leaning back she started the Jacuzzi which burbled into life. The jets of water massaged her and she luxuriated in the warm water, glass of champagne in hand. Her eyes closed.

She sensed him, rather than heard him, as he joined her in the Jacuzzi.

"You look very ... appetising," he said. "Enjoy your run?"

"Yes, thanks. I'm glad I have taken up running. I should have done it years ago. It's very therapeutic."

"This is one of those places that is completely therapeutic. I love the whole holistic approach that they have here. I think we should stay here another month, at least," he continued, sliding closer to her. "Your painting is looking good too."

"It must be the light here and all the wild beauty that inspires me. Going to Cesar Manrique's house in Tahiche the other day inspired me too. It reminded me how much I enjoy painting."

"You are a constant surprise. When did you learn to paint?"

"It was after Elisabeth died and I had my breakdown. I took classes to help me get over it. It helped but only for a short while. My paintings were quite different then. They were all crazy swirls and dark colours. Jim hated them. I seem to have found a new voice here though. So, what have you been up to while I was out?"

"I went to check out trips for tomorrow. I thought we might hire a car and go off to El Golfo. It looks like a moonscape there. Besides, it is also where they filmed One Million Years BC. That was one of my favourites. Probably because Raquel Welch was in it. I rather fancy strolling along the beach with my very own Raquel. Maybe you could wear a loincloth for me."

She flipped some water at him with a laugh. "You are incorrigible. What is it with you and older women?"

"Don't know. I am too mature for my own age, I suppose. Always preferred the company of older, gorgeous ladies. Fuelled all my schoolboy fantasies," he chuckled. "We could go to Timanfaya Park, ride a camel at the foothills then go and see the fuego. Bet you didn't know camels were used as transport here fifty years ago."

"You have been reading guidebooks again, haven't you? I'd like to go and see the volcanoes there though. I like it here at the hotel but to go and see real volcanoes would be even better. There is something so wild and savagely beautiful about it all."

"It's very fitting being here, what with it being a hot fiery volcano hotel and you being ... much hotter and more fiery than I imagined," he murmured into her ear, biting her earlobes gently and moving his hands down to caress her body. "You are perfect, everything a man could want. And, where did you learn those moves you practised on me last night?" he whispered kissing her neck.

She laughed again. "I don't know. You just bring out the bad in me, I guess."

"If that's bad, then bring it on. I think I like a bad woman," he mumbled, his head making its way along her neck and throat. "Seriously," he said, bringing his head up to gaze into her eyes, "I can't think of anyone else I'd rather be with. I know it's early days for us, but you are huge fun to be with, and you make life more interesting … spicier."

He stroked her shoulders. "Talking of spice, I have a confession to make."

"Uh-huh, what's that?"

"I looked at your passport. It was on the table staring at me, tempting me, and I just had to find out. I don't know why you don't use it. I think it suits you one hundred per cent."

"Do you?"

"It's definitely you. Spicy and fragrant," he said breathing in deeply. "I think I'll start calling you by your first name. It'll be our secret if you prefer. What do you think, Cinnamon?"

Dawn thought for a moment. "Yes, you are right. It's different now. I am different. I should start using my proper name. It probably suits me better than I thought it did. Inside, I have always been a Cinnamon." And with that, she put her arms around his neck and manoeuvred herself on top of him, kissing him deeply as the bubbles splashed playfully around them.

Later, Cinnamon and Jason lay side by side on the Balinese bed taking in the magnificent purple red sky. She reflected on how her life had changed dramatically in a few short months. She had no regrets. If anything, she felt renewed. She had a more exciting future ahead of her now. She lifted the glass beside the bed and raised it to the sky making a mental toast.

"To Cinnamon and her future. May it be full of spice."

About the Author

A graduate of the University of Keele in Staffordshire, Carol E Wyer is a former teacher, linguist, and physical trainer.

She spent her early working life in Casablanca, Morocco, where she translated for companies and taught English as a foreign language. She then returned to work in education back in the UK and set up her own language company in the late eighties.

In her forties, Carol retrained to become a personal trainer to assist people, who, like herself, had undergone major surgery.

Having spent the last decade trying out all sorts of new challenges such as kickboxing, diving, and flying helicopters, she is now ensuring her fifties are "fab not drab". She has put her time to good use by learning to paint, attempting to teach herself Russian, and writing a series of novels and articles which take a humorous look at getting older.

Carol lives in rural Staffordshire with her own retired Grumpy. It is little wonder that she is a regular blogger and social networking addict.

Award-winning novels
by Carol E Wyer

Mini Skirts and Laughter Lines

Amanda Wilson can't decide between murder, insanity, or another glass of red wine. Facing fifty and all that it entails is problematic enough. What's the point in minking your eyes when your husband would rather watch Russia Today than admire you strutting in front of the television in only thigh boots and a thong?

Her son has managed to perform yet another magical disappearing act. Could he actually be buried under the mountain of festering washing strewn on his bedroom floor? He'll certainly be buried somewhere when she next gets her hands on him.

At least her mother knows how to enjoy herself. She's partying her twilight years away in Cyprus. Queen of the Twister mat, she now has a toy boy in tow.

Amanda knows she shouldn't have pressed that Send button. The past always catches up with you sooner or later. Still, her colourful past is a welcome relief to her monochrome present—especially when it comes in the shape of provocative Todd Bradshaw, her first true love.

Amanda has a difficult decision to make – one that will require more than a few glasses of Chianti.

Surfing in Stilettos

Amanda Wilson is all geared up for an exciting gap-year, travelling across Europe. She soon finds her plans thwarted when she is abandoned in France with only a cellarful of Chateau Plonk, a large, orange Space Hopper, and Old Ted, the dog, for company.

Fate has intervened to turn Amanda's life on its head. First, Bertie, the camper van, breaks down. Then her dopey son, Tom, who is staying in their house in the UK, is wrecking it, one piece at a time. Next, the jaw-dropping video Skype calls that her irrepressible mother insists on making are, by contrast, making Amanda's humdrum trip even less palatable.

Finally, she discovers that her new-found, French friend, Bibi Chevalier, had engineered a plan to ensure that her philandering husband would never stray again; unfortunately, Amanda is unwittingly drawn into the scheme, becoming a target.

Meanwhile, on a beach in Sydney, a lonely Todd Bradshaw realises that his first true love, Amanda Wilson, is definitely the only woman for him. Can he get back into her good books and hopefully back into her arms with his latest plan? Or will fate intervene yet again and turn everyone's lives upside down?

How Not to Murder Your Grumpy

Is your Grumpy Old Man getting under your feet? Is he wrestling with retirement? Are you wondering if you should bundle him up and entrust him to basket-weaving classes? Then this book could be the answer to your prayers. This light hearted guide is packed full of lively ideas, anecdotes and quips. Not only does it set out to provide laughs, but offers over 700 ideas and ways to keep a Grumpy Old Man occupied.

From collecting airline sick bags to zorbing, you will be sure to find an absorbing pastime for your beloved curmudgeon. There are examples of those who have faced extraordinary challenges in older age, fascinating facts to interest a reluctant partner and innovative ideas drizzled, of course, with a large dollop of humour.

Written tongue-in-cheek, this book succeeds in proving that getting older doesn't mean the end of life or having fun. It provides amusing answers to the question, "How on Earth will my husband fill in his time in his retirement?" It offers suggestions on what might, or most certainly might not, amuse him. Ideal for trivia buffs, those approaching retirement, (or just at a loose end) and frustrated women who have an irritable male on their hands, this book will lighten any mood and may even prevent the odd murder.

CPSIA information can be obtained at www.ICGtesting.com
Printed in the USA
BVOW03s1313121113

336104BV00002B/8/P

9 781908 208224